P9-AZU-720

Zowee! Edie thought as she walked back across the campus to her mother's car. *Zowee! Zowee! Zowee!*

In the car she pulled off her jacket, tossed it onto the back seat, kicked off her heels, which had elevated her exactly to the level of Peter Darling's gray-green eyes, threw them into the back, too, and sat grinning idiotically at the cracked green vinyl-covered dashboard.

Zowee!

Shaking her head, she pulled down the driving mirror to look at her face: flushed scarlet. The car, she noted belatedly, was a furnace. She rolled down the driver's window, still seeing Peter Darling's face.

Zowee!

If every female in the place wasn't having indecent dreams about him, she'd…eat her press pass.

Dear Reader,

Sometimes I think that writing fiction is a little like making a patchwork quilt—you take a little of this, a piece of that and, oh yes, got to find a place for that little scrap. I felt that way as I wrote *Return to Little Hills*. While the characters, the situations and the locales are all fiction, I frequently found myself digging into the ragbag of my own life.

Okay, this is the time to say—I should probably underline this part—that my own elderly mother, while hard of hearing, is much more kind, understanding and all-around wonderful than Edie's mother. Are you reading this, Mum? And my sister, Kathleen, is—thankfully—nothing at all like Viv. Okay, Kaff?

That said, though, I really enjoy writing about the dynamics of family relationships. Families are a source of incredible joy and comfort and, let's face it, have the unique capacity to get under our skin in no time flat, as my heroine, Edie, discovers when she returns to her hometown of Little Hills, Missouri.

I hope you enjoy *Return to Little Hills*. Please write to me at Janice Macdonald, P.O. Box 101, 136 East 8th Street, Port Angeles, WA 98362, or visit my Web site at www.janicemacdonald.net.

Oh, one more thing. If, like Edie (and myself), you're a gooey-butter-cake aficionado, send me your recipes! I'll try to publish a few on my Web site.

Best wishes,

Janice

Return to Little Hills
Janice Macdonald

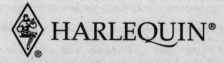

TORONTO • NEW YORK • LONDON
AMSTERDAM • PARIS • SYDNEY • HAMBURG
STOCKHOLM • ATHENS • TOKYO • MILAN • MADRID
PRAGUE • WARSAW • BUDAPEST • AUCKLAND

If you purchased this book without a cover you should be aware
that this book is stolen property. It was reported as "unsold and
destroyed" to the publisher, and neither the author nor the
publisher has received any payment for this "stripped book."

ISBN 0-373-71201-4

RETURN TO LITTLE HILLS

Copyright © 2004 by Janice Macdonald.

All rights reserved. Except for use in any review, the reproduction or
utilization of this work in whole or in part in any form by any electronic,
mechanical or other means, now known or hereafter invented, including
xerography, photocopying and recording, or in any information storage
or retrieval system, is forbidden without the written permission of the
publisher, Harlequin Enterprises Limited, 225 Duncan Mill Road,
Don Mills, Ontario, Canada M3B 3K9.

All characters in this book have no existence outside the imagination of
the author and have no relation whatsoever to anyone bearing the same
name or names. They are not even distantly inspired by any individual
known or unknown to the author, and all incidents are pure invention.

This edition published by arrangement with Harlequin Books S.A.

® and TM are trademarks of the publisher. Trademarks indicated with
® are registered in the United States Patent and Trademark Office, the
Canadian Trade Marks Office and in other countries.

Visit us at www.eHarlequin.com

Printed in U.S.A.

To Kaff, with much love

Books by Janice Macdonald

HARLEQUIN SUPERROMANCE
1060—THE DOCTOR DELIVERS
1077—THE MAN ON THE CLIFF
1132—KEEPING FAITH
1157—SUSPICION

Don't miss any of our special offers. Write to us at the
following address for information on our newest releases.

Harlequin Reader Service
U.S.: 3010 Walden Ave., P.O. Box 1325, Buffalo, NY 14269
Canadian: P.O. Box 609, Fort Erie, Ont. L2A 5X3

CHAPTER ONE

"DON'T SNAP AT ME," Edie Robinson's mother said as Edie maneuvered Maude's elderly Chevrolet Nova into the parking lot of the Little Hills IGA. "No one asked you to come back. You're busy, we all know that. You've got an important job. Nobody expects anything from you. All I said was I needed toilet paper—"

"You told me four times, Mom."

"Why would I have said limes?" Maude's voice was indignant. "I wouldn't know what to do with a lime if it bit me on the nose. I need toilet paper and...denture cleaner," she added in a conspiratorial whisper. "But if you're going to snap at me, forget it. Viv will take me. Viv can always make time, not that she isn't busy, too, but all I have to do is pick up the phone and—"

"Viv walks on water, Mom. I don't." *"Sarcastic,"* Maude would have shot back if she'd heard anything more than a muffled jumble of words. *"You've always been sarcastic, Edith."* With her right hand, Edie massaged the knot of tension in the back of her neck that usually only hit her when she procrastinated on a deadline, and cruised the lot for a parking space close to the market entrance. She watched a woman in pink tights and a maternity top load groceries and three small kids into a minivan. *God.* Three kids and the woman had to be at least fifteen years younger than she was. Edie glanced in the rearview mirror, frowned at the vertical lines around her mouth and thought to hell with it. When the van finally pulled away, Edie slid into the spot, switched off the ignition and turned in the seat to look directly at her mother.

Maude was eighty and, despite the late-summer Missouri heat, wore a black woolen cardigan over a cotton housedress blooming with improbably vivid peonies. On her feet, little pink ballerina-style slippers and knee-high support hose. For some reason, the sight of Maude's tiny slipper-clad feet and swollen ankles made Edie want to weep. She reached over and scooped up Maude's left hand in her own. Maude's felt soft and almost boneless, fingers clutched around a wad of tissue. "I didn't mean to snap at you," Edie said. "I'm sorry."

Her chin trembling, Maude scrabbled for the door handle. "You've always had a short temper, Edith. I said to Viv just the other day, I never know what's going to set Edith off. You'll have to come and open this door for me, it sticks. You're just like your father in that way." She pushed ineffectively at the door. "Viv said she'd have Ray look at it—"

"Mom, leave the door alone. I'll open it for you. You need to get rid of this damn car. Unless," she muttered facetiously, "you're going to start driving again."

"Ham." Maude clutched her purse close to her chest. "They've got that sliced ham on sale. I like a slice of ham for dinner. Can't eat anything too heavy before I go to bed, or I'm up all night with heartburn. Viv tell you about the new principal at Ray's school?"

"She mentioned him." An understatement. From the moment Viv picked her up at the airport the night before, her sister had talked about little else. *Peter Darling: English, wife died of cancer, four small children, collects butterflies, Ray says he won't last. Too pie-in-the sky.*

Twenty years of journalism had trained her to isolate and retain the salient facts of any information she was given. She'd retained these particular snippets because the idea of raising four small children with or without a spouse appalled her and because she'd probably meet Peter Darling tomorrow when she gave a talk to students at the school. Her brother-in-law, the assistant principal, had hit her with the request late last night and she'd agreed before she realized she didn't particularly want to do it.

Too late now. She grabbed the keys, got out of the car and walked around to the passenger side. Waves of heat rose up from the parking lot. A line of sweat trickled down her back, pasting her cotton shirt to her skin. It had been nearly midnight when she'd stepped out of the airport and the warm, moist temperature had hit her like a slap in the face. This morning, the relentlessly cheerful weatherman on Maude's ancient Magnavox had announced that the day promised to be another scorcher, even hotter than yesterday. She'd snapped off the set as he'd been yammering on about the misery index.

No one expects anything from you. She pulled open the heavy door and leaned inside to unfasten her mother's seat belt. Maude's hair, soft and fine as cobwebs, brushed against her cheek. Edie caught a whiff of mothballs and peppermint candy. *But you're glad I'm here, aren't you, Mom? You miss me sometimes. Don't you?*

"Okay, there you go." She stood back and extended her hand; Maude ignored it. "Going to be another hot day," she said as Maude slowly swung her legs around. "You're going to bake in that sweater. Want me to help you off with it?"

"Don't rush me." Maude's little pink slippers were gingerly touching down on the asphalt. "I know you're in a hurry, you're always in a hurry, but it takes me a while these days."

"Take your time, Mom. I'm not going anywhere." Her mother's face was flushed with heat and exertion and, as she helped her out of the car, Edie slid her palm under the shoulder of Maude's black sweater and felt damp warmth. "Let me help you take it off, Mom. You'll be more comfortable."

Maude shook off Edie's hand. "The store's air-conditioned. I'll need my sweater."

"You got it." Her arm linked in Maude's, they made their way slowly across the parking lot. "Okay, toilet paper, denture cleaner and ham. Is that it?"

"Yams?" Maude shook her head. "Get some for yourself if you want, I won't eat any." She turned her pale blue eyes on Edie. "You probably ate that sort of thing in…where was it you were last? I can't keep up with all the places you're off to. I said to Vivian, no wonder Edith never married. What man would want to go traipsing around the world after her?"

"I'll get you a basket." At the entrance to the store, Edie separated a cart from the line and wheeled it over to Maude. "There you go. Want me to push it for you?"

"I need it to lean on." Maude elbowed Edie aside. "Now, I'll be as quick as I can," she said as they progressed sedately along the dairy aisle. "Just don't lose your temper with me. There's no call for it. Vivian doesn't snap at me the way you do, she knows it takes me longer these days. She said to me when we knew you were coming, she said, 'Mom. Edith's just going to upset you the way she always does.' Viv thinks about these things."

Edie bit the inside of her lower lip very hard and sent a prayer aloft. *Please, please give me patience. Half of*

*my sister's saintliness would help, too. And please,
please, I know it's too late to expect much in the way of
mother-daughter bonding. I know we're not going to
snuggle up in bed for heart-to-heart talks over mugs of
cocoa, but please, please, let this be a...pleasant visit.
And please,* please, *don't let me snap at her. Even
though I didn't snap at her in the first place.*

"EDIE ROBINSON!" the cashier shrieked some forty-five
minutes later when Edie followed Maude with her brimming basket to the checkout line. "My God, I don't
believe it. When did you get back?"

"Last night." A package of toilet paper in one hand,
Edie grinned at the woman she'd last seen at their
twenty-year high-school reunion which—she did a quick
mental calculation—was nearly three years ago. Honey
Jones, she immediately observed, was probably fifteen
pounds heavier than she'd been back then and her blond
hair was gray at the roots. God, you're shallow, Edie
scolded herself as she began piling stuff on the conveyor
belt. Yeah, but when you're barreling along the road to
middle age, she justified, you notice these things. "So,
Honey," she said. "What's going on with you these
days?"

Honey grinned broadly. "Same old, same old. Get up,
go to work, come home, get dinner for Jim and the kids.
Go to bed. Do it all over again the next day. But what
about you?" She glanced at Maude, who had dug a fist-
ful of coupons from her purse and now held them close
to her face as she slowly inspected each one. "The last
I heard, your mom said you were in…"

"Afghanistan," Edie said when it became clear the
answer wasn't on the tip of Honey's tongue "Before
that, Bosnia." *Chechnya, Somalia, Rwanda. She'd cov-*

ered them all. Dangerous, difficult, complex, frustrating. But a piece of cake compared to Little Hills, Missouri.

"Doing okay, Mom? Want me to help you sort through those coupons?"

"Frozen peas," Maude said. "Too much sodium in the canned ones."

"So you're just back for a visit?" Honey asked.

"A month. Mom's decided the house is too much for her, living alone and everything. My sister thinks Mom would be happier in a…more structured environment, so I'm back to help her find something."

"Viv's such a doll," Honey said. "So patient. Always a smile. I don't know how she does it."

"Yeah." Edie forced a smile of her own. "Mom's lucky to have her living close by."

"Edie's giving a talk at Ray's school tomorrow," Maude said. "Ray's the principal. He's married to my daughter Vivian."

"I know, Mrs. Robinson," Honey said, kindly as though to a child. "I was a bridesmaid at their wedding." She looked at Edie. "*Assistant* principal, right? My kid's a junior there. I guess you've heard all about the new principal, huh?"

"Yeah. Viv filled me in. Everyone seems all agog."

"That's small-town life for you," Honey said and shook her head. "I can't even imagine your life. The farthest I've ever been is New Jersey. Do you get scared? I mean, all that shooting and everything."

Edie shrugged and thought about the bullet in Sarajevo. She'd left her room for five minutes to talk to a photographer about the story they were working on. She returned to a cloud of dust and a .50-caliber slug embedded in the wall behind the desk she'd been using. If she'd been there, the bullet would have gone right through her forehead. She'd kept the bullet. "You take your chances," she said. "It's part of the deal."

"I've got coupons," Maude announced. "Here, Edith, you sort them out. Don't know why they make the writing so small. Did Edith tell you about her big award?" she asked Honey. "Twenty-five cents off the coffee, the coupon is here somewhere. And the canned salmon is two for three dollars. Edith, look at these coupons. I know you can't be bothered with that sort of thing, but it's a savings, let me tell you. My daughter thinks money grows on trees," she said with a glance at the cashier. "Always been that way. I remember Vivian used to save her allowance until she could get something she really wanted, but not Edith. As soon as she got it, she spent it. Still that way."

Edie exchanged glances with the cashier, who smiled sympathetically.

"In your mother's eyes you never grow up." Honey scanned a roll of paper towels. "Doesn't matter if you're fifteen or fifty, you're always this kid who doesn't have sense enough to cross the road." She reached for a can of pineapple chunks. "So. Tell me about your award."

"Oh…" Edie started sorting Maude's coupons into little piles. "I got a Pulitzer for a series on the rebels in El Salvador." She picked up a ten-cents off coupon for grape jelly and checked the contents of the basket to see if she'd actually picked up the jelly as Maude had asked her to. "It was a team effort though, three other reporters and myself. I couldn't have done it without them."

"Wow." Honey's eyes were shining. "I am so proud of you, Edie. But, hey, we always knew you were smart. So…no husband on the horizon?"

"You got grape jelly." Maude shoved the jar under Edie's nose.

"I know, Mom." She looked at Maude, whose eyes, brimming and clouded by cataracts, could look frighteningly hostile. "You said that's what you wanted."

"I said strawberry."

"You said grape."

"Strawberry," Maude said. "That's my daughter for you," she said with a sigh. "Never listens. Never has. Snaps at me too."

Edie held her breath. *I won't snap again if it kills me. And it might.*

Honey winked at Edie. "So, no handsome man in your life?" she asked, rephrasing the question this time.

"No man, handsome or otherwise." Edie took the grape jelly from Maude. "Wait right there, Mom. I'll go back and get the strawberry. Anything else while I'm at it?" Maude didn't answer, but as Edie walked away, she could hear Maude's voice telling Honey, "Edie'll never marry. Too darn independent and set in her ways."

LUTHER HIGH SCHOOL principal Peter Darling stood in the sweltering heat at the side of the quad watching the faces of the assembled students for signs that they were actually listening to the tall woman up at the podium. To his vast relief, he saw no signs of the pushing and snickering and not-so-muffled yawns that had turned last week's spotlight-on-careers program into an embarrassing fiasco. The assistant principal, openly skeptical about a weekly spotlight on careers, had smirked afterward that maybe they should line up hookers and pimps to discuss their work, with possibly a spotlight on auto theft and strong-arm robbery—the lines of work for which most Luther High kids were destined. Then to Peter's surprise, Ray had done an apparent about-face and suggested that his sister-in-law would be willing to speak.

Peter watched the kids who, from their intent expressions, all appeared to be contemplating a career in journalism. Of course, Edie Robinson—with her sleek toffee-colored hair and photogenic smile—was no doubt part of the appeal.

"What do I like best about my job?" she'd just asked in response to a question thrown out by a girl in the front row. "*Everything.* The excitement, the variety. I think people often become unhappy because they're just dissatisfied with the way things are in the place where they live. That doesn't happen to me. I'm always going somewhere else. If I don't like my current circumstance…oh well, tomorrow I'll get on a plane and be on the other side of the world. New situation, new country, new experiences. I live in hotels. I eat in restaurants. I leave my laundry in a plastic bag in the hall outside my door. Almost all my friends are other journalists. My life is exclusively travel and work. And that's exactly the way I like it."

"Or to put it another way," Ray Jenkins muttered in Peter's ear, "Edith never has to think about anyone but herself. Which she never did anyway, even before she got to be a hotshot journalist. Kind of explains why she's forty and never been married. You wanna hear about the stuff she's not telling you, ask me. I used to go with her before I came to my senses and married her sister."

Apart from mild surprise that the assistant principal might have anything at all in common with the woman at the podium, Peter had no interest in Ray Jenkins's personal life, so he ignored the remark and made his way over to the stage just as Edie, having wrapped up her talk, was stepping down. He motioned for her to stay put and addressed the students himself, inviting them to show their appreciation for the interesting and informative talk. They complied with great enthusiasm, punctuating their applause with a few whoops and whistles.

He followed Edie off the stage, where she was now regarding him with very faint amusement in her light, amber-colored eyes. Her face and throat were lightly tanned and she wore an off-white trouser suit in a thin material that draped gracefully on her tall, angular figure. There was a cool confidence about her that made it quite easy for him to imagine her calmly reading in a bathtub as mortar shells flew around. The image intrigued him.

"Riveting talk. The students were captivated and, trust me, they're a tough audience."

She eyed him for a moment. "North of London, but not as far north as, say, Birmingham. Lived in the States for…oh, ten years or so. Long enough to have lost a little of the accent."

He laughed, taken aback. "Very good. Malvern, actually. And I've been here twelve years. You've spent time in England, have you?"

"Five years in the London bureau, some time ago, though. I used to be a whiz at identifying regional accents. I thought I might have lost my touch."

"Clearly, you haven't."

"I'm sure there's an interesting story about how a man from Malvern, England, came to be a high-school principal in Little Hills, Missouri, but—" she glanced around "—I see a line forming to talk to you, so I'll just…invent my own version of the facts."

"Or you could call me," he said, surprising himself. "And we could exchange life stories over dinner."

"Thank you," she said. "But I think I'll stick with my invented version."

"Pity," he said. And then as he was about to let her

go, he said, "I've noticed that your brother-in-law calls you Edith. Is it Edith, or Edie?" he asked.

"Edie," she said. "Only my family calls me Edith…and I tolerate that very poorly." A moment passed. "I've noticed that my brother-in-law calls you Pete. Is it Peter, or Pete?"

"Peter." He grimaced slightly. "I suppose it sounds terribly formal, doesn't it?"

"It sounds fine," she said.

ZOWEE, Edie thought as she walked back across the campus to Maude's car. *Zowee. Zowee. Zowee.* In the car, she pulled off her jacket, tossed it in the back seat, kicked off her heels, which had elevated her exactly to the level of Peter Darling's gray-green eyes, threw them in the back, too, and sat grinning idiotically at the cracked, green vinyl–covered dashboard. *Zowee.* Shaking her head, she pulled down the driving mirror to look at her face: flushed scarlet. The car, she noted belatedly, was a furnace. She rolled down the driver's window, still seeing Peter Darling's face. *Zowee.* If every female in that school wasn't having indecent dreams about him, she'd…eat her press pass.

THE OLD BLACK DIAL PHONE in the hallway was ringing when Edie let herself into Maude's house some thirty minutes later. Her mother, Edie thought as she picked up the heavy receiver, should at least have a portable that she could carry around the house, but Maude wasn't about to go easy into the digital age. The old one suited her just fine, thank you very much. Edie dragged the phone to the stairs and sat on the bottom step, listening to Vivian describe the pot roast she'd just put in the oven for dinner that night. Edie should bring Maude over at about six, Viv said.

Edie leaned back against the stairs and stifled a groan. Family gatherings ranked low on her list of ways to spend a pleasant evening. Viv would outdo herself with the food, then complain of being exhausted. Ray would be smarmy and insinuating. She'd lost touch completely with her nephews. And Maude would spend the whole time telling everyone that she didn't know what she'd done to deserve the way her youngest daughter was always snapping at her.

Home sweet home. Thank God it was only for a month. Looking on the bright side, Viv would probably continue her rant about Peter Darling. Funny how much more interesting that prospect was, now that she'd met him.

''Mom doesn't feed herself properly,'' Viv was saying now. ''And I'm sure you've probably forgotten all you never learned about cooking. I'll do the roast and then I'll wrap up what's left and you can take it back to Mom's. That way, you'll both have something decent to eat.''

From the stairs, where she remained after hanging up the phone, Edie could see Maude at her chair by the window. ''She spends hours there,'' Viv had complained on the ride from the airport. ''Just staring out at the street. That's why she needs to get out of that house and into a place where she can be with other people her own age.''

Elbows on her knees, Edie sat for a while watching her mother from the dim and musty hallway. Maude, at her lace-curtained window post, in a fusty room crammed with knickknacks, crocheted mats, knitted cushions, cuckoo clocks and all the detritus accumulated over a lifetime, seemed so organic to the house that Edie found herself wondering whether uprooting her might cause Maude to just wither and die sooner than she might if she were left to live out her life at home.

But when she mentioned the thought to Vivian that night, her sister looked impatient.

"Edie, trust me, I spend a lot more time with Mom than you do. She needs to get rid of that house."

Edie, sprawled on the massive off-white leather couch in Viv and Ray's cavernous family room, channel surfing on their massive TV because Vivian had laughed incredulously at her offer to help out, conceded that Viv was probably right. Still, she would sound Maude out anyway, just to be certain in her own mind. "Are you sure I can't do anything to help?" she called to Viv, who hadn't left the kitchen for the past hour.

Vivian laughed. "Thanks, but no thanks, Eed. I can manage better without your help. Trust me. Just relax."

So she tried. She channel surfed some more, but found herself critiquing the correspondent's performance on every new station. It was hard to forget her vocation, even when she wasn't working. Finally, she let her thoughts drift. She thought for a bit about her sister in the kitchen, whom she normally thought very little about. Coming home always brought the old memories flooding back. Viv. *Poor* Viv, the pretty but asthmatic child. She could still hear Maude scolding, *"Oh Edith, don't be so selfish. Let Viv have the doll."* Or the candy, or the book or whatever else it was that Viv might want. *"You're such a lucky girl, you have your health. Look at poor Viv."* And Edie would look at Viv and feel not sympathy but envy because Viv had Maude's attention and she didn't.

All that old, bitter stuff that she hardly ever thought

about now. But, deep inside, she still felt it, that same need for her mother's approval and acceptance. Love *me*. Need *me*. Ben, she reflected, had failed badly in that regard. Don't look for commitment from me, he'd said. Pretty much the last significant thing he'd said, as a matter of fact. If other events that night hadn't overshadowed everything else, those words would have plunged her into a dark void of gloom. Instead, she'd developed a sort of emotional amnesia. Ben would escape or be released; she knew that much for sure. After that, who knew? Her thumb on the button of the remote, she gazed at the flickering images. A perfume ad with heartbreakingly beautiful people locked in dreamy embraces. Happy women folding diapers, mopping floors, sending happy kids off to school.

"So you really like the house?" Viv called from the kitchen. "We love it, but sometimes I get freaked at how much we had to go into debt… Want a glass of wine?"

"Maybe later." Edie called back. Viv and Ray had bought the house two months ago. It was a sprawling mock Tudor that sat amidst similar houses on the edge of what Edie remembered had once been bean fields. It had struck her, as she'd trailed Viv around earlier, dutifully oohing and aahing, that everything about the house—from the sweeping driveway and mirrored guest bathroom with its elaborate gold-plated fixtures, to the cream-and-gold master bedroom—seemed new, immense and designed to impress. Fleetingly, she'd wondered what assistant principals made these days, but it wasn't a question to ask. "What's not to like about the house?" she answered rhetorically as televised images flickered hypnotically across her line of vision.

"We like to entertain," Viv, still in the kitchen, was saying now. "It's something Ray and I both enjoy."

"Well, you've got a great place to do it in." A cartoon bird gave way to an anchorwoman's face and Edie's thumb paused on the remote. "...*and the search continues,*" the announcer said, "*for American freelance journalist Ben Morris, captured last month on assignment in Iraq. Morris and three other journalists came under fire when the jeep they were riding in was ambushed by gunmen...*"

CHAPTER TWO

EDIE STARED transfixed, but the announcer's dry recap of that nightmarish ride told her nothing she hadn't relived endlessly ever since. "Hold on to your hat, Eed," Ben had said. "We're going to outrun them." She remembered the way his teeth had gleamed in the dark night. The roar as he'd gunned the jeep, the terrifying careen up the dark mountainside with no headlights on. He loves this, she remembered thinking. It's his essence. I'm an idiot to even think about commitment... And then the jeep had flipped.

"Carrot sticks, cauliflower and a no-fat dip." Vivian set a tray on the chrome-and-glass coffee table and flopped down on the couch beside Edie. "I'm not real sure about the carrot sticks, they have a bunch of carbs and I'm on this low-carb diet. Doesn't it seem weird to think of carrots as a no-no? I mean, carrots and cottage cheese used to be what you'd eat when you were trying to drop a few pounds, but supposedly now they're off limits. Too high carb. If you want some wine, let me know. It's not on the diet...*beaucoup* carbs, although gin's okay. Want some gin?"

Edie blinked, staring at Viv as though she'd been roused from a dream that still seemed real. Viv smiled. Kitchen warmth had flushed her face and her shoulder-length hair, hardly faded from the strawberry blond it had been in high school, fell into a smooth bob. "Vivian's the pretty one," Maude would say. "But you're smart, Edie."

Edie rubbed her eyes. "Sorry. I'm miles away. Where's Mom? I thought she was out in the kitchen with you."

"Ray ran her down to the IGA to get denture cleaner. I didn't want to tell you, but she'd worked herself up into quite a tizzy about it and—"

"I took her to the IGA this morning," Edie said. "We got denture cleaner. I remember taking it off the shelf."

Viv reached over to pat Edie's knee. "It was the wrong kind, sweetie," she said maternally. "Don't blame yourself. How would you know that? I've got beer too. Beer, wine, gin, you name it. I'm not drinking, though. If I don't get this extra weight off I'm going to kill myself. What do you think about these jeans?" She jumped up, turned to present a rear view. "Do they make my hips look kind of wide? Tell me, I won't be mad, honestly."

"You look fine, Viv." Edie said, her mind still on Maude's shopping trip. "So why didn't Mom say something?"

Viv sat down again. "She's scared of you, sweetie," she said softly as though there was a chance Maude might overhear. "She says you snap at her. You know, I might cheat a little and have some wine. Want some?"

"I'm fine." Edie shook her head. "No, I'm not. I'm furious. God, it kills me. I tried to be so patient with her. I *was* patient. For me, anyway. And I didn't snap at her in the first place. Maybe I overreacted slightly when she told me for the fourth time that she needed toilet paper, but—"

"Hey, Eed." Viv reached for a carrot stick. "Can we not talk about Mom for a minute? You're going to be here for a while, we'll have plenty of time to discuss her. Trust me. Come on, eat something.''

Edie took a carrot stick. ''Will the boys be here for dinner?''

''Absolutely,'' Viv said. ''They're always talking about their glamorous Aunt Edie.''

Edie gave her sister a skeptical look.

''Really. One of them—I think it was Eric—was asking something about you just the other day,'' Viv said. ''Frankly though, Edie, you haven't exactly been a big part of their lives.'' She dunked her carrot stick in dip, twirling it for a second. ''Back to Mom, though. She's a novelty to you, but—''

''She's my mother, Viv. And trust me, I don't find her much of a novelty.''

''Well, you know what I mean. In a couple of weeks, you'll be flying off to Boogawongabooboo, or wherever, but I'll be right here listening to Mom tell me about the little sore up her nose. Eat something, Edie.'' She reached for a cauliflower floret. ''You're making me feel like a pig. How come you stay skinny when everyone else balloons up as soon as they hit thirty?''

''Clean living,'' Edie said.

''Yeah, sure.'' Vivian eyed her for a moment. ''Frankly though, and please don't take this wrong, I think having a little fat actually makes a woman look younger. Personally, I wouldn't want to be too skinny. It gives you this drawn, dried-up look.''

Edie smiled politely. ''You think so?''

''Ray thinks so too. Scrawny chickens, he calls them.'' She reached for a napkin and dabbed at a spot of dip on the glass coffee table. ''I mean in general, of course.''

''Of course,'' Edie said. ''What little sore?''

"Little sore?" Vivian looked momentarily confused. "Oh, Mom's little sore. She's always got one up her nose. I swear to God, the minute I sit down to breakfast, the phone rings and it's Mom going on about how the little sore bleeds every time she blows her nose. I can't even look at strawberry jam these days."

Edie laughed. Despite everything, she wanted, suddenly, to embrace her sister. The perfunctory little hug at the airport had been disappointing. On some level, she realized now, she'd been looking to Viv for the same thing she sought in Maude. *Love me, need me. Tell me not to leave again.* Ironic, this need, when she would battle to the death anyone who tried to wrest away her shield of independence and self-sufficiency. Odd, too, that the need only seemed to trouble her when she returned home.

"You know what?" Vivian said. "I *am* going to have some wine. How often does my little sister honor us with her presence? Be right back."

When she returned a moment later, she had two glasses and a bottle of wine. Blush, Edie observed with a surreptitious glance at the label. Snob, she scolded herself. Ben had once used a UN transport plane to ship two cases of Italian wine to Sarajevo. "Nearly broke my back carrying it to the car," he'd said as he'd poured her a glass. "But it beats the hell out of the local plonk."

Edie watched Viv fill two balloon-shaped glasses with pale pink wine. "So," she said. "Shall we make a toast?"

Vivian hooted. "*Shall* we make a toast? *Shall?* Jeez, Edie, when did you start using words like *shall?* You sound like Peter Darling. That's one of the things Ray hates about him, one of many things. Apart from the fact he's younger than Ray and gorgeous." She downed half her wine and refilled the glass. ''Talk like everyone else, for God's sake. This is Little Hills not Buckingham Palace.'' She paused for a moment. ''Sorry. I didn't mean to get started, it's just that I hear enough about Peter Darling from Ray.'' She touched her glass to Edie's. ''To my little sister with her hoity-toity voice being home again. *Joking,* Eed.'' She patted Edie's knee. ''Don't look at me like that. It's great to have you here. Really.''

''It's great to be here,'' Edie said, averting her eyes.

Vivian glanced over her shoulder and moved fractionally closer. ''I'm in a quandary, Edie. A *real* quandary. Remember Beth Herman?''

Edie thought. ''Beth Herman from high school?''

Viv nodded. ''She works at Luther now. Peter Darling hired her to run this new teen mother program—which Ray says is a complete waste of money. All it does is encourage kids to have sex, but anyway, she's in love with him.''

''Ray?''

Viv smacked Edie's knee. ''Peter Darling, doofus. I mean, she's gaga over him and she keeps coming to me for advice. I'm happy for her, of course—I mean, Beth's such a sweet girl, she deserves to find someone—but I'm torn. I hear Ray going on about what an idiot the guy is and Beth telling me how he's so wonderful and I don't know whether I should be encouraging her or what.''

''Hmm.'' Edie took a carrot stick and tried to think of something to say. ''Well, he seems very nice,'' she said neutrally. ''Interesting. Attractive.''

''Attractive.'' Viv hooted. ''Did you see him? He's gorgeous. I mean, drop-dead gorgeous. He's like a cross between Ralph Fiennes, Daniel Day-Lewis and…who was that poet I had to study in high school? Myron, or something?''

"Byron?"

"Yeah, I guess. I don't know what Byron looks like, but that's what Beth says. I tell you…'' She sighed loudly. "If it's not one thing, it's another. Any idea what I should do?''

"Well, Viv, it's not really your problem, is it? Peter and Beth are adults.'' A thought occurred to her. "Is it mutual?''

"Who knows? Beth isn't sure, but she's so sweet and nice and they're both in education. How could it not be? And she'd be a wonderful mother to his little girls. I mean, how many women would want to take on four kids?''

"Certainly not me,'' Edie said. Although, having met Peter Darling, she felt quite sure he'd have no shortage of candidates. "Sounds like a nightmare.''

"Well, you've never had the maternal streak.'' Viv poured more wine. "Anyway, enough of that. I'm worried about Ray. Here he's been knocking himself out for years, nothing he wouldn't do for those kids. And everyone just knew he was a shoe-in for principal once Frank Brown retired, but then what happens? The school board brings in this Peter Darling, who's probably five years younger than Ray—which, trust me, doesn't help things—and so damn pie-in-the-sky you wouldn't believe it.''

Edie stifled a yawn. Except for the Beth Herman element, they'd been over essentially the same ground on the ride home from the airport. She hadn't been particularly interested then and, despite the new principal's considerable appeal, time hadn't increased her thirst to know more. What she wanted to do was collect Maude, drive back to her mother's house and then sink into oblivion. *Selfish, selfish,* Maude's voice scolded deep in her brain. *You've always been selfish, Edith.* She drank some wine and tried not to grimace at the flowery sweet taste.

"What exactly do you mean by pie-in-the sky?" she asked in a tone that made her think she should have a pen in one hand and a notebook on her knee.

"Oh…" Viv reached for the wine again. "You know what? The hell with this rabbit food, I need salt and fat." She jumped up again and returned a moment later. "Actually, it's some sort of artificial fat," she said as she dumped a bag of chips into a yellow bowl. "Don't ask me how, but they say your body doesn't recognize it, so it passes right through you. God, that sounds gross, huh? Come on—don't make me feel like a pig. Try one. Have some more wine." She reached to refill Edie's glass, and then the front door slammed.

"Shh." Viv flashed Edie a warning look and drained the last of her wine. "Here's Ray. Don't mention Peter Darling's name or the whole evening will be ruined."

"Hey, *Edith,*" Ray said with a glance at the wine bottle. "Been leading my wife astray? Nothing changes, huh?"

"Now, Ray, be nice." Vivian gathered up the wine and glasses. "Poor Edie's been with Mom all day, she needed a little drinky. She was just telling me about her job. God, you'd better be glad you've got me. Listen, babe, you stay and talk to Edie while I go into the living room and make Mom pretty. Her hair needs a trim," she said to Edie, "And, naturally, she won't let anyone but me work on it." She winked at Edie. "Now, be good, you two. I'll be back in a jiff to finish dinner."

"Let me give you a hand." Edie extracted herself

from the billowing contours of the couch. "What can I do?"

Ray hooted. "You mean you've learned to cook, Edith? What you going to feed us, stewed yak or something?"

"*Ray.*" Viv who had disappeared into the kitchen, reappeared in the doorway, grinning widely as she shook her head at her husband. "I told you to be nice. Ignore him, sweetie," she told Edie. "He's just showing off. Could you maybe make a salad?"

"I'll give it a try," Edie said, biting back a sarcastic response. In the kitchen, she eyed the wineglasses Viv had set in the sink. Her own was still full. Perhaps she'd just hold her breath and gulp it down; anesthesia against the rest of the evening. And then Ray was behind her, his arms around her waist. She removed his hands and turned to look at him. "Lettuce," she said, increasing the distance between them. "You wouldn't know if Viv has any tomatoes, I guess." She pulled open the refrigerator's stainless-steel door. Cold air hit her face. "Lettuce, lettuce, lettuce," she said. "Bottom drawer. Crisper. God, I've never seen a refrigerator this big. You could chill a…yak. Okay, lettuce."

"So how long has it been since I saw you last?" Ray asked. "Five years?"

"Six." She pulled out the lettuce and closed the door. Ray leaned against the sink, arms folded across his chest. She'd taken his measure, too; he had lines around his eyes now, the thick blond hair had faded and thinned, and the smile that had made her knees weak in high school struck her as goofy now. Her face colored, anyway. "When I came back for the high-school reunion, you and Viv were on vacation. Before that it was Mom's heart attack. That was the last time."

He nodded. "Sorry I couldn't be at the airport to meet you. School board meeting. New principal's big on everyone attending. What do you think of him? Kind of out of place with Luther kids, isn't he?"

"Oh, I don't know." She took the lettuce to the sink and began separating leaves. "He seemed fine to me. What do you see as the problem?"

"Aagh." Ray shrugged. "Don't even get me started. He won't last long, that's all I know. I could have had the job if I'd wanted it. School board practically begged me, but I wasn't interested—too much work. I've got a family. The boys. More important things in life than chaining yourself to a desk." He laughed. "'Course, I'm probably telling that to the wrong person, right, Eed?"

Edie felt the knot in her shoulders ratchet up another notch. Salad. Could she possibly do a Caesar? She'd once spent half a day putting together a Caesar salad for Ben. Finding the necessary ingredients in a shattered Belgrade marketplace had been a challenge, but he'd confessed to a nostalgic yearning for the kind of Caesar salad he'd enjoyed at a certain Los Angeles restaurant. He'd been unimpressed, less by the salad than by what the effort said about her priorities. "Don't go getting domestic on me, Edie," he'd warned. "It's not what I need or want."

She took a couple of eggs from the fridge and set them in a pan of water to simmer. Back at the fridge, she dug around for anything resembling Parmesan. She could feel Ray's eyes on her back.

"So what time will the boys be here?" She thought again about the nephews she'd watched grow, mostly through pictures sent by Vivian, from cute, wide-eyed babies to strapping, athletic teenagers and felt a stab of remorse. "I will get to see them, right?"

"Oh sure," Ray said vaguely. "Hey, Eed, remember that day after school when we were goofing around in your mom's kitchen and I squeezed Thousand Island dressing into your mouth?"

Edie watched his face for a moment. "Not a day goes by that I don't relive that experience, Ray. It haunts my dreams."

Ray's forehead creased. "You being sarcastic?"

"Bingo."

"You ever try not being sarcastic for more than five minutes?"

"Once. I was bored."

Ray shook his head. Clearly, there was no hope for her. He took a beer from the fridge, popped the top, and stood with his back against the granite countertop watching her move around the kitchen.

"You were pretty hot back then," he said.

"Thank you, Ray. So were you. Back then."

"You ever think about the way things might have turned out if we'd stayed together?"

"No, Ray." She looked directly at him. "I don't. I'm happy with my life. And it looks like you're doing well too. This house, by the way," she said with a sweeping gesture at the kitchen, "is amazing."

"You like it? Viv give you the grand tour?"

"She did." Behind the jars of mayonnaise and bottles of ketchup and mustard, Edie found a green tub of grated Romano cheese. "It's huge. You guys must get lost going from one room to another." She set the cheese down on the center island. Out in the living room, she could see the top of Maude's white head. Her mother had all but disappeared amidst the massive pillowy cushions of the couch. The coffee table on which Maude's feet rested was several feet of mirrored glass atop a low chrome cylinder. "Very elegant," Edie said. "Impressive."

Ray gave her a look that seemed to calculate her sincerity. "But it isn't what you'd buy, right?"

"What does that matter? It's your house."

Ray smiled. "But you'd buy something down in the Historic District, wouldn't you?" he persisted. "If you ever settled down and came back home, I mean. Every time Viv and I go down Roosevelt, we see this old Victorian place that's been for sale forever and she always says, 'That's what Edie would go for.'"

Edie shrugged, thinking of the astronomically priced bungalow off Sunset Boulevard she'd once been tempted to buy, mostly because it reminded her of some of the older homes in Little Hills. For what it cost, she could have bought two of them and had change to spare.

"It's a moot point, Ray, because I'm not about to settle down and come back home. Married to my work," she said. "Kind of like your new principal."

"Goddamn butterfly collector." His expression darkened. "Thanks for mentioning him again, Edie. Now you've ruined my mood altogether. Head stuck up in the clouds. Hasn't figured out that we're dealing with a bunch of loser kids. They're not going to be Rhodes scholars, for God's sake. Get 'em in, get 'em out, that's the best you can do with them."

"So what?" She asked and then, too late, remembered Vivian's admonition. She pushed on, anyway. "He thinks some of them might have potential or something?"

Ray narrowed his eyes at her. "You haven't changed a whole lot, have you?"

"I guess not," she said. "Neither have you."

"See, that's what I mean. With you, everything has

to turn into some goddamn battle. You really don't give a damn whether I'm right or wrong about this guy. You just want an argument. Well, I'll tell you. Give Peter Darling six months around some of those kids at Luther and I bet you a six-pack he won't be collecting butterflies for long.''

"God, Edie,'' Vivian said from the doorway. "I told you not to get Ray fired up. Now you've ruined the whole evening.''

"THE LAST THING I want to do is interfere in your life,'' Peter's sister, Sophia, said as they sat on a park bench watching the children play. "But it's nearly two years now and, quite honestly, as much as I adore the girls, I do have a life back in England. This popping back and forth for extended visits is getting a bit much.''

"Has George complained?'' George was Sophia's longtime companion, but Peter gathered that the relationship was problematic. So much so that when Sophia first volunteered to come and look after the girls, she'd intimated that it would be a relief to put some distance between herself and George. In the last few weeks though, George had been calling quite frequently.

"He's grumbling a bit, but it's not that, really. I don't quite trust anyone to handle the nursery as well as I can. It's silly of me—I'm sure Trudy does a perfectly competent job—but I envision the assistants selling half-dead flowers and not offering the kind of variety people have come to expect.''

"I don't expect you to stay forever, Sophia. The girls know that, too.''

He stretched his legs out. His oldest daughter, Natalie, was pushing the twins on side-by-side swings. Natalie was eight; Abbie and Kate were four. Delphina, the seven year-old, sat off to one side, her expression wistful. A quiet and solitary child, she seemed always in the shadows of her sisters' play. He worried about Delphina. He worried about them all. Natalie was saddled with too much responsibility for a child of her age; the twins still sucked their thumbs. Last night, Abbie had wet the bed—the third time in a week.

"Peter—" Sophia knocked on his temple "—are you in there somewhere?"

"Thinking," he said.

"Not about a sudden sighting of the swallow-tailed thingamajig, I hope."

"Painted swallowtail." He grinned. "Actually it *was* rather unusual to spot one so far north this late in the year…but no, I was thinking about what you were saying. You've been an incredible help with the girls, but I do understand that you need to go home."

"What will you do?"

"Look around for a live-in nanny, I suppose. I'd planned to do that after Deborah died…"

Sophia rubbed his arm.

"I'm fine."

"Still miss her?"

"Of course."

"Life goes on, though."

"Please spare me the homilies, Sophia. I'll work things out in my own way."

"I'm sure you will."

"Deborah was always very pragmatic and unsentimental," he said. "As soon as we knew how ill she was we discussed what would happen with the girls. She was convinced I'd be married within the year. Quite adamant really that I *should* be married, that it would be better for us all."

"I always did admire Deborah's intelligence," Sophia

said. "Pity that her husband is less gifted in that regard."

Peter shot her a sideways glance.

"Well, for heaven's sake, Peter. Look at that Amelia woman you were so besotted with. The girls didn't have the foggiest idea what to make of her. And she was obviously quite bewildered by them. Honestly, sometimes I want to grab your shoulders and shake you very, very hard. How could you not have seen that this woman was all wrong for you? It was apparent to me the moment you introduced her."

"Perhaps you should have warned me."

"I did."

"Oh." He grinned. "Perhaps I should have listened."

"Why *won't* you find a nice woman?"

"Amelia was nice."

"Amelia was an actress."

"Actresses can't be nice?"

"I wouldn't know firsthand, Peter, my life being considerably less exotic than yours, but Amelia struck me as…a tart."

"Sophia," Peter said, "Amelia wasn't a tart. Perhaps not a candidate for marriage, but not a tart."

"Well, that's as may be," Sophia said darkly. "But why are you drawn only to unsuitable women?"

"Because," Peter said honestly, "as much as I'd like to meet a woman who could love the girls and create the sort of home Deborah and I had, I want more than a mother replacement. *I* want to be in love."

"Of course you do," Sophia said. "And?"

"And I've discovered that I'm not particularly attracted to nice women who want to settle down and have children."

"Rubbish." Sophia dismissed the comment with a flap of her hand. "You simply have to put your mind to it. What we need,'' she said briskly, ''is a plan. Now, wipe that stupid grin off your face and think very carefully. Not about the kind of woman to whom you've typically been attracted… We're looking for wife material. Start naming names. We're thinking sweet, potentially maternal and absolutely not flighty. Come on, there must be someone at school. Think hard.''

''Betty Jean Battaglio,'' he said after five minutes of not very hard thinking.

''Good.'' Sophia smiled. ''Tell me about her.''

''She's my secretary,'' he said.

Sophia looked dubious. ''Hmm. Not always advisable to dip the pen into the company inkwell, as it were, but if you're discreet… What does she look like?''

''Dark hair, blue eyes. Pictures of cats all over her desk.''

''Loves animals.'' Sophia nodded. ''Sounds promising. What else?''

''Won a gold medal at the Little Hills fair for her cherry cobbler.''

''Enjoys cooking. Perfect,'' Sophia said. ''And she's single?''

''Widowed.''

''Widowed?'' Sophia arched an eyebrow. ''How old is she?''

''Sixty-five,'' Peter said. ''We're in the process of planning her retirement party.''

Sophia gave a snort of disgust. ''You're just not taking this seriously.''

''Yes, I am,'' Peter said and, just to prove it, the following morning he called Edie Robinson to invite her to the theater.

CHAPTER THREE

"THE THEATER?" When the phone rang, Edie had braced herself for another sisterly self-improvement lecture. Now she sat on the floor in the hallway of her mother's house talking to Peter Darling. "Let me guess. *Madame Butterfly.*"

Peter laughed. "No, unfortunately. I don't think it's playing anywhere. But will you join me, anyway?" he asked. "Saturday night."

She shifted the phone to her other ear. Peter's voice was almost inaudible. "You know what, Peter? I can hardly hear you. Are you whispering or something?"

"Just speaking softly. I'm over at the teen mother center and—"

"Is that where Beth works? Is she there?"

"She's talking to a student."

"Can she hear what you're saying?"

"No, of course not."

"Why of course not?"

"Because I don't as a rule broadcast details of my private life. What does my asking you to the theater have to do with Beth, anyway?"

She's in love with you, Edie thought. Besotted, infatuated, head over heels—at least according to my sister, who also thinks you're gorgeous and could, of course, be doing a little projecting. God, it was so much easier to fly in and out of trouble spots. Perhaps she should drop a hint to Peter about Beth's feelings for him. Maybe Beth wouldn't appreciate it, though. She herself would definitely not appreciate someone intervening on her behalf, especially with a co-worker. Better to say nothing.

"Edie?" Peter said. "Are you still there?"

"Yes, sorry, I was thinking."

"And what's the verdict?"

"No, I'm sorry, Peter. Thank you for asking, but I really can't."

"A jealous boyfriend in a safari suit?"

"Safari suit?" She laughed. "You've seen too many movies."

"But a jealous boyfriend nevertheless?"

"Essentially."

"Perhaps we could take your mother as a chaperon," he said. "I'll buy another ticket."

"Thank you," she said, "but no. Here's an idea, though. Beth absolutely loves the theater."

"Does she?" Peter asked with no discernible enthusiasm. "Hmm."

Don't tell me I've never done anything to make a difference in someone's life, Edie thought as she replaced the receiver. And give me some credit for generous self-sacrifice. A night at the theater with Peter Darling has a whole lot of appeal. A whole lot of appeal.

PETER HAD JUST HUNG UP and was nursing his rejection, when Beth Herman dropped by his office with a picture of a butterfly. Beth wanted him to identify the butterfly before she hung the picture in her classroom.

"Hmm." He lowered his head to peer closely. "It looks rather like *Heliconius charithonius*. Note the long narrow black-and-yellow stripes on the wing. Although, of course," he added solemnly, "the *charithonius* is not exactly indigenous to the state of Missouri."

"I just assumed they were painted ladies," Beth said. "But then that's pretty much the only butterfly I know of." She turned and retrieved a paper-wrapped package from her tote bag. "A little gift for you." Her face colored as she handed it to him. "Nothing much. I just saw it and thought of you."

"How kind." He smiled at her. Beth had curly brown hair flecked with gray and wore a long gauzy skirt and the sort of knobby woolen cardigan his aunt Beatrice used to knit. Actually, she rather reminded him of his aunt Beatrice—same gentle demeanor and low, patient voice. A thought hit him like a thwack to the side of the head. He took a closer look at Beth. Although not his type, which he supposed was the good news, Beth was really rather...sweetly attractive. He realized he was staring.

Beth, blushing wildly, smiled at him. "Open it," she said.

He tore through several layers of paper and tissue. Shortly after he'd accepted the position at Luther, the school district had sent over a press-information person to interview him for the newsletter. Foolishly, he'd mentioned his avocation. Now a day didn't go by in which someone didn't present him with a butterfly knickknack. His classroom shelves were, embarrassingly, full of the sort of cups, plates and assorted trinkets that had once collected dust in his grandmother's parlor. What he couldn't bring himself to mention was that while he derived a great deal of pleasure from observing the insect in its natural habitat, he had no interest at all in painted depictions. Still, he felt quite certain that Sophia would approve of Beth.

As he removed yet another layer of paper, he glanced up briefly to see that Beth had been joined by a couple of other teachers, three students and the school security guard. All were grinning expectantly.

"Ah." He removed a mug emblazoned with spring blooms and, of course, a dozen or so garishly colored butterflies, none of which bore the faintest resemblance to anything he'd ever seen in nature. "Ah," he said again.

"What kind are they, Mr. Darling?" one of the students asked.

"Not absolutely certain." He turned the mug this way and that and frowned as though in deep thought. "Possibly something indigenous to Hong Kong. Intriguing design. Thank you, Beth. You're very kind." Perhaps we should have dinner, he thought. With everyone milling around though, it struck him as a less-than-opportune moment to extend an invitation.

"Well…" She smiled. "I'm glad you like it."

"Absolutely." He tried to picture Beth with the girls. Perhaps she would draw Delphina out of her shell. He thought she might. "Well," he said. "Thank you. Again."

She left then and he relegated his marriage quest to the far recesses of his brain. He spent an hour monitoring the performance of a newly hired English teacher, then headed back to administration. On the way, he encountered several people requiring his attention. A student who assured him she would literally die if she couldn't get her schedule changed, a math teacher who wanted to explain the failing grade she'd been forced to give, a parent alleging her son was being unfairly singled out for discipline just because he'd dyed his hair blue. Peter listened and nodded and made assurances that he would look into the matter, even as part of his mind was formulating a program to completely redesign the school grounds and provide entry-level job training in landscape design and horticulture for a group of particularly hard-core senior boys.

Throwaways. That was the term often used to describe Luther students—children who, for one reason or another, failed to thrive in their regular high school and transferred to Luther to accrue the credits needed to graduate. The view of Luther High, more commonly known as Loser High, as little more than a way station on the road to a life of drug dealing, petty crime and welfare was surprisingly entrenched. He intended to change all that.

"Mr. Darling. Mr. Darling."

In the reception area of the administration building, a girl with a swinging ponytail and silver hoops at her ears waylaid him.

"Mr. Darling, I need to talk to you." Her eyes widened. "It's real important."

"Mr. Darling." The security guard had also found him. "Just so you know, the hinge on room 220 is still broken."

"Peter," a counselor called from the copier machine. "Got a problem I need to discuss with you."

"Hey, Pete." Ray Jenkins, the assistant principal, clasped Peter's arm. "We're still on to meet at two?"

Peter nodded. He didn't often instinctively dislike someone, but just the sound of Ray Jenkins's plaintive nasal twang irritated him. Equally irritating were Jenkins's overly chummy insistence on addressing him as Pete, his habit of parking the bloody great monster of a truck he drove in a way that took up half of Peter's own space, and the assistant principal's stunning familiarity with, seemingly, every section of the Missouri Educational Code.

In his office, Peter sat down behind his desk, folded his hands and regarded the girl with the silver earrings who had followed him in. Melissa Fowler wore the unofficial Luther girls' uniform. Jeans that, threadbare knees aside, might have been sprayed on, a minuscule pink shirt and enormous clunky black shoes.

"How are you, Melissa?"

"Good."

He met her eyes for a moment and her face went red.

"Well, my Mom got fired, so it's been kind of crazy. I have to baby-sit my little sisters—"

"They're how old?"

"Two and three. And my brother's four. My mom had this really cool bartending job. She was making a ton of money, but then I guess she got into this thing with her boss—he's this huge jerk—and now she's looking for another job." Her face worked and she twisted one leg behind the other one. "See, the thing is, I know I didn't do so good last semester…"

"Well," Peter corrected.

"Well, I didn't." Melissa said. "But now I'm doing really good, right? And now, like, I really want to graduate from my old school, Stephen's High, with my friends." She hesitated. "I want to be like that lady who came to talk to us yesterday. The reporter? She was really interesting. I'm thinking that's what I want to do. I feel really, like, inspired."

"Good." Peter sat back in his chair. "Very glad to

hear it. You've seen the error of your ways, as it were, and are eager to diligently apply yourself.''

She grinned. "I guess."

Peter swiveled his chair to face the computer, tapped in her name and brought up her record. Melissa was luckier than most of the students at Luther. No father in the picture, but a mother who at least cared enough to attend the teacher-parent nights. Which did little to alter the reality that Melissa was essentially a fourteen-year-old substitute mother who, between meal preparation, child care and other domestic responsibilities, had precious little time left for schoolwork.

As her record came up, Peter reminded himself, as he did on a daily basis, of the parting advice the former principal had offered. "These kids can get you right here." He'd tapped his chest. "You can care deeply. You have to care. But at the same time, you must keep an emotional distance. If you don't, you'll destroy yourself. And you won't do the children much good, either."

"Right, then," Peter said. "You need one hundred and twenty credits to graduate. So far, you only have fifty. Shall we talk about what we need to do?"

Fifteen minutes later, Melissa was gone and Ray Jenkins was sitting in the chair she had occupied. Ray was, Peter guessed, at least five years his senior and had thinning fair hair, faded blue eyes and a pallor that suggested most of his waking hours were spent indoors. Peter had seen framed pictures on Ray's office wall of his two sons in football uniforms. Both had the tall, blond, athletic looks that Peter imagined Ray had once possessed. And, something else about Ray, a weary sort of bitterness about the assistant principal made Peter suspect that not being promoted probably wasn't the first disappointment in his life.

"She's basically a goof-off," Ray said after Peter described the course he'd laid out for Melissa. "Don't let her con you. The real reason she's so hot to go back to Stephen's is she started hanging around my son again."

"She has a boyfriend, doesn't she?" Peter thought for a moment. "Yes, I know she does. Marcus Adams. I managed to get him into an auto-shop program and he was absolutely rhapsodizing about her. No driver's license yet, but he rides his bicycle over to her house and helps her baby-sit."

Ray's lips curled slightly. "That's this week. All I know is she's always calling the house to talk to Brad. He said he felt sorry for her once and took her to a movie. Now he can't get rid of her."

"Yes, well," Peter said. "I'm sure we all dimly remember what fourteen was like." He got up from the desk and wandered to the window, where out on the quad, a vigorous game of basketball was under way. After a moment, he turned to look at the assistant principal. "Melissa is a bright, resourceful girl and I personally have a great deal of confidence in her."

Ray smirked. "Well, good for you. I guess I've just been around these kids a lot longer than you have."

Peter said nothing, and they moved on to other matters. Twenty minutes later, Ray stood as though to leave. Hands in pockets, he hesitated at the door.

"So what d'you think of my sister-in-law, the hotshot foreign correspondent? Ms. Been-Everywhere-Done-Everything?" His tone invited criticism, but when it wasn't forthcoming he smiled. "Still, the kids seemed interested. She knows her job, I'll give her that."

Peter allowed the remark to drift into a vacuum of silence, broken after a while by the sound of Ray jingling change in his pockets. As he filed away a couple of folders, Peter recalled the assistant principal's whispered remark after Edie's speech, and decided that it was unlikely that the relationship had ended in the way Ray had described. What he found remarkable was that it had ever gotten off the ground in the first place. It would be interesting to know the real story, he thought, picturing Edie again. "I've had four students express an interest in a journalism career since her talk," he told Ray. "In fact, I'm turning over the idea of starting a campus newsletter—"

"Won't work," Ray said. "Waste of time and money, I'm telling you right now."

Peter eyed the assistant principal. Pity it was so damn difficult to fire state employees, he mused.

"GIRLS' NIGHT OUT," Vivian said when she dropped by Maude's around six that evening. "Pitchers of margaritas, waiters in tight black pants. Move it, Edie. Drag yourself off the couch. You're turning into an old woman. Speaking of which…"

"She's upstairs resting." Edie pushed her glasses over the top of her nose and looked at Viv, all dressed up in snazzy designer jeans and a leather bomber jacket. "Count me out," she said. "I'm exhausted. A bubble bath, a glass of wine and a book in bed strikes me as the perfect way to spend the evening. Old woman or not."

"Oh, come on, Eed. How often do we see you? Come on, go upstairs and fix yourself up. It'll be fun. You might meet Mr. Right, fall in love and have half a dozen children in quick succession.''

''I hate to break it to you, but that scenario does nothing for me.''

''Get up.'' Viv pulled at her fingers. ''Make yourself pretty, and when you're done I'll tell you Peter's latest crazy idea. Ray just got through ranting about it. Anyway, I want you to get together with Beth. We can all drink margaritas and reminisce about the days when we were all young and sexy. There's going to be a whole bunch of us...''

As Vivian began to name names, Edie tried to think of a convincing reason not to go. She hated girlie gabfests, mostly because they invariably involved too much self-revelation, something she considered an unwise indulgence. What was the point of sitting around talking about your fears and insecurities? She'd never yet heard of anyone's life changing as the result of one of these sessions. Mostly you drank too much, got maudlin, and then toddled on home to behave the same way you always had.

Anyway, she'd spent too many years creating her self-protective coloring. If she started yammering about how she really felt inside, in no time others would see her that way too. Once at a conference, she'd had drinks in a hotel bar with a colleague whom she had always seen as supremely confident but a little cool and aloof. After a third glass of wine, the woman had confessed to being scared to death much of the time; the cool exterior really masked a basic shyness. Edie never saw her the same way again and, she hated to admit, she had lost confidence in the woman's decision-making skills.

But she dragged herself up off the couch, anyway.

"Sue Ellen Barnes?" Edie asked several hours later as she dipped a tortilla chip into a bowl of salsa and glanced from Viv to Beth. They were in Casa Julio's, perched on stools pulled up to tall tables. Vivian had ordered a pitcher of strawberry margaritas that sat, nearly empty now, in the middle of the table. The others had left and it was just herself, Viv and Beth. "Who did she marry? That guy with the red hair? What was his name?"

"John Yardley," Beth and Vivian shouted in unison.

"Now she's Sue Ellen Barnes-Yardley." Edie giggled. She'd eaten nothing but bar snacks for hours, and the margaritas were making her feel slightly buzzed. "What about Helen Anderson?"

"She's on her second husband, I think," Beth said. "And so is Frana Van Bergen."

"You know who else just got married again?" Elbows on the counter, Vivian looked at Edie. "That really stuck-up girl who transferred from Ladue, Karen something-or-other."

They all shook their heads, baffled that snotty Karen could even snare one husband, let alone two. Earlier, the focus had been shoptalk—problem students, mostly. All the women except for herself and Viv worked at Luther; Edie had just tuned out. Every so often, a fragment of chatter from the dressed-for-success crowd had risen above the ambient noise, drifting over to where she sat. "A hundred grand in five years, that's my goal." "You gotta be focused. If you're not, there's someone right behind you who is." "Nah, she's lost her edge."

She'd tuned back in to hear Beth, her face impassioned, say, "But the whole goal of the program is to help the next generation of students get off to a healthy start.''

Around the table, heads had nodded in agreement. ''...difficult for anyone who isn't in this field to really appreciate how fantastic it is just knowing that you've truly made a difference in the course of a student's life,'' one of the teachers had said with a glance at Edie. And then, ''You must be bored, huh? Bunch of teachers sitting around talking shop.''

And then Vivian, apparently sensing a need to draw Edie more fully into the conversation, had said, ''Almost anything would seem boring compared to what Edie does. She's the family success story. I married her reject and stayed home and had babies. Edie went off to live a glamorous life in New York.''

And Edie had protested that it wasn't all that glamorous, but all the women had been looking at her and, she knew damn well, imagining a life that bore little resemblance to their own reality. She'd felt fraudulent, envious of these women who could talk so passionately about changing lives. Suddenly, feeling profoundly alone, she'd excused herself and found the rest room. Two women had stood at a bank of mirrors, laughing and talking as they applied lipstick.

She had a glimpse of loose blond hair and red lips as she'd slipped past them and into a cubicle. They were at least a decade younger and she'd thought, I hate them. I hate them because the tarnish and weariness haven't set in. They don't know yet that they won't always be beautiful; that they won't conquer the world, marry the man, have the babies. Make a difference. She'd draped the toilet seat with a paper cover and sat until she heard them leave. Stood then and leaned her forehead against the cool metal surface of the door. I need, she'd thought. I need, I need, I need. But what?

"Earth to Edie," Viv was saying now. "She's in a foxhole," she said with a wink at Beth. "Shoulder to shoulder to a hunky marine."

"Right," Edie said, rallying. "And I haven't showered for a week and neither has he." She drained the margarita, tasting the gritty strawberry seeds, the sweet, fruity ice. "So, Beth," she said. "How come you haven't joined the married-with-children club?"

Beth smiled sadly. "I don't know, really. One minute it seemed as though I had all the time in the world, and I just knew I'd have children and a husband, the whole thing. And then I woke up and I was forty and there was no one even on the horizon."

Vivian gave a small, conspiratorial smile and leaned slightly toward Beth. "Except for Peter," she whispered.

"Oh, Peter." Beth's expression turned dreamy. "Be still my heart. Today, he told me about his little girl's dance recital. Delphina, the quiet one he always calls her. I've met them all. Delphina's this solemn little thing with huge dark eyes. The twins, Kate and Abbie, are adorable blond angels, and Natalie is an absolute sweetheart. She's the little mother."

Vivian arched an eyebrow at Edie. "Kind of sounds like Beth might be more in love with the girls than she is with Peter, doesn't it?"

"I just love children," Beth said. "And Peter's so sweet when he talks about them. He came in this morning with this big stain on his shirt pocket where Natalie had put a sandwich. Some men would have been embarrassed to walk around all day like that. He's the principal, after all. But Peter's much more focused on the idea that his little girl made him lunch.'' Her face colored. ''I just think he's really a sweet, sweet man... I just want good things to happen for him.''

''You'd be a good thing,'' Vivian said.

Beth smiled. ''Edie, if you haven't noticed, your sister is trying to set me up with Peter. She thinks we'd be perfect together. And your sister, in case you haven't noticed that, either, happens to be very determined when she sets her mind to anything.''

Viv hooted. ''Me, determined? You don't know determined until you know Edie. Once she makes her mind up on something, nothing's going to change it.''

''A family trait,'' Edie said, thinking of Maude. ''So, are you interested in Peter?'' she asked Beth. ''Personally.''

''Of course she is,'' Viv said. ''How could she not be?''

Edie looked at Beth, waiting for her to answer. With her nondescript brown hair pulled into a straggling ponytail, no makeup and an unflattering orange knit sweater, Beth looked like the before picture of a makeover candidate. Not without potential, but at the moment, clearly untapped.

An assessment Beth confirmed a moment later. ''I don't think I'm exactly Peter's type,'' she said. ''A few weeks ago I was in administration and this tall gorgeous woman came in. Everyone was looking at her. The security guard's jaw just about dropped. She asked for Peter, and Betty Jean let her into his office. Apparently, she's this actress he was dating.''

''But he's not dating her now,'' Viv said. ''Ray heard Peter telling her not to bother him anymore.''

"Well, it doesn't matter," Beth said. "Clearly, that's the type of woman he's interested in."

"Beth." Elbows on the table, Viv looked at her friend. "He needs a mother for those children. Betty Jean told Ray. He's not looking to marry an actress. You just need to work at it, let him see you're interested."

"But I don't know if I am," Beth said. "I think I might feel...inadequate."

"No, no." Viv shook her head. "You and Peter would be perfect together. Men are just sometimes slower to catch up. Although," she said with a little smile, "sometimes you do get that gut feeling. I remember with Ray. Everyone said, 'Oh he's still in love with Edie, he's just marrying you on the rebound,' but I knew."

Edie clasped her hands. A pain that had started at the top of her scalp was gathering strength. "The thing is," she said. "It's sometimes difficult to know what guys are thinking. You know how you can kind of read things into situations? See what you want to see?" Edie really wanted to go home and stick her head under the covers. "All I'm saying is, Beth, a friend of mine told me years later that she really wished someone had told her right from the start that this guy was never in love with her. It was just a difficult call, though."

"Excuse me," Beth said as she hurried from the room.

"What the hell is with you?" Vivian glared at Edie. "Beth has been glowing all evening and it's like you just poured a bucket of cold water over her. Why don't you keep your damn cynical opinions to yourself and quit spoiling things for everyone else?"

"I honestly didn't mean to rain on her parade," Edie said. "I was just telling her—"

"Next time, try telling yourself to butt out," Viv snapped.

Edie returned home to find a message from Maude scrawled on a note under the phone.

Gone to bed. A man called I told him he had the wrong number but he kept calling back and asking for Fred so I wrote down his number just to get some peace and quiet you better call him we need more toilet paper and don't get that thin stuff again my fingers go right through it. Love Mom.

CHAPTER FOUR

WITH A SMILE, Edie folded the note and put it in her pocket. The infrequent letters Maude sent her were written the same way; long, garbled, stream-of-consciousness missives without a hint of punctuation. She dialed the number she knew by heart and reached a colleague and friend she'd known since their days in the *Times* London bureau. A grizzled bearlike man approaching retirement, Fred Mazare had probably reported from every country in the world during his forty-odd years in journalism. A gold mine of information on anything from overseas press clubs—he knew them all—to public transport in Bangkok—he recommended *tuk tuks*—Fred was mentor, father figure, confidant and friend all rolled into one untidy, overweight, cigar-smoking curmudgeon. He picked up the phone on the first ring.

"Where the hell have you been?" he demanded, "And who was that old bat who answered the phone?"

"Out with the girls," she said, grinning because it felt so damn good to hear his voice. "And watch how you talk about my mother."

"How're things going?"

"Oh…" She rubbed her eyes. "I'm home. Does that tell you anything?"

"Yep. It tells me you're about as out of place as a nun in a brothel."

She laughed. "Hmm, I'll have to think about that one." Her back against the wall, the phone cord wrapped around her wrist, she slid down to the floor. "Why do I feel so…weird whenever I come home, Fred?"

"One, you don't belong there anymore. Two, you're trying to convince yourself into believing that you do."

"I am?"

"Sure you are. Probably hooked up with an old boyfriend and he's trying to talk you into settling down—"

"Wrong."

"Okay. Your biological clock's ticking."

She groaned. "Oh please, if you can't come up with something more original…"

"Okay, Edie. Tell Uncle Freddy the problem as you see it."

"I just…have this empty feeling inside."

"You going soft on me?"

"No." She swiped the back of her hand across her nose. "Maybe I've had my fill of moving around. Maybe I need to settle, put down some roots." She swallowed. "Maybe you're not really so far off the mark about the biological clock."

"Highly possible," he agreed.

"But I'd hate to settle down in a place like Little Hills." She thought of Viv and her off-white leather couches and her endless chattering about Ray and the boys. She thought of Peter with his little girls. Beth all shiny-eyed as she'd called them angels. "I have nothing in common with these people."

"My guess is that you would if you decided Little Hills is what you're looking for," he said. "Ready for some news about Ben?"

She leaned her head back against the wall, closed her eyes. "Yeah."

"State Department's arranged for his release. Could be any day now."

She breathed a sigh. "Thank God."

"I spoke to his wife."

"Ex-wife."

"Tell her that."

"*He* told me that."

Fred laughed. "Ever strike you funny how people can be so cynical and hardheaded about things they want to believe and so damn gullible and stupid about other things?"

"Not so much funny as pitiful," she said. You're not breaking up my marriage, Edie, Ben had told her. It was broken long, long before I met you.

"Hey, Edie." Fred was saying, "Cut out the whiny broad stuff."

"I'm not whining."

"You're feeling sorry for yourself."

"Bull." Tears burned her nose. "I'm fine. Terrific."

"You've always had Ben's number..."

"I said I'm fine."

"Yeah well...listen, here's something that'll put a smile on your face. I heard your name mentioned the other day. How does Edie Robinson, Asia bureau chief, strike you?"

"ASIA? Wow, Edie, how exciting," Vivian enthused the next morning when Edie told her about the bureau chief job. "You know what, though? I don't envy you one bit. I tell you, when Ray and I got back from New York after our tenth anniversary, I was never so glad to be home."

"Yeah, I can imagine." Edie stuck the phone between her ear and shoulder and, as Viv rattled on, searched the refrigerator shelves for breakfast material. Another trip to the IGA seemed likely. She wanted to get off the phone with Viv, who was seriously beginning to get on her nerves. Irritation, like a small yappy dog kept on a tight rein ever since she'd hauled her bags into the back of Vivian's gleaming new SUV, was tugging hard at the leash. She bit experimentally into a withered apple, decided it was too far gone and dumped it into the trash.

Maude, upstairs clomping around, would be down any minute and they were out of coffee creamer, which would inevitably get the day off to a shaky start. I don't want to be here, Edie thought. I don't want to hear my mother tell me she needs prunes and I don't want to listen to my sister bitching to me about her hot flashes and her gourmet club. I am cold, unlovable and I *vant* to be alone.

"I know Little Hills seems boring to you," Viv was saying now. "But as far as we're concerned, there isn't a better place to raise kids. And that sort of thing matters to me and Ray," she said. "We're very serious about our kids."

"I know you are, Viv." Edie stuck her head in the fridge. The gas oven was also an option. Why didn't the prospect of a bureau chief job strike her with quite the sense of elation she'd thought it might? She'd stayed awake half the night trying to figure that one out. That and Ben's release—which she'd never had any doubt about—and the three years she'd wasted with him. "Don't expect commitment from me," he'd always say. Something she'd have understood much more readily had he also mentioned a wife back in the States.

Her mood didn't improve much that day and it wasn't much better the next, when someone from Maple Grove Residential Living called to inquire whether Maude was still interested in having her name added to the waiting list for residential apartments.

Edie, pacing the hallway with the black receiver lodged between her ear and shoulder, moved too far in one direction and the phone clattered to the floor, knocking over the spindly table it had been standing on. "Damn it."

"Excuse me?"

"Nothing." Edie stood the table up again and replaced the heavy black phone on its crocheted doily. "I was talking to the phone."

"Of course." The administrator cleared her throat. "When your sister and mother paid us a visit recently, they were both very impressed. Your sister did say that there were other places they wanted to investigate, but we were under the impression that they were definitely leaning toward Maple Grove."

Literally or figuratively? Edie wanted to ask. "I don't think my mother's made a decision yet," Edie said. "In fact, I'm sure she hasn't, but let me check with my sister."

"That would be Vivian Jenkins?" the administrator asked.

"That would be," Edie said, irked by the woman's officious tone. In the mood she was in, Mother Teresa would have irked her.

"I was under the impression, from Mrs. Jenkins, that the decision had been made. Mrs. Jenkins is concerned that your mother is no longer capable of living alone. Your mother was so taken with Maple Grove, she wanted to move in on the spot."

"Well, that may be," Edie said. "As I said, I'll check with my sister."

"We have very few vacancies," the woman said. "In

fact, that's why we were forced to create a waiting list. I would hate to see your mother lose out. She was so impressed—''

''I'll call you,'' Edie said and slowly replaced the receiver in its cradle. Tinkerbell, the most persistent of Maude's three cats, watched her balefully, his eyes the color of grapes. ''I hate salespeople,'' she told him. ''Actually, this morning, I hate everyone.''

The cat mewed and moved to snake its long orange body along Edie's bare calf.

''That will get you nowhere, trust me.'' On tiptoe, Edie reached for a jar of Ovaltine, thinking for a minute it might be coffee. Maude appeared to be out of coffee, which wasn't helping matters. She took down the jar, unscrewed the lid and peered inside at the dried-up cake of brown powder. ''Yuk.''

''Meow.'' The cat rubbed its ear against Edie's leg.

Edie nudged it gently with her toe. ''Look, if you want to get into my good books, run down to the corner and get me a double latte, okay? Maybe a bagel, too.''

Still musing on the phone call, a niggling sense that she'd somehow been shut out of an important decision prompted her to dial her sister's number. As usual, Vivian sounded harried.

''I'm trying to do a million things,'' she said, ''and the phone keeps ringing off the hook. Brad spilled root beer all over the family-room carpet and I've got someone coming in to clean it. Ray's in a permanent funk. By the way, I'm sorry I jumped at you the other night about Beth. You know I didn't mean it, right? I swear when I'm on a carb diet, I get the worse sugar withdrawal and—''

''Viv, some woman called from Maple Grove—''

''Oh right.'' A pause. ''I meant to tell you about

that… Look, if the carpet cleaners don't take too long, how about I drop by right after and we'll talk. Where is Mom, by the way?"

"A woman from church dropped by to pick her up. They were going to a potluck, or something. Mom was up before me this morning, making macaroni and cheese."

"Damn." Vivian exhaled loudly. "Dixie Mueller, right? Little tiny thing with white hair? Well, they're all little tiny things with white hair, but Dixie's…first of all she shouldn't be driving, so every time she takes Mom out, I have to worry about whether they'll get into an accident. And then Mom goes to these potlucks and eats too much and ends up calling me in the middle of the night convinced she's having a heart attack…"

Edie held the phone away from her ear as Vivian railed. I am completely out of my element, she thought. This is my mother, but I have no idea what's really in her best interests. "I'm sorry," she said after Vivian finally wound down. "Mom seemed really jazzed to be going out and I didn't know about—"

"It's not your fault, Edie. Don't blame yourself. It's just that I'm with Mom and you're not. And that's why she needs to be in a place like Maple Grove. She can't look after herself and I'm honestly worn out with looking after her."

"But there are other options besides a residential facility," Edie said. "She could have someone come in to help her. A live-in assistant, maybe. That way she could stay in the house—"

Vivian laughed. "Edie, Edie. You have no idea, do you? Live-in assistants cost money—"

"So do residential facilities," she pointed out. "I

might not be with Mom on a day-to-day basis, but I'm not entirely out of touch with the real world.''

"I didn't mean to suggest that you were," Viv said. "It's just that…well, I hate to keep saying the same thing over and over, but I'm here, Edie, and you're not.''

A theme that was beginning to sound so familiar, Edie thought, she could almost predict the moment Vivian would say it. Almost as predictable as Vivian's breathless complaints that she had a million things to do and really didn't have time to talk about this right now.

"…And I'm going out of my mind," Viv was saying now. "Do you have any idea at all how much food two teenage boys can consume?''

"Of course I don't," Edie said. "I don't have children.''

A moment of silence from the other end of the line. "Are you being sarcastic?" Vivian wanted to know. "Because if you are—''

"I was just stating a fact," Edie said. "You have kids and I don't.''

"I know, but you get that snippy tone in your voice… Anyway, I really don't have time to argue. I don't *want* to argue, let's put it that way. I don't see you often enough to spend time when you *are* here bickering with you.''

Having established the moral high ground, Viv then went on to complain about the paintwork in her newly finished upstairs bathroom, her neighbor's obnoxious dog who barked half the night and the ridiculous price of the boneless pork roast she'd bought for tomorrow's dinner with some friends who probably wouldn't be impressed, anyway.

As she listened, Edie wondered whether it would seem insufferably self-righteous if she attempted to lend some perspective to her sister's problems by describing the young girl she'd seen in Sarajevo—all dressed up in high heels and full makeup as she picked her way through the rubble from a recent mortar attack because, war or no war, life goes on. Or the women who sent their children to school during shell fire with the reassurances that they were probably safer at school than at home. Yeah, it would be insufferable, she decided, not to mention hypocritical. *You've never dwelled endlessly on your own petty problems?*

"By the way," Viv said, "I really am sorry for jumping on you lately. You must think I'm a total bitch. When I'm on a low-carb diet, I swear I get sugar withdrawal. Anyway, look, bottom line is we both have Mom's best interests at heart."

"Exactly," Edie agreed, "Which—"

"I'm sure it isn't easy for you to be back here, feeling that you're doing everything wrong, but face it, Eed, that's reality. You made your choice to go off and lead...your kind of life."

"But—"

"And I have no problem at all with looking after Mom. I mean, I told Ray, I said I don't even know why Edie's coming back, as busy as she is...but look, sweetie, I know you're concerned. Tell you what, how about we take Mom out to Maple Grove tomorrow and you can see the place for yourself?"

Meanwhile, Edie decided as she hung up the phone, she would have a little talk with Maude when she got back from her visit with Dixie—just the two of them. She might never know or understand Maude the way Viv did, but she could at least try to get to know her a little better.

Tomorrow, she would take Maude to lunch.

PETER'S PHONE RANG during the middle of a parent conference. Since he'd told Betty Jean to hold all calls other than emergencies, his first thought as he excused himself to pick up the receiver was that it was one of the girls. "Your sister," Betty Jean said. "She insisted that I put her through immediately."

Peter exhaled. "Yes, Sophia?"

"I'm calling for a progress report."

He frowned. "On what?"

"The wife search. What else?"

"Oh, that," Peter said, irritated. "Do you honestly think that I have nothing else... Listen, I'm in a meeting—"

"I just thought you might have given it a little thought."

"I have," Peter said without thinking first.

"And?"

"We'll talk about it later."

"A teacher?"

"No."

"What then?"

"A foreign correspondent."

"A foreign... Oh, Peter, that's ridiculous. They're gone all the time. You read about their lifestyles. How can that possibly work?"

"Not quite sure." Especially since she's now declined two invitations, he thought as he hung up on Sophia.

"Anyway, as I was saying, Mrs. Black...Patricia's academic progress would be enhanced considerably if she attended school more than two days a week. Let's talk a little about what we can do to ensure she gets up in time to catch the school bus in the mornings. An alarm clock would be an obvious first step..."

Sophia's second call came just as he was leaving his

office to head across campus. "Please forget about the foreign correspondent," she said. "It would be an enormous mistake. As soon as the girls begin to trust her, she'll be whisked off to Timbuktu, or somewhere, only to be shot at and God knows what else. Please tell me you weren't serious."

EDIE HAD ENVISIONED somewhere a little more celebratory for her getting-reacquainted lunch with Maude, but her mother had insisted on Mrs. Brown's Burger Bar: pumpkin-colored vinyl booths and anthropomorphic dancing pies painted on the windows. Maude liked Mrs. Brown's early-bird dinners. Edie glanced at the menu. A little insert offered a free slice of apple, chocolate or cherry pie with any order over six dollars.

"I don't want anything spicy," Maude was saying. "What are you having?"

"Salad." Edie set the menu down and looked at Maude. So far today things had gone quite smoothly. She hadn't slapped her forehead in exasperation, or sworn or wanted to shake Maude silly. I am becoming a better person, she decided. If not a paragon of saintly virtue, more patient and understanding. Compassionate, even. Earlier, as they had been getting into the car, she'd taken a second look at her mother's headgear and refrained from asking why Maude had chosen to go out wearing a tea cozy.

And last night, after her mother returned from the visit with Dixie Mueller, Edie had listened with a degree of patience she had no idea she possessed to Maude explain that she only ate eggs on Tuesdays except if it rained and then sometimes she'd have a banana, not because she was hungry, mind you, but because of the potassium, but if you stopped to think about it, she'd lived this long so if she wanted to eat eggs on Wednesdays, too, how could it hurt?

"This was nice, Edie," Maude had said when just before midnight she'd announced she was ready for bed. "It's been a long time since we've had a talk like this." And actually, Edie thought as she'd drifted off to sleep, it had been kind of nice. Not exactly the heart-to-heart, mother-daughter chat she'd once dreamed about, but peculiarly contenting, anyway. Of course, she'd had a couple of glasses of wine.

"What can I get you ladies?" The waiter, a tall gawky kid who appeared to be about twelve, thirteen max, looked from Edie to Maude, then reeled off a list of specials.

"I didn't get that," Maude told him. "Can you read them again?"

"Mom, what difference does it make?" Edie asked. Vivian had already warned her that Maude, when dining out, would eat nothing but fish and chips. "You're going to have fish and chips, anyway."

"Where's the chicken potpie?" Maude had picked up the menu again. "How much is it?"

"We don't have chicken potpie," the kid said.

"Chicken potpie," Maude said. "And a cup of coffee."

"They don't have chicken potpie," Edie told Maude. "Why don't you just have fish and chips like you always do?"

Maude eyed Edie, a tad suspiciously. "What are you having?"

Edie felt her hand move almost involuntarily to her head. She restrained it. "I'm having salad, Mom. I already told you."

Maude screwed up her face as if she'd just learned

that her daughter was going to dine on stewed yak.
"Salad?"

"Salad."

"I don't want salad. I'll have chicken potpie."

Edie slapped her head. "Mom! Look at me. *They
don't have chicken potpie.*"

"Don't shout at me." Maude raised her eyes to the
waiter. "See how my daughter talks to me?"

"Want me to come back in a few minutes?" he said.

"No," Edie said. "She'll have fish and chips."

"I don't know though." Maude was browsing the
menu again. "The last time I had chicken potpie here it
had bits of green pepper in it. I think I'll just have the
fish and chips. Edie, that man across the street keeps
looking at you."

Edie looked beyond the dancing pies to see Peter Darling leaving the hardware shop, smiling broadly. She realized with irritation, now back and in plentiful supply,
that her hair was lank and unwashed, she had on no
makeup and that she was wearing tatty elephant-colored
sweats. She drank some water and slouched down in the
booth as Peter approached. The life of the foreign correspondent wasn't always glamorous and exotic.

CHAPTER FIVE

As HE APPROACHED the booth where Edie sat opposite an elderly woman in a natty white knitted hat, Peter acknowledged, reluctantly, that Edie did not appear overjoyed to see him. By contrast, her companion was all smiles as she patted the booth beside her.

"Didn't recognize you from across the road," she said. "You're that assistant principal at my son-in-law's school. Saw you when my other daughter took me there so she could drop off Ray's lunch. He's on a low-sodium diet. You met Edie? She's a foreign correspondent, got shot at last year. I'm having the fish and chips. Edie's having the chicken potpie."

"Mmm." He met Edie's eyes across the table. As he remembered, they were amber, only slightly lighter than her hair. "I wasn't really hungry, but I quite like chicken potpie."

"They don't have chicken potpie." Edie looked as if she might have a headache. "I'm having a salad."

"If you don't mind the green peppers, the chicken potpie is good," Maude said.

"I think I'm going to sit here and go quietly insane," Edie said. "Hi, Peter. This is my mother, Maude Robinson, in case you weren't previously introduced. Mom—" she leaned across the table to Maude "—you remember Peter Darling?" She looked at Peter again. "School day over already?"

"No," he said. "I just came for the chicken potpie."

"Don't do this," she said.

"You ever seen Edith slap her head?" Maude asked. "That's what she did just before you got here. I said I wanted fish and chips and she slaps her head. She shouted at me, too."

"I should be locked away," Edie said. "What *are* you doing here?"

"I placed two students at the hardware shop across the street," he said. "It's a great arrangement. The school district partially subsidizes the shop owner. He gets a couple of assistants and the students get some real work experience while earning credits toward graduation."

She eyed him for a moment. "That must be gratifying."

He looked straight back at her. "It is. Very."

"I meant it sincerely," she said. "I wasn't being facetious."

"I didn't suspect for a moment that you were," he lied. Edie disquieted him. It was nothing overt; an enigmatic smile, the faint whiff of cynicism about her. He imagined that she saw him as painfully earnest, which he supposed he was. Well, earnest—not painfully, he hoped. Perhaps he should cultivate a new persona. Cavalier and brutish. *Take that insolent smirk off your face, wench, and get thee to the bedchamber.*

"My daughters both think I'm a senile old woman who doesn't have a clue in the world what's going on right in front of her eyes," Maude said. "They're trying to put me in a home."

Edie set down her water glass. The air went still. Peter tried to think of something to say. At his side, the old woman was sipping water, seemingly unaware that she'd just sparked a match to the conversational tinderbox.

"Edith hasn't been back here for donkey's years," the elderly woman said. "Too busy with her high-powered job. Now she decides it's time for poor old mom to be put away, so she comes out here to drag me around to these fancy high-priced places that are nothing more than storage rooms where you sit around and wait to die."

"Are you living in your own home at the moment?" Peter asked, trying only to defuse the tension. He didn't look at Edie, but he could feel her presence, glowering across the table. Beside him, Maude fiddled with her ear.

"Sorry. It's not that I'm deaf. I only wear my hearing aid when there's something I want to hear. Do I rent? No, I own my home. My husband and I bought it when our oldest daughter, Vivian, was born. Both the girls were raised in that house and now they're trying to make me move out—"

"Mom, that's absolutely not true," Edie said. "That's what we've been talking about. That's why I'm back. Viv said you want to move—"

"I didn't until she started showing me all these fancy brochures and then you come back and…" She looked at Peter. "Now they're both on at me. I never said stick me in a warehouse though, did I?" She glared at Edie. "I didn't say come out here and turn my life upside down—"

"Ah, food," Edie announced as the kid waiter approached. "Too bad I'm suddenly not hungry."

HALF AN HOUR, still shaking with anger, Edie helped Maude back into the car. As she walked around to the driver's side, Peter caught her arm. He'd gamely sat through the meal, engaging Maude in small talk about roses and gardening and preventing an incendiary situation from erupting into a wildfire. As they were leaving the restaurant, Maude had invited him and his daughters to dinner. Edie had been too furious to even listen for his reply. She looked at him for a moment, not trusting herself to speak.

"So." She forced a bright smile. "Here you have the real truth. Heartless daughters evict poor old mother...no, daughter. Singular. As Maude would have told you if you'd waited a little longer, Viv would never be so cruel. But then Viv didn't kill her father. Funny how Mom's never quite forgiven me for that." She stopped, appalled at what she'd just said. She could see confusion in Peter's face and something else, something tender and soft that made her want to run. "Sorry for that little outburst," she said. "Could we please rewind the tape?"

"Consider it done." His hand was on the top of the car now. He hadn't taken his eyes from her face. "It would be an understatement to say you've got a tricky situation, and I don't want to interfere in a family matter. But, if you need someone to talk to, you know where to find me."

"Thanks."

"I mean that." He reached into his pocket, pulled out a card and scribbled something on the back. "That's my number at home." He handed the card to Edie. "You're likely to get one of my daughters, and if it's Delphina, she'll want very much to read you a poem. She's quite talented. Of course, she'll be too shy to tell you that...but with a little coaching, you can draw her out."

"Thank you," she said again. She would never call, she knew that, but it was a sweet gesture. "I appreciate it."

"I mean it sincerely. The offer. I'm a very good listener. I also used to have an elderly mother…"

She smiled.

"I don't know why Ray doesn't like him," Maude said as they drove away. "Seems very nice to me. 'Course, you can never tell."

PETER HAD FELT some misgivings as he watched Edie drive away with Maude in the car. Perhaps he should have done more to calm her down. He could imagine the headlines in tomorrow's *Little Hills Union*. Noted Foreign Correspondent Throttles Elderly Mother. He'd felt the tension radiating off her.

He stood in the quad now, almost an hour later, watching a troupe of young actors, all dressed in black, perform for the assembled students. Perhaps he would ring her this evening, just to make sure everything was all right. He remembered that he'd meant to tell her how inspired the students had been by her talk. She'd like to hear that, he was sure.

Sophia might be right about the unsuitability of a foreign correspondent as a wife, but it would be very agreeable to get to know Edie as a friend. That said, how could it hurt to call? He did wonder, though, at the remark about killing her father. What was that all about? Bit of melodrama, maybe. One would hope.

On a stage across the quad, an antidrug message was being conveyed through mime, dance and ear-splittingly loud rap. His temples throbbing, he snaked a hand down over the shoulder of a boy in the back row and plucked a bag of sunflower seeds, forbidden on campus because of the mess they created, from the surprised boy's grasp. He wondered if, at forty-one, he was too old for this sort of thing.

And then Beth Herman tapped him on the arm. He shot her a quick sideways glance and did a double take. Normally, he didn't pay a great deal of attention to women's clothes—a shortcoming of which Amelia had frequently complained—but Beth's blouse was really quite extraordinary, patterned with brilliant butterflies that danced over her entire upper body. Another surreptitious glance revealed small black script identifying the various species. By then, mercifully, the music had stopped and he turned to take an even closer look, realizing as he did so that he was ogling her left breast.

"Sorry," he said, although Beth did not seem at all offended. "Very nice blouse." The students were now ambling off to their classrooms and Beth was smiling and it seemed necessary somehow to say something else. Would you like to be a mother to my children? seemed a bit peremptory. "Very nice cupcakes, too," he said instead.

"Cupcakes?"

"The cakes you brought in this morning with the little silver balls. Quite delicious."

"Oh," she said. "They weren't mine. One of my aides brought them in. I'll thank her on your behalf," she said. "Actually though, I do love to cook."

"And I'm sure you do it very well," he said, trying to imagine Amelia's response if he were to suggest she bake cakes. Probably about the same as if he were to suggest they marry and raise a dozen children together. Edie would react similarly, he suspected. But he must stop thinking about unsuitable women. Which reminded him of Edie again—or, rather, her mother. "I have a proposal," he said.

"A proposal?" Beth's face reddened and the pile of

papers she'd been carrying like a baby slipped from her arms and fell to the ground. "Sorry."

Peter joined Beth on the grass to help retrieve some papers that had been scattered by a sudden breeze. For a moment or so they were both on their hands and knees, and he glanced up to find Beth's nose inches from his own.

"A proposal?" she said again.

"A proposal." Peter held out his hand to help her up. "You seem a little…flustered."

"Flustered?" She raked her brown curls. "Oh no, no. I'm fine. I mean, this is the way I always am. Sorry. Um, what can I do for you?" She laughed. "Sorry, that didn't come out right—"

"Beth, you've just apologized for the third time in as many minutes," Peter said. "Stop it. You're making me feel like an ogre."

"An ogre? Oh no, I'm sorry I…"

Peter shook his head. She'd caught her lapse and was looking at him with such dismay that he couldn't help laughing. "I'm sorry…" He grinned. "God, you've got me doing it. Look, all I wanted to suggest—"

"Would you like some tea? I could make some if you'd like to walk back to the center. Peppermint? Apple? Chamomile?"

"Oh no, thank you." He loathed tea, particularly the herbal variety, but people were always offering him cups of it. "About my proposal, though. You do know Edie Robinson? I met her mother today and I rather had the sense that time hangs heavy on occasion and she becomes depressed. I know you're always short of volunteers and—"

"Perfect." Beth beamed. "The girls would love having a surrogate grandmother to help with the babies, and if Mrs. Robinson is anything like my mother, there's nothing she'd enjoy more than being surrounded by babies and young people."

"Good. I'll ring Edie today," he said, quick to grasp at any excuse. Perhaps he could determine whether there really was a safari-suited boyfriend, or if that was just a polite excuse, in which case... He realized that Beth was watching him as though she had something more to say. He smiled and she glanced down at her feet, then up at him.

"By the way, Peter..." She hesitated. "There's a butterfly exhibit at the Arboretum coming up soon. I have two tickets. I bought one for a friend who...uh, he can't make it. I wondered if you'd like to go."

"WHAT DID YOU GET?" Maude peered at the ice cream cone in Edie's hand. "Mine tastes like coffee. I wanted chocolate. I think they switched them and you've got the chocolate one."

"They're both chocolate, Mom. That's what we ordered." She bit into the ice cream, disposing of it quickly before it melted in the hot afternoon sun. They had driven downtown so that Maude could buy a knitting pattern and were sitting on a bench in the cobbled and historic Riverfront section, watching a troupe of street performers cartwheel and careen and toss what looked like bowling pins at one another. Red and yellow flowers bloomed in wooden tubs all along the street, more bouquets hung in moss-covered baskets from Victorian-era lampposts and a mild breeze blew off the river. It was all very pleasant, Edie thought, and if she weren't sitting there thinking about Maude's remarks to Peter, she might have enjoyed her surroundings.

"Let me taste yours," Maude said. "I know I've got the wrong one."

Edie took a breath. "They're *both* chocolate, Mom." Maude said nothing, but her disgruntled expression showed she was unconvinced. She sat there on the bench, a tiny, white-haired presence absolutely unshaken in her belief that she'd been cheated out of the flavor she really wanted. Exasperated, Edie wanted to grab the damn cone, throw it to the cobbled street, and stamp up and down on it. It was her mother's quality of implacable certainty that drove her nuts. Maude was right and that was that. *You're never wrong, are you, Edie?* she heard Ben saying. She glared at her own dripping cone and then thrust it at Maude. "Here. Take mine. We'll swap."

Maude took a tentative lick of the exchanged cone. "Told you," she said. "Now, this one *is* chocolate. I knew that wasn't chocolate. I might be old but I haven't lost my sense of taste."

"Good. Enjoy it." Edie counted slowly to ten before she turned on the bench to look at Maude. "Turn your hearing aid up, okay?" she said in a low, distinct voice. "I want to talk to you."

"I've got if off," Maude said. "When you shout, it hurts my ears."

"I'm not going to shout," Edie said. *Fat chance.* "Please leave it on, okay?"

"I can hear without it." Maude licked her ice cream cone. "It's only you and Vivian that think I need a hearing aid. I just thought of something. We need to stop at the IGA. They've got bacon on sale. I like to put it over the top of the meat loaf, it makes it nice and juicy. Vivian says she never uses bacon, but that's why her meat loaf is always so dry, a little bacon won't hurt I say but she's always watching her weight—''

"Okay, we'll stop." Edie polished off her ice cream, licking her fingers as she glanced around for a napkin. "Mom. I want to talk about Maple Grove—"

"I turned off the stove," Maude said. "You saw me."

"Mom." Edie caught Maude's free hand. "Please turn on your hearing aid, okay?"

"Going to get it all sticky." Maude had also finished her cone and, fingers wriggling, was glancing around as though for something to wipe them on. Edie jumped up, grabbed a handful of napkins from inside the store, came back and handed them to Maude. Her mother used them and then, with a great show of reluctance, raised her hand to her ear. Forehead creased in concentration, she twiddled for a moment.

"What?"

"Mom, I'm very upset—"

"Oww." Maude flinched as though she'd been struck. "See, that's what happens. You shout."

"I wasn't shouting," Edie said. "But I'll speak even softer. Look at me though, okay? This is important." Maude turned, a smear of chocolate ice cream on her lower lip and a tiny white hair sprouting from her chin. "I want to know why you said that to Peter, about being forced out of your house."

Maude's chin trembled.

Edie leaned forward to dab the chocolate from her mother's lip. "Is that what you think, Mom?"

"I'm too much work for Viv," Maude said. "She can't be running over every day to take me places. It's better if I'm somewhere else."

"But Viv doesn't have to take care of you. We can arrange for someone to come in and do the things you need help with. You *can* stay in your own house, Mom. If that's what you want. Nobody is forcing you out. I want you to understand that.''

Maude nodded, seemingly deep in thought. ''That's the last time I let you talk me into having ice cream,'' she said after a moment. ''I've already got heartburn.

''MOM'S JUST BEING MELODRAMATIC,'' Vivian said when Edie called her that night to relay the details of her talk with Maude. ''I've never said she's too much trouble for me. No offense, Edie, but I wish you would just leave things alone. You breeze in and after less than a week, you think you understand the whole situation. Well, you don't. But if you want to move back here and deal with Mom calling every day with a new emergency, fine. Be my guest. And I'd appreciate it if you didn't go telling Peter Darling everything. Ray works with him and we don't want our personal business spread all over the school.''

Edie waited a full ten seconds before she trusted herself to speak. ''I merely questioned whether Mom—''

''No, you didn't *merely* question. You're trying to second-guess me because you think you have all the answers, which is the way you've always been. You know, when I picked you up at the airport, I thought, okay, this is my only sister. I haven't seen her for six years. No matter what she says, I'm not going to get in an argument with her. I bit my tongue, Edie. I literally bit my tongue.''

Edie pictured this. An amazing feat, she reflected, since it had been her impression that Viv had done most of the talking. On the other hand, she could be wrong.

''The minute you got in the car,'' Vivian was saying now, ''you were condescending and patronizing, but I thought, I'm not going to say anything. It's not worth a fight…'' Her voice broke. ''You're just impossible, Edie, you really are.''

Five minutes later, she'd called back to apologize. ''I'm sorry, Eed. I know my problems probably don't sound like much to you, but…well, I've just got a lot on my mind, what with Ray and all. Still, I shouldn't take it out on you. Forgive me?''

''Let's just drop it, Viv.''

''What are you going to do now?''

''I don't know.'' Talking to Vivian made her feel suffocated, smothered by the past and by a problematic relationship that she suspected troubled Viv more than it did her. ''Go for a walk. I could use some fresh air.''

''But it's nearly ten, Edie. Don't you think it's kind of late to be going for a walk? Where are you going? Don't go down by the river, okay?''

''Why?''

''I don't know—it's dark. I always think it's kind of spooky.''

''But nothing's ever happened? No one's been mugged or anything?''

''Not so far, but there's always a first time.''

Edie hung up the phone, wandered into the living room and found Maude channel surfing in front of the TV. Curious about what she might settle on, Edie waited. ''What are you looking for, Mom?'' she asked a few moments later when Maude was still flicking through the channels.

''Go for a walk if you're bored.'' Her hand on the remote, she turned to look at Edie. ''You don't need to baby-sit me, you know. I'm capable of taking care of myself.''

Edie breathed deeply. "Good idea, Mom. I think I will take a walk."

"I'm not upset, I just don't want to talk. I've been talking all day. I'm sorry I can't be more entertaining, but coming back here was your idea. Like I told Vivian, I fell once, but that can happen to anyone. I can take care of myself."

"Fine, Mom, you're on your own," Edie said, then just to be safe, called Vivian, anyway. "I'm going for a walk," she told her sister. "Mom said she's fine by her-self."

"I'm sure she is," Vivian said. "I hope I haven't given you the idea that you need to check in with me, because you don't."

After she hung up, Edie stood for a minute thinking about an alternative to the riverbank, which was where she'd planned to walk. Then she ran upstairs, changed into sweats and walked down the hill to the river, any-way.

It was dark in a way it never seemed to be in Cali-fornia, the air still and warm. Music from a paddle wheeler docked a few hundred yards away floated over to where she stood, summoning carefree romantic im-ages that bore no relation to any reality she knew. Maybe that was the whole problem, she mused as she cut across a grassy field to the water's edge. Life was life, whether you lived it in Missouri or Rome. Not all good, but not all bad, either. Maybe her problem was an inability to let go of the dream of a perfect life where moments of contented bliss were as abundant and available as the apples on the trees in Beth's backyard. If she could let go of that notion, maybe everything would just fall into place.

Maybe.

"Edie," a voice behind her said.

She turned to see Peter, tall and silhouetted against the paddle wheeler's panoply of colored lights. They were standing in the middle of a gravel towpath that meandered downriver for miles, eventually reaching farmlands and open country. She registered the pale oval of his face, the escalated beat of her heart and the sound of footsteps behind her. And then Peter caught her arm, removing her from the path of an oncoming runner, a swift burst of neon-nylon in the dark night.

"Wow," she said. "I was so deep in thought I didn't hear you or him."

"I spotted you from a good way back." He was smiling. "Well, at first I didn't know it was you, but then as I drew closer I felt almost certain that it was. Fortunately, I was right, because I'd have felt like a bit of an idiot calling out to a strange woman."

She smiled back at him, her mood lifting. "What are you doing down here?"

"Jogging. I wait until the girls are asleep and then I run off the tensions of the day."

"You leave the girls alone?"

He looked at her for a moment. "Of course not. My sister looks after them. She's living with us, temporarily, until…well, until things work themselves out."

Exactly what that meant, Edie couldn't guess. He'd seemed flustered for just a moment. *Hmm.*

"I live a block or so up there." He waved toward the lighted shops on Main Street. "Actually, I'm down here quite often with the girls. They adore the gooey butter cake at Olde Towne Bakery. As do I."

Edie smiled. "Gooey butter cake is a St. Louis tradition. I have a definite weakness for it, too."

Peter glanced over at the shops, then pulled back the

sleeve of his red nylon windbreaker to glance at his watch. "Pity, I think the place is closed, otherwise I'd suggest we indulge in some over coffee."

"Yeah, too bad," Edie said, thankful that she hadn't been put in the position of having to decline so as not to ruin Beth's chances of a long and blissful life with Peter. A moment passed in which she caught herself about to say, "Some other time." Peter, she reflected, had that combination of sweetness and out-and-out sexiness that could turn her into a convert to marriage and family. A dog barked somewhere. Behind Peter, the river lay dark and silent. "Well," she said finally, "I suppose I should hit the trail again."

"Are you finishing your walk, or just starting out?"

"Halfway through," she said.

"May I join you?"

She smiled. And saw Beth's face. "Actually, I can feel this blister starting on my heel. It's pretty painful. Shoes not broken in, I guess." They both glanced down at her well-worn sneakers and she felt her face grow warm. "I usually wear a different pair. Anyway, I should probably cut it short…"

"I was meaning to call you, anyway. After I left you and your mother, I took the liberty of talking to Beth Herman about Maude volunteering at the teen mother center. Helping the girls with their babies and so forth. Do you think it's something she would enjoy?"

They'd started walking, and Edie glanced up at him. "I'd never have thought of it myself, but now that you mention it, I think she would enjoy it. I remember when my nephews were babies, my mom took a real delight in them. She's always dropping hints about more grandchildren…"

God. Her face went from warm to hot. Talk about a

leading remark. Peter said nothing, though, and they walked in silence for a little while. The weather, which had been so steamy for the last few days, had turned brisk. She'd noticed, that morning, a few of the trees in Maude's backyard had started to change color. Autumn was her favorite season, but she couldn't even remember the last time she'd seen the yearly blaze of autumn gold and red on the streets and slopes of Little Hills. Last fall, she'd been in Afghanistan.

"I also had a favor to ask of you," Peter said. "Since I came to Luther, I've been trying very hard to help the students make relevant connections between school and their future employment. We've started a landscape program, and one of the teachers just came up with a terrific idea to help the kids fulfill English requirements by becoming storytellers for children in local hospitals." He laughed. "A rather long-winded way of asking whether you would be willing to talk to the students on a weekly basis about careers in journalism."

"I'd be happy to talk to them, but I'm not sure about the weekly basis. I'm only here for a month."

"Well, yes...I realize that."

They walked along in silence for a few minutes. Edie shoved her hands in her pockets and thought about the way he'd just said what he had. She wondered whether the short duration of her visit had crossed his mind before. Hmm. *Quit projecting.*

"Perhaps you could come in a couple of times, though," he finally said. "Just to get things off the ground. I've got so many plans. I also want to start up a campus newspaper. Any help and advice you can offer us there would be most welcome."

Edie listened as he went on to explain his ideas, his voice low and impassioned. After a while she found herself so caught up in his enthusiasm that she almost forgot that the man walking at her side was also the man who inspired fevered dreams in most of Luther Kidd High School's female population. Almost. He'd shoot her a sideways glance, or his arm would brush hers, and she'd feel torn between wanting him to kiss her and fearing that he would.

Mixed in with all that now, though, was a huge slice of admiration and more than a sprinkling of envy. *She* wanted to feel that dedication and enthusiasm.

"I empathize completely with these kids," he was saying. "I went through school, bored stiff and underachieving, but ravenous to learn. By high school, I was constantly banned from the classroom for being disruptive. No one at home paid very much attention, so when I was sixteen I just dropped out."

"No kidding." She absorbed this piece of information, surprised. She'd imagined expensive schools and model parents. "Was this in England?"

"Just before we came to the States. My parents had divorced and my mother had an aunt in St. Louis who was always writing about the wonders of America. My mother sold everything we had to buy plane tickets for the three of us. My sister, Sophia, came too."

"She's older or younger?"

"Older. She was seventeen. It was a huge adjustment for both of us. Sophia actually ran away, she hated it so much. I hated it, too. I'd dream about England and it would seem so real. Even though I knew it was a dream, I somehow thought that if I tried hard enough I could hold on to it and make it real. I can still recall the sense of loss I felt when I finally opened my eyes."

"Like dreaming about someone who has gone," Edie said and felt a sudden chilly dread, the source of which she couldn't entirely identify. "That was quite a plunge for your mother to make. How did she support you?"

"She got a job as a nurse's aide. She had absolutely no experience, so she'd come home from the late shift and wake us up, taking our blood pressure and sticking thermometers in our mouths." He laughed. "Practice."

They kept walking, the night dark around them. Occasionally, she'd think of Maude, waiting up perhaps, and consider turning around. She'd think about it, then Peter would offer another detail and she'd find herself absorbed once more.

"And then what?" she asked. "Did you and your sister go to school?"

"Sophia did for a while, but she eventually returned to England. She's back here now, has been on and off ever since my wife died. She takes care of the girls while I'm at school. I tell her that I don't know what I'd do without her and she tells me that I'd jolly well better learn how because she wants to go back to England."

"And what will you do? Hire a nanny?"

He laughed. "Sophia feels that the only answer is for me to marry again. She's becoming quite insistent about it."

"And…" Edie thought about Beth Herman. "Why haven't you?"

"Because I haven't found anyone," he said.

Edie, still thinking of Beth, decided she'd felt more comfortable when they were talking about less personal matters. "So did you ever go back to England?" she asked, picking up the previous thread.

"After college. And then I met an American woman in London. My wife. After our first daughter was born, Deborah very much wanted to come back home to the

States. Anyway…'' He stopped walking. ''I've rattled on long enough. Perhaps we should turn back.''

''I was thinking the same thing.'' She laughed as they turned around and started back along the pathway. ''Not about you rattling on. I found it all very interesting. My mother's probably calling the police, though.''

''I like your mother,'' he said. ''I suspect that the two of you are very much alike.''

She looked at him. ''Oh please.''

''I meant that you both strike me as determined,'' he said. ''Probably quite stubborn. Very strong personalities. I admire those qualities.''

''Thank you,'' she said. ''Except that I don't know any women who really want to be like their mothers. Same with me. I see all my mom's faults and she irritates me to distraction. But then I remind myself I'm genetically predisposed to do exactly the same kind of thing and I swear I'll watch out for it. If I see myself doing something she does, I'll nip it in the bud.''

''Tell me something about her that you don't like but see in yourself.''

''Hmm, that's a good question.'' She thought for a moment. ''Right now I can't come up with anything. Everything with my mom is so complicated and mixed up, all my feelings about her. I love her and I'm sure she loves me, but we're always on edge with each other. I tell myself she's eighty and to let it go, but she just gets under my skin.''

''Do you admire her?''

''Admire her?'' She thought about it. ''That's a strange question. I guess I do. As you said, she's pretty strong-minded and determined…''

''Like you.''

Edie shrugged. ''I know she's proud of me, but she

doesn't like me. We've never really gotten along and now she's old and I keep hoping things will be different, but we just rub on each other's nerves. And then I feel guilty as hell." She took a breath. "Sorry, none of this is really your concern. You just seem to bring out the Aunt Blabby in me."

He smiled. They'd reached the town again and they stood on the deserted sidewalk, the shop windows that had blazed with light earlier shuttered now.

"The dinner invitation still stands," he said. "As does the theater invitation."

"Sorry. The answer is still no." Beth's face wouldn't go away. "I'm expecting a call from my boyfriend and—"

"He's given to maniacal fits of jealousy?"

"Difficult to imagine, isn't it—that I'd inspire fits of maniacal jealousy? But you've pretty much summed it up. I don't want to risk his wrath."

"God forbid," he said. "But perhaps I could give you a note to take back to him, confirming the chasteness of our encounter. If that isn't sufficient, I'll…challenge him to a duel. Meanwhile—" he touched her arm "—would Thursdays work for you and your mother to come to school?"

"Thursdays?" She considered. Would her mere presence on campus threaten Beth somehow? Come on, a voice in her head mocked. You think you're some kind of femme fatale? Get over yourself, why don't you? "Barring an emergency trip to the IGA, Thursdays would work just as well as any other day."

He smiled. "Brilliant. I'll let Beth know. While your mother is at the teen mother center, you can come over and meet the journalism students. I'll call you when I've set up a date."

CHAPTER SIX

EDIE COULD SEE Vivian and Maude waiting at the living-room window when she walked up the front steps. As she fished for her key, the door swung open and Vivian stood glaring at her under the blazing hall light. Edie blinked, her eyes still adjusting from the dark street.

"Where were you?" Vivian hissed. "Mom's in a complete tizzy. I couldn't calm her down. She wanted me to call the police to go look for you."

"I went for a walk." Behind Vivian, Maude had appeared, wraithlike in a cream silk robe. "What's the big deal?"

"You nearly gave me a heart attack." Maude clutched the front of her robe. "Tell her, Vivian, tell her how frightened I was. First I couldn't find the phone—"

"Mom, the phone is where it always is," Edie said.

"You moved it," Maude said. "You took it off the stand where I always keep it and I went to pick it up and nearly tripped on my robe and—"

"I could have sworn I did put it back," Edie said, trying to remember.

"Why did she need to move it?" Maude asked Vivian. "What's wrong with leaving it where it's always been?"

"Mom." Edie took her mother's hands. "I promise I'll never move the phone again."

"Complain? What have you got to complain about?"

Maude snatched her hands from Edie's and moved past her into the kitchen. "If you're going to start staying out all night, you can pack your bags and leave right now—"

"God." Edie smacked her hand to her head. "I can't stand this."

"See!" Maude pointed an accusing finger at Edie. "That's what she does. Slaps her head and swears at me."

"Mom, it's *her* head." Vivian, bustling around the kitchen, poured milk into a brown mug and set it in the microwave. "If she wants to slap it, that's her business. Be thankful it's not your head she's slapping."

"Don't tempt me," Edie muttered.

Vivian shot her a warning look and turned to Maude. "Edie's back now and everything's fine, Mom." She put her arm around Maude's shoulders. "I'm making you some hot milk and we're going to get you up to bed, okay?"

"I don't like her shouting and cursing," Maude said. "And I don't like her hitting her head."

"Mom." Edie took her mother's hands again. In order to look directly into Maude's eyes and say what she wanted to say, she had to get down on her knees. For a moment, she saw the three of them as a sort of tableau. The ancient queen with her flowing silk robe, the faithful servant at her side and herself in supplication at her mother's feet, begging forgiveness for a transgression she hadn't even been aware of committing. The thought that it had always been that way filled her with a sudden anger that made it difficult to meet Maude's eyes, but she swallowed and summoned strength from somewhere deep within herself. "I'm sorry I shouted and hit my head. I'm sorry I worried you by staying out late. I shouldn't have gone out and I truly apologize.''

Her chin trembling, Maude nodded. ''I love both my daughters,'' she said. ''I don't know what I'd do if anything happened to either of you. Vivian, help me up to bed, will you?''

''SO YOU WERE JUST OUT for a walk?'' Vivian asked after Maude had been tucked into bed and she and Edie were in the living room drinking white wine from a bottle Edie had bought the day before at the IGA.

Edie drank some wine and considered. If she lied about seeing Peter, it would give the whole thing more significance than it deserved.

''I ran into Peter Darling,'' she said.

Vivian set her wine down. ''And?''

''And nothing, really. We walked for a while. He told me about things he's doing at school. He wants Mom to volunteer in the teen mother center and he asked if I'd help set up a journalism group.''

''What?'' Vivian shook her head, clearly astounded. ''See, that's exactly the sort of thing Ray's always complaining about. This guy gets these ideas that are so damn impractical, it's not even funny. Mom has no business volunteering…you told him no, I hope.''

''I told him it sounded like a good idea. Mom loves babies. I think it would be good for her to have something to do.''

''Well, you're wrong.'' Viv folded her arms across her chest. ''Once she moves into Maple Grove, how is she supposed to get over to the high school? Are you going to be here to drive her? I certainly don't have the time.''

"I hadn't thought about that." Edie shrugged. "I'm sure someone could give her a ride. I'll talk to Beth—"

"No you won't," Viv snapped. "You've screwed up enough as it is. Why the hell can't you just look beyond the moment, Edie? Think things out a little. Did you mention Beth, by the way?"

"Mention Beth?"

"To Peter."

"No." Edie gulped down half the wine in her glass. Viv could destroy a pleasant evening in no time flat. "Beth's name didn't come up."

"Edie, you're good with words. I'm pretty sure you could have worked her name into the conversation somehow. Or you could have if you'd wanted to."

Edie yawned and rose to her feet. If she left right this minute, she could avoid locking her hands around Vivian's throat. She smiled. "Well, as pleasant as these sisterly little chats are, Viv, I think I'm ready for bed."

"Oh sure, walk away. The truth's always painful, isn't it? You know what, Edie? I see right through you. Beth's this small-town schoolteacher, you're some big-shot reporter who breezes into town. You know damn well Beth's infatuated with Peter, but you've just got to prove that all you have to do is lift your little finger and he'll be all over you."

"Yep, that's me." Anger tingled, effervescent on her tongue. In a moment, rage would erupt in tears and she wasn't about to give Viv that satisfaction. Casually, she stooped to pick up her wineglass from the coffee table. "I've got him panting all over me. Asked me out twice already, but I'm letting him dangle—"

"He asked you out?"

"Twice. Dinner, the theater…"

Vivian sighed. "Well, just don't say anything to Beth.

He probably just thinks you're…I don't know, available or something. But Beth's much more his type. I'm thinking maybe we should give her a makeover…''

''Good night, Viv.'' As she walked up the stairs, Edie decided she didn't want to be around when her sister learned that their mother had invited Peter and his daughters to dinner. Her preference, she thought, would be not to be around, period. Right now, she wanted to get on a plane and fly far, far away from Little Hills, Missouri.

THE NEXT DAY, Maude went out with Dixie Mueller again. This time Edie questioned Dixie's daughter so thoroughly that the woman got a little snippy and intimated that if Edie was that concerned, perhaps she shouldn't allow Maude to go. Maude went, anyway.

Alone in the house and relishing the quiet, Edie spent the morning working on her laptop at the kitchen table, drafting an article she planned to sell as a freelance piece. War correspondents—does gender make a difference? She was of the opinion that it did. War was dangerous for all journalists, but women war correspondents faced what female war victims faced, including the threat of sexual assault. And, some of her female colleagues complained, it was difficult to get high-ranking officials to take them seriously. She worked steadily for an hour or so. Sitting in her mother's kitchen, she had taken a while to properly focus on the article. But before long, she'd become so engrossed that when she heard a clap of thunder, she thought momentarily it was gunfire.

When she heard the second low rumble, she got up to look through the kitchen window. The sky had turned an ominous green, the leggy rosebushes black silhouettes in the neglected backyard. She'd forgotten Midwest weather: the weird green color the sky got during a storm; the still, heavy air.

As the first drops of rain, heavy and furious, began to fall, she ran around the house closing windows, then sat down to write again. But her concentration was gone and after ten minutes or so of erasing everything she'd written, she got up again to look outside. If she craned her neck, she could see, almost hidden in the tall grass, the wooden hutch she'd built for Jim Morrison, the French Lop rabbit she'd had when she was about fourteen.

Jim would be standing on his hind legs behind the wire mesh, waiting for her to take him out, when she got home from school. Around the same time, Ray Jenkins, whom she'd had a crush on forever, began to notice her. Instead of coming home to feed Jim, she would hang out at Ray's house. One day, she'd found Jim dead in his little cage, his water bowl bone dry.

Twenty-six years later, the memory could still make her weep; a lot of memories out there in that small backyard. One winter, her father had turned the lawn into a skating rink for her and Viv. He'd flooded it with the hose before they went to bed, and the next morning it was frozen solid. In the summer, the grass had always been green and clipped. Now it bloomed with dandelions and the rosebushes had huge orange hips that looked black as olives in the strange light of the storm.

Maude had once taken great pride in the garden. She'd tie a wide-brimmed straw hat under her chin and pull on white gardening gloves patterned with tiny yellow roses. Summer evenings, she'd be down on her knees tying up the peonies that always flopped, stems too slender to support their extravagant frilly blooms. Peonies. Edie turned from the window. She probably hadn't thought of peonies since she'd left Missouri.

She wandered about the house. In her head, Vivian was telling her to stop interfering, to leave things alone. And then Maude was saying, *I don't even know why you came back.* She wandered back into the kitchen, where Tinkerbell eyed her balefully. "I know," she said. "You don't need me here, either. Trust me, *I* don't want to be here."

Odd how different she felt right now than she had the day she first met Peter Darling at the high school. She'd stood on the podium that day basking in the kids' admiration as they looked up at her, hanging on to her words. She'd felt good—the successful foreign correspondent wowing them with her exotic adventures. And she'd seen the admiration in Peter Darling's eyes. Seen herself through his eyes and liked what she saw.

But only a month ago, she'd stood in a hospital in Kabul feeling about as useless and irrelevant as she did right now. She had no medical skills. She wasn't bringing anything anyone needed. Why would she? She was a journalist. Patients all around with horrendous injuries imploring her: *Do something.* Harried nurses trying futilely to stop armed militia from stealing medical supplies. Unarmed, she could do nothing to help. In the midst of all the chaos and suffering, she found herself apologizing to a nurse for being in the way.

What the hell am I doing here? she'd wondered then—and she did now. Later though, she'd decided there was a good reason. She was there to observe and then to honestly communicate what she had observed. And if something she wrote helped someone to better understand, or brought about change, then she could believe that her work mattered.

But standing in her mother's kitchen, it wasn't so easy to answer the same question. Why *was* she here?

"Meow." Poochie—or was it Panda?—rubbed its ear against Edie's leg.

"Yeah?" She stroked the cat gently with her toe. "You're saying that it's because I'm a great joy and comfort to my mother? Because my very presence is like sunshine in the midst of her day? Is that what you're saying?"

Its tail twitched and, with great dignity, the cat exited the room.

"You don't buy that, huh?" She sighed. "Yeah, well, neither do I."

In the hall, the stentorian chime of the grandfather clock told her it was now three o'clock. The house felt quiet and claustrophobic, with the seconds, minutes, hours stretching on endlessly until the moment she would climb the stairs and fall into bed. Ben had once said they were both adrenaline junkies, one reason they were drawn to war reporting. She had no doubt that it was true of Ben.

She exhaled. "There is nothing you can achieve by staying on," her bureau chief had told her after Ben's capture. "It's too dangerous. At the very least, you'll get in the way, and you could wind up in trouble yourself."

She dropped into one of the flowered green-and-orange vinyl chairs that surrounded her mother's simulated-woodgrain kitchen table, curled her legs up and picked at the polish on her toenails.

Okay, kiddo, time for some straight talk. Grit your teeth because it's gonna hurt.

NO ONE NEEDS YOU.

And that's not being maudlin or anything, it's just the truth. It was your idea to come back. Yours. And here's another thing. If you're not needed, it's your fault. You've brought it all on yourself. So what are you going to do about it? Mope around and feel sorry for yourself, or find some way to keep yourself occupied for the next few weeks?

She got up and glanced at her watch. Maude should be home soon. She decided to make dinner. Maude might not need her in the way Maude needed Viv, but Maude would appreciate a hot meal waiting for her. She opened the freezer, dug out a package of chicken breasts from under the boxes of fish sticks and potpies, and stuck them in the microwave to defrost. While she rummaged around in the cabinets for something to serve with the chicken, she had another idea.

Half an hour later, the chicken was in the oven and Edie, from the laptop on the kitchen table, was cruising the Internet for information on retirement facilities. By the time the chicken was done, she'd amassed enough information that she had a good idea of the questions to ask and the things to look for when she and Viv took Maude out to Maple Grove. Viv claimed to have already done plenty of research, but this would be additional insurance. As she printed out the material, it occurred to her that Viv might also consider this an example of micro-managing. Edie shrugged. So be it. She glanced at the clock again just as the phone rang.

Maude was calling to say that Dixie's daughter was taking them both to the movies. *Doesn't need you, doesn't need your chicken,* a cruel voice in her head taunted. Edie set the chicken aside along with the soft-focus fantasy in which she confided in Maude all her doubts about Ben, work and life in general. She set that aside along with the scene of Maude confessing that she hadn't wanted to burden her because she knew what a busy and successful life Edie led, but... In the fantasy, Maude's chin trembled, her eyes shone with unshed tears. "I need you so much, Edie," she would say. "I've always needed you. *Viv snaps at me.*" Small, but Edie couldn't resist. Anyway, it was her fantasy.

"So what time do you think you'll be home?" she asked Maude.

"Something about Las Vegas," Maude said. "Dixie said her other daughter saw it and it was hilarious. There are some fish sticks in the freezer if you want to fix those for yourself.

"HOME, Mom," Edie said. "What time?"

"No, no bones. They're fish sticks. Anyway, I like them. You suit yourself."

After she'd hung up, Edie wondered whether she should have checked with Viv before giving Maude permission. Except that Maude hadn't really called for permission and Edie was wearying of Viv's patronizing assurances. *"Don't blame yourself, sweetie."* She could hear Viv's voice in her head. *"It's not your fault."* Subtext: You can't help being the selfish and irresponsible one.

She wandered into the living room where all three cats were asleep on the sofa.

"Want to join me for a gourmet feast, guys?"

Tinkerbell opened one eye, the other two cats ignored her.

"Looks like I'm dining alone," she said.

And then Peter Darling called.

CHAPTER SEVEN

"JUST A SECOND…" Peter told Edie as he switched the receiver to his other ear. A squabble had broken out between the twins, who sat on the floor of his office, crayoning pictures of butterflies. "Abbie. You have your own butterfly to color. Let Kate color her butterfly."

"But she put brown on my butterfly," Abbie cried. "And it doesn't have brown." She scrambled up from the floor and thrust her coloring book in front of Peter's face. "See, it should be all blue and she put a brown spot on it and now she's ruined it."

"Sorry," Peter apologized into the phone. "You know, Ab," he told his daughter, "with that brown spot it looks rather like a blue morpho. Here—" he reached for his *Guide to North American Butterflies* "—look through this. I think you'll find the blue morpho has a brown spot."

"Mr. Darling," the janitor said from the doorway. "It's after six. You gonna be here much longer?"

"Mmm?" Peter glanced up. "Sorry. Is it that late? I was trying to catch up on paperwork—"

"Take your time," the janitor said. "Just lock up when you leave. And, Mr. Darling, there are three kids hanging around outside the gate. Said something about waiting to go for a walk with you. You gonna go in all this rain?"

"Rain?" Peter said distractedly. "Sorry again, Edie."

He held a hand over the mouthpiece and addressed the janitor. "Would you mind telling them that I'll be outside in about fifteen minutes and then we'll all walk down to the river."

"Daddy…" Natalie sidled up to the desk and brought her face to his ear. "Tell the twins they can't swim in the river," she whispered. "They're both wearing their bathing suits under their shorts."

"You want to call me back?" Edie inquired. "Sounds like you've got your hands full."

"I do, but that's all right. Hold on." He turned to speak to Natalie, "I'll take care of it, sweetheart," he said and then spoke into the phone again. "All right. I'm trying to reduce a mountain of paperwork that I can never find time to tackle during the day," he told her. "And my daughters are here—"

"You bring them to school?"

"Not during normal hours. They're just keeping me company while I work. It's rather nice, really. Companionable." As he spoke, Abbie pulled Kate's hair, causing Kate to squeal loudly and launch a retaliatory attack. "Girls," he said. "Companionable," he told Edie, "if not tranquil."

"It sounds chaotic," she said. "I can't imagine trying to write with a bunch of kids in the room."

Peter felt a mild stab of disappointment. "The reason I called," he said, "was to let you know what a success your talk was with the students. I'd meant to mention it before, but the days get a little hectic. Anyway, I think we have at least three or four fledgling journalists, all eager to hear more from you."

"Terrific," she said, sounding genuinely pleased. "Right now, that's exactly what I need to hear." A pause. "You caught me in the middle of a massive attack of self-pity."

"Really?" He could see her, tall and supremely self-assured, the glint of sun on her hair. The admission startled him, until he thought of her outside the restaurant that day. "I can't imagine it. What on earth would produce that?"

She laughed. "Oh…I let my rabbit starve to death."

He hesitated a moment. And then, "Before or after you killed your father?"

Silence. "I feel like an idiot."

"Therapy's always a possibility."

"You're saying I'm crazy, is that it?"

"I'm saying that you appear to be carrying around an awful lot of guilt. Needlessly, I'm sure."

"Thanks," she said. "It would have been kind of awkward if you'd believed me. That I'm this maniacal killer, or something." Another pause. "Listen, forget this whole conversation, okay? I'm fine. Too much time on my hands is the problem. Fortunately, I'm usually too busy for introspection. Socrates was wrong. The unexamined life is really the way to go."

"I think you're wrong," Peter said. "And I'd love to pursue this, but my daughters are getting restless and three students are waiting outside for me to walk them down to the river. An impromptu, after-hours field trip. We're all going to spot butterflies, if you'd care to join us."

EDIE AMBLED SLOWLY along the narrow cobbled streets of Little Hills' historic downtown, thinking about Peter's invitation and the excuse she'd given him: polite, careful not to hurt his feelings, something about work to do.

Would I like to spend a few hours with four small children and a bunch of hulking adolescents? Hmm, let me think about it. Nah, I think I'll chew my toenails. Difficult choice, though.

Still, it was sweet of him to call and say kind things. She did feel better. He was a nice guy. Attractive and interesting. Just not attractive and interesting enough to compensate for the fact that he had four small children. No man alive was that attractive or interesting. Just her opinion, of course—obviously, one not shared by Beth Herman. Good for Beth, though; tall, handsome widowers with four small children were created for women like Beth. Women who were warm, generous, unselfish. All the things I'm not, she thought. Which was fine. Like Popeye, I yam what I yam.

She stopped to look in the window of Ye Olde Little Hills Bookstore, all done up with back-to-school posters and books artfully displayed in red and green knapsacks. Moved on, past Gently Used, an upscale secondhand clothes boutique that had been a small general store when she was in high school. Past Olde Towne Bakery and Granny's Sugar Plum Treats, where she and Maude had bought their ice cream cones. Even the newer shops along River Street were designed to suggest Little Hills' origins as a Missouri River trading post, although Edie observed that Victoriana had improbably infiltrated the neighborhood.

As a kid, she'd truly thought Little Hills, with its steep streets of old-world houses running down to the river, was the best place in the world anyone could live. The exhilarating thrill of careening down the hills on a bike—an activity that, literally, came to a screeching halt when Vivian flew over the handlebars and broke two front teeth. Long, warm summer days with fireflies and sweet white peaches and the mysterious allure of the river. A proud past and a promising future, according to the chamber of commerce brochures. By her last year in high school, though, Edie had been less than convinced about the future the town promised.

On Elm she glanced up at a French Colonial where her best friend in grade school had lived. Megan something or other. No idea what happened to Megan. Three kids, probably. Everyone her age seemed to have three kids. And there was the late Victorian mansion where she'd taken ballet lessons in a chilly studio that had once been a conservatory. Lots of architectural variety, she reflected. German here, Greek Revival there. What would her life have been like if she'd never left Missouri?

She crossed Elm and started down the grassy slope to the river. When she saw Peter Darling surrounded by kids, another small blond child on his shoulder and a butterfly net held aloft, she swore to herself that she'd forgotten he said he'd be down here.

"WELL, a butterfly's wings are actually clear." Peter looked around at the circle of faces, scanning the periphery of the group to make sure Delphina hadn't wandered off, as she was apt to do. He spotted her, dark and bespectacled, standing beside Natalie. Both girls wore red shorts and striped T-shirts, and Sophia had braided their hair that morning. But while Natalie appeared engaged and interested, Delphina's eyes were distant, her face so forlorn that he momentarily lost his train of thought. He would have a talk with Sophia tonight, he decided, although of course she'd insist that what Delphina needed was a mother, which would start up the whole find-a-wife matter again. "Right," he said. "Where were we?"

"Butterflies come from a chrysalis," Abbie announced. With her arms locked in a stranglehold around his throat, her sandal-clad feet beat against his chest. "It's also called a pupa." This struck her as hilarious and she kicked harder. "Poo-pa," she shrieked. "Poo-pa, poo-pa, *poo-pa*."

Peter grabbed her ankle. "Stop it, or I shall have to put you down."

"Mr. Darling," a boy with purple hair yelled. "Come over here. I think I spotted a blue morpho."

"I rather doubt it." Peter started over to the cluster of maples where Eric, the purple-haired boy, was waving his net into the lower branches. "Blue morphs are mostly found in Mexico and Venezuela, occasionally Costa Rica."

"I saw one this morning," Abbie, still perched on his shoulder, announced. "It sat on my finger."

"Daddy." Kate tugged at his fingers. "*I* want to sit on your shoulders."

"No. I am." Abbie kicked again. "You're a pupa. That's why you can't sit here. Pupa, pupa, *pooooooo-pa*."

"Right, that's enough." Peter set her down on the grass and peered up into the maple where Eric was still brandishing his butterfly net. "Can you still see it?"

"Nah." Eric lowered the net. "Probably took off chasing a lady butterfly."

Peter rejoined the circle of students standing under a tree, studying their guidebooks. "As I was saying…" he started again. "A butterfly's wings are actually clear. The color you see is the result of pigments on the underside of the tiny scales that cover the wing."

"I'm thinking now that wasn't a blue morpho after all." Eric's purple head was bent over his book. "There's this picture of one and its wings look kind of like metal, or something."

"Iridescent," Delphina said shyly from the sidelines. Eric turned to glance at her. "Whatever."

"Delphina," Peter said, encouraged by his daughter's unusual show of participation, "can you tell us what makes the wings appear iridescent?"

Her face flaming, she wrapped her arms around her knees and pressed her mouth into them. "Don't know," she said indistinctly.

Peter felt the familiar tug at his heart. Certain that she knew the answer, he'd hoped to draw her out. Clearly a mistake. The students—laughing, boisterous fifteen-year-olds who must seem like another species to a quiet, withdrawn child of seven—were chasing one another with butterfly nets now and straggling off up the hill. Time to wrap things up, he decided as he got up and went over to Delphina. Natalie and the twins sat nearby, making daisy chains. He'd just crouched down beside Delphina and started to say something, when he saw Edie Robinson leaning nonchalantly against a maple.

He grinned. "How long have you been standing there?"

"Long enough to want to know why a butterfly's wings look iridescent."

Peter put his arm around Delphina's shoulders. "Any idea?" he asked softly.

"I know." Kate inserted herself between Peter and Delphina. "Because it makes them look pretty."

"Butterflies have a proboscis," Abbie said. "Daddy told me. That's how they drink nectar."

Natalie placed a circle of daisies on his head. "I crown you King Daddy."

"And they have pu-pas," Kate said.

"It's an optical illusion," Delphina said so softly it seemed meant for only Peter to hear. "Because of the light."

"Exactly." Peter squeezed her close, kissed the top of her head and then looked up at Edie, who wore the cool, faintly amused look that he was starting to recognize. He'd seen it slip after the Burger Barn incident, but it was back in place now. Natalie was shooting her shy glances and the twins were flinging themselves around in an obvious attempt to gain her attention. He stood, remembering suddenly the daisy-chain crown on his head. "My daughters," he told her, naming each girl. "And this is Edie Robinson."

Edie smiled at the girls but remained standing beneath the tree. After a moment or so, the girls, perhaps sensing her disinterest, dispersed. Peter felt a momentary letdown, a cloud drifting lightly across the sun. He remained standing, arms folded across his chest—mirroring, he realized after a moment, Edie's stance.

"I decided to take a walk after all," she said after they'd stood in silence for a moment or two. "I like the way the air feels after a storm. I'd sort of forgotten it." She glanced over at the girls, then back at him. "And I also have to tell you that I was quite fascinated watching your students—kids I would probably cross the road to avoid if I saw them approaching me after dark—utterly captivated by what you were telling them. I'm very impressed."

"Thank you," he said. "Actually, it took quite a leap of faith to suggest to a kid with purple hair and a nose ring that the study of butterflies might be a good science elective, but he's one of the most enthusiastic in the group.''

Delphina came back then, sidling up to his hip. He put his arm around her. "Delphina writes really good poetry,'' he wanted to tell Edie, but found himself reluctant to expose his daughter to the woman's cool amber gaze. "By the way,'' he said instead, "I've got a date set up for the journalism group. Are you still interested?''

"Sure,'' she said. "I have to warn you, though, that I can talk your ear off about journalism, but I know nothing about working with kids.'' Her gaze lit briefly on Delphina and then returned to him. "They're like a foreign language I have absolutely no interest in learning.''

HOURS LATER, in the darkened bedroom next to Maude's, Edie punched her pillow into submission, turned onto her stomach and tried to make her mind a blank. *They're like a foreign language I have absolutely no interest in learning.* She shot up, raked her hair back, lay down again. *Why* had she said it? You said it, she answered, because it's true. Still, she'd noticed something in Peter's face that she hadn't wanted to see there. It was nothing like the way he'd looked at her after she spoke at the school. Then she'd seen respect. In the park, with his daughter beside him, a crown of daisies on his head, he'd looked at her and she'd seen…pity.

To hell with it. She gave the pillow another thrashing, yanked the quilt around her shoulders and curled up on her side. He was the one who needed pity: four kids, pulling at his fingers, climbing over his shoulders, each demanding her share of attention. Who wouldn't pity him?

The whole incident left her feeling surly and unsettled, a mood that lingered the next morning as she stood in the kitchen making Maude's breakfast. Maude had probably never been served breakfast in bed, Edie reflected as she cooked three strips of bacon. This would be a treat.

"See, I do have the potential to be kind and generous," she told Tinkerbell, who was snaking sinuously against her leg. "It just doesn't shine forth very often." For some reason, she kept seeing Peter's dark-haired child—she'd forgotten all their names—standing at his side, Peter's arm around her. The girl was probably seven or eight and obviously shy. For a moment, she'd found herself wanting to do something to connect to the child, but she could think of nothing and that's when she'd blurted out that idiotic remark.

She took the bacon from the pan, set it on a plate in the oven and beat two eggs into a bowl. Then she melted butter and poured the eggs into a pan. *Kids are like a foreign language I have absolutely no interest in learning.* Okay, put the damn remark out of your head. You said it and there's nothing you can do about it. She glanced at the eggs, puffing nicely in the pan, then ran outside, picked a couple of pink rosebuds, found a vase in the kitchen, arranged everything on a tray and carried it upstairs.

Maude's bedroom door was pulled to but not closed. The tray in her hands, Edie nudged the door with her hip. Daylight coming from behind long chenille drapes hit the middle of the swaybacked old double bed. A clock ticked on the dresser, lending an oddly dreamlike quality to the room. Edie set the tray on the floor and pulled open the drapes. Maude lay on her back, her hands folded across her middle. Sound asleep still, cheeks sunken, lower jaw slack. Her teeth sat in a pink plastic cup on a wooden nightstand next to the bed. Edie's heart skipped with the fleeting thought that Maude was dead. Then she saw her mother stir slightly, lips mumbling something indecipherable.

"Surprise," Edie whispered, setting the tray down on the bed.

Maude's white-lashed eyes opened and she looked blankly at Edie, shrieked and bolted up in the bed. "Who is it?" she breathed, her gaze darting around the room. "Who is it?"

"It's me, Mom." Edie grabbed the tray, too late to stop the vase of roses from overturning and spilling across the food. "Damn." She blotted the water with the folded napkin, straightened the rose vase and smiled brightly. "Hungry?"

"I better take a blood pressure pill." Maude had one gnarled hand across the front of her starfish-patterned nightgown. Wisps of white hair, not caught up in the pink foam-rubber curlers that lay like fat little pigs across her scalp, stood at attention in vertical tufts "You frightened me. Never creep up on me like that."

"I didn't creep up on you. I whispered very quietly. Look." She eyed the cooling omelet. "I made you breakfast."

"What's that?" Maude frowned at the breakfast tray. "Where did those roses come from? You didn't pick them from next door's bushes, did you? She's always complaining about people picking her roses. Don't think it's me picking them, I always tell her, I've got plenty of my own, or I did until Vivian pruned them to a fare-thee-well, hardly any blooms this year. Last year, you couldn't see the leaves for all the roses—"

"Mom." Edie nodded at the food. "It's an omelet. Doesn't it look good? Eat it now before it gets cold."

"I always have oatmeal. Every morning I have a bowl of oatmeal, been doing it for years. The doctor said that's why my cholesterol is so good. Oatmeal, it's good for you. Wouldn't hurt you to start eating it, too, I said that to Vivian, I said—"

"I thought you'd enjoy a change." Edie picked up the fork, wrapped Maude's fingers around it. "I don't think you've ever had breakfast in bed before, have you?"

"I'm not an invalid. I'll get up and eat it downstairs."

Edie felt her patience ebb. "Mom, just eat it here, okay? By the time you get downstairs the food will be cold."

"I might be old—" Maude swung a leg off the bed "but I'm not an invalid. I never eat breakfast in bed."

"Well, how about making an exception, just this once?" Maude had set the fork down and Edie picked it up again and stuck it in Maude's hand. "Come on, take a bite."

Maude surveyed the omelet with suspicion. "That a green pepper? I can't eat green pepper, you ask Vivian. Makes me belch, I'll be belching all day. Never liked green pepper anyway, can't see the point of it. Tasteless, if you ask me, and it repeats. Belching like a trooper if I eat—"

God, give me patience. Edie snatched the fork from Maude, flipped open the omelet and scraped away the green pepper from the congealing egg and cheese. "There, no green pepper."

"Still smell it though." Maude had a note of triumph in her voice. "Can't hide that smell."

"Oh yes you can." Edie swooped the green pepper

up in her hand, carried it into the bathroom next door and flushed it down the toilet. Back in the bedroom, she looked at Maude. "There, no green pepper. Now eat."

"D'you wash your hands?"

Edie slapped her forehead, her patience gone. "Goddamn it, Mom—"

"Don't you swear at me," Maude said. "And don't hit your head like that, you'll get a brain tumor. You're not the easiest person to get along with, either, I'll tell you that. And I don't like being made to feel that I'm some helpless old woman who can't do a thing for herself. I get up every morning at six, you ask Vivian, she'll tell you. Get up and fix my own breakfast. And I won't put up with you shouting and taking your bad moods out on me."

"I'm sorry." Frustration subsided into something more complex, a dark jumble of feelings that brought her close to tears again. She sat on the bed. "I wanted to do something nice for you. I didn't do it because I think you're helpless or an invalid. I just thought you'd enjoy breakfast in bed, but I guess I was wrong."

"I used to walk to the market every day." Maude, still looking aggrieved, had not touched the omelet. "You can ask anyone, up to the market and back, sometimes with a bag of groceries. Oh Vivian always says she'll take me, but she has a busy life. I don't need her running around after me. Besides, she's got problems with Ray and that new principal. Seemed nice enough to me, though."

"Well, let's not think about that right now." Edie was still focused on the omelet, its appetizing brown puffiness sadly deflated. "Are you going to eat this, or not?"

"Peter Darling." Maude cut a small piece of omelet and lifted it to her mouth. "Don't know what made me think of him right now. Funny name. That's the boy in *Peter Pan,* isn't it?''

Edie watched Maude chew. ''What do you think?''

''Ray doesn't like him, Vivian said. Says he's got his head in the clouds.''

On the verge of slapping her head again, Edie counted to ten instead. ''Good omelet, huh, Mom?''

''Wife died, Viv said. Left him with four little girls. When are you going to settle down, Edie? Leave it too long and you'll be too old to have kids.''

''I said, good omelet, huh, Mom?''

''Eh?'' Maude cut another piece. ''Nice. I can still taste green pepper, though.''

From the hallway, Edie could hear the clanging ring of the old black phone. ''Eat,'' she said as she darted downstairs to catch the phone. It was Vivian.

''Just leaving,'' she said. ''I hope you gave Mom plenty of time to get ready. She moves pretty slowly these days. See you in fifteen minutes.''

''Edith,'' Maude called from the bedroom. ''Come here, I want to show you something.''

Edie hung up the phone and returned to the bedroom. ''That was Viv. You need to get dressed. We're going out to Maple Grove.''

''Viv said she set up an appointment,'' Maude said.

''I know, Mom. That's what I'm saying.'' She sat down on the edge of the bed. ''Remember what I told you, though. This is your decision. You don't have to do it.''

''Look.'' Maude held up her fork. ''Green pepper. Told you I could smell it.''

''MR. DARLING.'' Betty Jean regarded Peter fondly but with obvious exasperation, as though he were an inat-

tentive child who had once again forgotten his home-
work. "Have you heard anything I said?"

Peter stopped thinking about Edie and summoned a
suitably involved expression. "You said, I believe, that
the copier is on the blink again."

"And…"

"Hmm. Refresh my memory."

"You have a parent meeting in twenty minutes. And
here's a list Mrs. Adams gave me of things she wants
to discuss with you." She set the list on the desk in front
of him. "Is everything all right, Mr. Darling? The girls
and all?"

"The girls are fine, Betty Jean. Thank you for asking."

She left and Peter tried to focus on the list.

"Well, perhaps children are like a foreign language
to her," Sophia had said the night before when he'd told
her about Edie's comment in the park. "All women are
not, by definition, maternal candidates. I'm not myself.
As much as I adore the girls, I can't say I've ever had
any particular desire to have children of my own."

"Natalie thought she seemed haughty," Peter said.

"Well, perhaps she did."

"And she gave Delphina a rather cold look, I
thought."

Sophia looked exasperated. "Peter, what on earth do
you expect? You've said quite clearly that you're not
attracted to warm cuddly women who want babies. Now
you've met the type of woman you are attracted to, but
you expect her to embrace your children with open arms.
That's very unrealistic of you."

Peter had conceded that he supposed it was unrealistic. He'd felt disappointed nonetheless.

"Perhaps this woman has no interest in you," Sophia

said. "Could that be the case? Has she given you any reason to suppose her feelings are reciprocal?"

"Not really. So far she's turned down every invitation I've extended."

"Well, there you are then," Sophia said. "She's probably involved with someone else."

"Actually, she did mention a boyfriend."

Sophia had been leafing through a magazine and she threw it at his head. "Peter, you are so thick, you're driving me mad. Pull yourself together, for God's sake, and look elsewhere. Or I shall be forced to take matters into my own hands."

CHAPTER EIGHT

"GUESS WHAT?" Vivian said later as they drove Maude out to see the Maple Grove place. "Peter asked Beth for a date."

In the back seat, Edie had been thinking about Peter, comparing again the look he'd given her at school that first day with last night's look in the park. She had almost succeeded in convincing herself that perhaps, instead of last night's remark making her seem cold and unfeeling, it actually spoke of a willingness to learn. In fact, she wasn't sure now whether she'd said, "…a foreign language I have no desire to learn" or "…a foreign language I'd like to learn." Vivian's announcement jerked her out of her reverie. "A date. When?"

"Next weekend, I think. They're going to the butterfly exhibit. He asked her a couple of days ago. I forget when exactly."

"Good, that's great." Edie picked at her thumbnail. So here she was beating herself up for some stupid remark when, by the time she'd made it, Peter had already invited Beth out and was no doubt viewing her as a New Mommy candidate. Well, good. Beth would make an excellent mother. Probably a good wife, too. Loving, warm, generous. A drop of blood appeared on Edie's cuticle and she stuck her thumb in her mouth, tasting salt as she watched the Missouri countryside flash by through the tinted windows of Vivian's car.

"Edith made me breakfast this morning," Maude told Vivian. "In bed."

"Well, that was nice." Vivian turned to smile approval at Edie.

"Gave me heartburn," Maude said. "And then she rushed me to get ready."

"Mom." Swallowing irritation, Edie leaned over to talk straight into her mother's ear. Maude, disgruntled that she'd been rushed, had refused to wear her hearing aid. No one was likely to say anything she wanted to hear, she'd announced.

"This first place, Mom," Edie said, "is Maple Grove. Then we're going to—"

"I've seen it already," Maude said.

"I know, but I haven't. After that, we're going to see Sunset Manor, and then—"

"Banana," Maude shook her head. "I'm still full from that breakfast you made me eat. I can feel those green peppers coming up," she said and then, as if to demonstrate, belched loudly. "I told you I can't take them, but you never listen. Poor old Mom, that's what you both think. Poor old Mom, she won't know—"

"I scraped away every bit of the damn peppers, Mom." Edie met her sister's eyes in the rearview mirror. Looking amused, Vivian slowly shook her head. Edie leaned back in the seat, close to tears for the second time that day. Why did Maude always leave her feeling defeated? In the front seat, Vivian was extolling the virtues of Maple Grove.

"You're going to love it there, Mom." Vivian kept turning her head to look at Maude. "I just know you'll be so much happier there than in that big old house that's always needing something done to it. Edie and I both feel that way. We want what's best for you."

"You do something to your hair?" Maude stretched up a hand to touch Vivian's smooth reddish-blond pageboy. "Looks nice. Doesn't it look nice, Edith?"

"Yes, it does," Edie agreed, looking at Vivian. "I like it that length."

"Makes you look younger than your sister," Maude said. "I think so, anyway."

Edie eyed the patch of pink exposed skin on her mother's neck. She is old. She has cataracts. What the hell does it matter what she thinks? She leaned forward again. "What we want you to know, Mom, is that there are other alternatives. You don't have to give up your house. I called this visiting nurse—"

"I've got my purse." Maude patted the beige vinyl handbag on her lap. "Like it? Selma got it at that thrift shop on Main Street." Twisting around in the seat to look at Edie, she snapped open the purse. "It's clean, see? Not even used."

"Edie's right, Mom," Vivian said. "There are other alternatives, but you and I both know that keeping the house wouldn't be a good idea. Besides, you'll just be happier with other people your own age." She pinched Maude's arm. "Who knows, you might meet a handsome gentleman."

"It's one option, Mom," Edie said. In the rearview mirror, she caught Vivian's irritated expression, but plowed on, anyway. "When you've seen all these places today, we'll make a list of pros and cons and compare those with the good things and not-so-good things about staying in your house."

"Where you could trip over a rug, break your hip and end up in hospital," Viv said in a low voice, clearly intended just for Edie. "Edie won't be here to visit you every day, of course. She has a big important job—"

"I just want to make sure it's what Mom wants," Edie said in the same low voice, "and not what we're forcing her into."

"As I said, Edie…" Vivian braked behind a crossing guard who was leading a line of children across the street. "You are more than welcome to take over the reins from me. Of course, now that you've suddenly become the expert on what she needs, it shouldn't be any problem." One hand off the wheel, she reached over to pat Maude's knee. "I bet it's nice to have Edie back home for a while," she said loud enough for Maude to hear. "Too bad we don't see her more often, huh? Gets kind of lonely for you, doesn't it? You start getting depressed."

"I know I do." Maude fished in her purse for a tissue, dabbed at her eyes. "You're a good girl." A moment passed, then she turned her head to look at Edie. "You too," she said.

"Well, here we are," Viv said as she pulled in to the long driveway of Maple Grove. "Jeez, Mom, it looks so nice I kind of wish I was old enough to be going there." She winked at Edie. "Don't you think so, Eed? I think Mom's going to be really happy here."

"MR. DARLING." Betty Jean crooked her finger at Peter as he was walking into the staff meeting. "Come here." She glanced at his shirtfront. "I'm kinda worried about you today. Were you stabbed in the heart or something?"

Peter glanced down and saw the purplish-red stain over his shirt pocket. Natalie had shoved something in there when he saw her off to school. "I made you lunch, Daddy," she'd whispered.

"Hmm." He removed it. "Appears to be another one of Natalie's jam sandwiches, a little worse for wear."

Betty Jean held out her hand. "Want me to toss it for you?"

"Of course not," Peter said. "What would I eat for lunch?"

"...and I'm a firm believer in teacher autonomy," he was saying some twenty minutes later to the assembled teaching staff. "I will leave you alone unless you show that you're unable to handle a class of normal human beings—"

To his left someone snickered and Peter turned to see Ray Jenkins shaking his head.

"Point of clarification, Pete." Ray wore the look of someone confident he was about to publicly make a fool of someone else. "Kid comes to school with a gun. That's normal? Another kid rapes a girl in a stairwell. That's normal? Gangbangers? Kids whose old ladies turn tricks? That's all normal in your book?"

"Your point?"

Ray laughed. "Hell, Pete, none of these kids are normal. If they were, they wouldn't be at Luther in the first place."

Peter leaned back in his chair. The room was suddenly quiet and heavy with tension. Gunfight at the O.K. Corral about to erupt between the principal and his sidekick. "Perhaps you would define normal for me, Ray."

Ray's face colored, but his grin didn't fade. "Normal." He scratched his head, appeared to think for a moment. "Okay, I'll tell you what I see as normal. Not to brag or anything, but I consider my two sons pretty normal." He laughed. "Pains in the ass at times, but I'd say they're normal kids."

"And what makes them normal, in your opinion?"

Peter paused. "Other than their impeccable parentage, of course."

Ray laughed again, as did a few of the teachers. "Good one, Pete. Okay, they go to school every day, no cutting class or anything like that. They make decent grades. They're not into drugs and gangs. They both play sports…"

"And they have two parents at home, both actively involved in their lives," Peter added. "When they arrive home from school, someone is there to encourage them, to help put their problems and frustrations into perspective. They're not left to fend for themselves, to judge what's important and what isn't…" He looked at Ray. "I could go on, but is that essentially correct?"

"Yeah, well, my wife's always stayed at home. We both think it's important."

"I'm sure you do. Unfortunately, most of our students don't have that advantage. School is the only stability many of them know, the only safe place where there are rules to follow and obligations to meet. Our students are intelligent, talented and articulate, but, for a variety of reasons, the traditional setting hasn't worked and…" The secretary had stuck her head around the door. "Yes, Betty Jean?"

"A fight's broken out in the parking lot, Mr. Darling."

Ray sprang from his seat as if propelled. "I'll handle it."

"Where's security?" Peter asked the secretary.

"He's trying to break it up."

"Does he need help?"

"I don't think so. I just thought you should know."

"Thank you, Betty Jean."

"I better check it out, anyway." Ray stood at the door, clearly eager to make a break. "You never know."

"I'd prefer that you stay here." Peter glanced at his watch and trotted out all the housekeeping details and sundry matters necessary to hold the meeting until the very last minute. "And let me just say," he added finally, "that I'm looking to all of you for creativity and innovation. Take risks. Teach on the edge. Don't rely solely on what has worked in the past," he said, making it a point to look at Ray Jenkins, livid with anger at the end of the table. "Toss out the dog-eared notes. Come to me with new ideas. If they work, we'll build on them. If they don't, we'll toss them out. Fine-tune, tweak, change something here, add something there. Spice it up. I'd like each of you to think about a different approach to the subject you're teaching and be prepared to discuss it with the group at our next meeting."

As he returned to his office after the meeting, Betty Jean buzzed to say he had a call. "One of your little girls," she said.

It was Delphina.

"Daddy, there's going to be a dance recital and I'm going to be a butterfly."

"A butterfly." Peter sat on the edge of his desk, smiling as he pictured Delphina's solemn little face. "That's wonderful. Did you choose to be that, or—"

"I chose it. We could be birds or bees and I asked if I could be a butterfly. But they don't have butterfly costumes, so the teacher said I have to make one. I need big gauzy wings that flap around."

"Big gauzy wings? Well, I'm sure Auntie Sophia can come up with something."

"She said she can't." A note of distress in Delphina's voice now. "She said she can't even sew buttons on..."

"Hmm." Beth Herman had come into the office and Peter motioned that he'd be right with her. "Well, look, we'll just have to put our thinking caps on."

A silence on the line. "Will it be all right, Daddy?"

"Of course it will," Peter said. "I promise. Bye-bye darling. See you this evening."

"Would you know anything about making butterfly wings?" he asked Beth.

"OKAY, are you convinced now?" Vivian asked Edie as they took Interstate 40 back to Little Hills with Maude asleep in the back seat. "You've seen each place. I wasn't too jazzed with Sunset Manor, but the second one was okay, and Maple Grove…well, what can I say?"

"Nothing," Edie said, then had a thought. "What about her cats?"

"Her cats?" Viv dismissed the question with a wave of her hand. "I'll find somewhere for them. I'm always worrying about her tripping over the damn things, anyway. You know how they're always under your feet? They drive me nuts. I'd never have a cat, let alone three."

From the backseat, Edie could hear Maude snoring. Small, soft, sputtery sounds that made her feel tender and protective. The way she felt only when Maude was asleep. Given its rocky start, she reflected, the day had gone quite well. After her latest tour of Maple Grove, Maude had been so enthusiastic and adamant that it was exactly where she wanted to spend the rest of her years that she'd refused even to consider the fourth place Vivian had lined up for her to see. "My mind's made up," she'd told her daughters. "Go ahead and start packing my things."

"I knew you'd be sold once you saw it," Viv said.

"And Edie, I'm sorry if I got snippy with you earlier. Everything's so…I don't know. I told you about Brad and this new girlfriend of his, right?"

"Mmm," Edie said. She was suddenly feeling weirdly sad about Maude's cats and she couldn't imagine why since she'd never been a big fan of cats, either. "I'm not sure."

"Oh, it's this little trampy girl who goes to Luther. Melissa. She's trying to get transferred back to Stephen's, only so that she can be with Brad again. Ray knows that's why, but he says she's got Peter wrapped around her little finger. She told Brad she's going to earn extra credits for some newsletter thing Peter's trying to start. Ray says he's practically given up talking any sense to Peter, since he just doesn't listen."

"Peter mentioned the newsletter. He asked if I'd be an adviser."

Viv turned her head. "Peter asked you? How did that come about?"

"I ran into him when I went for a walk yesterday. He was with his daughters and a bunch of kids from the school."

"That was it? He just asked you, like that?"

"Yeah." Edie heard something in Viv's voice. "What? You sound surprised."

"Oh, I don't know…" Her fingers tapped on the wheel a moment. "You're not…like, attracted to him or anything?"

"Viv, he has four children."

"So?"

"So, can you picture me being a mommy to four children?"

Vivian grinned. "Not exactly."

"Well, there's your answer."

A moment passed. "You never think about having children?"

Edie shook her head. "They wouldn't fit into the kind of life I lead."

"You could do something different."

"Never. My work is who I am. I can't even imagine doing anything else."

"I used to envy you sometimes," Viv said. "Here's me stuck in Little Hills with a husband and two kids and you're out doing all these exciting things. But you know what? I wouldn't trade my life. A little more money might be nice, but I'm happy. Ray's a good guy and I've got two great kids. I think about you sometimes and wonder how it would have been if I'd just taken off and done my own thing. And then I think, no, I couldn't be that way."

Edie said nothing. It was always there in her conversations with Viv, that little barb. Pick up on it, and Viv would laugh and accuse her of being overly sensitive—which, Edie conceded, might be true. Maybe it was the moment to whip off the mask and proclaim, "Hey, the person you think is me isn't really me," but she felt weary. Things were settled with Maude now, it seemed. If she could survive the rest of the visit without turmoil, it would be enough.

In a dream that night, she wore a hideous yellow bridesmaid dress covered with butterflies and little green worms. Maude and Vivian wore similar dresses, except their dresses had no worms. Maude was complaining that her feet hurt and Vivian wanted the wedding to be over with because she had gingerbread in the oven. They were all standing at the end of the aisle waiting for Beth to appear. Then things got kind of weird and Peter was holding his hand across Edie's mouth and Beth kept whispering that formaldehyde was her favorite perfume and if Edie would just hold still everything would be fine, but then Maude started screaming, loud shrill screams that wouldn't stop. When Edie sat up in bed it was morning and the phone was ringing. Vivian's daily seven-thirty call.

"I realize that it's just your way, Edie," Vivian started out. "But sometimes, sweetie, you can be a touch heavy-handed and insensitive."

"No!" Edie said, weary already. "Me?"

"And sarcastic," Viv said. "Also, I hate to bring this up, but mom just called me. She said you screamed at her last night."

Edie rubbed her eyes. On the table beside her bed was the article she'd fallen asleep reading the night before. "An Analysis of Political Sensitivities in Southeast Asia." She leaned back against the pillows. "I didn't scream at her," she muttered.

"Mom said you did."

"I didn't scream at her," Edie repeated. "I asked her if she had an alarm clock and she didn't understand what I was talking about. I said it four times and then I finally pantomimed a damn alarm clock, *brrrrbrrrbrrr*. Little bell on the top of my head. And she kept saying, 'Boat dock? Boat dock?' Finally, I just brought my mouth up to her ear—"

"And screamed at her."

"I didn't scream. I raised my voice."

"Mom said you screamed."

Edie slowly banged her head against the pillow. "Okay, Viv, I screamed. I'm a wicked, horrible person. I screamed at a poor defenseless little old lady."

"Don't be sarcastic," Vivian scolded. "Just remember she's old. Maybe she seems energetic and capable to you, but trust me, if you'd spent any time around her, you'd appreciate how frail she is. By the way, if you're not doing anything today, we really need to get a start on packing her things.''

Edie considered the day ahead, the highlight being a promised trip to the IGA for Maude to buy toilet paper. ''Sure,'' she said. ''When are you coming over?''

Viv sighed. ''I can't, Eed. The gourmet group wants to do Japanese for the next dinner and guess who's been assigned sushi? Wasabi powder. That's one of the ingredients. First, I have no idea what wasabi powder is, but I know damn well the IGA won't stock it, so that means I'll have to drive into St. Louis. So, anyway, if you could just get started with her closets. Make her toss out the clothes she doesn't wear and…oh, by the way, I meant to warn you about this before…remember when we all went out for drinks and Beth was talking about Peter?''

Edie shook her head, dizzied by the sudden topic change. ''Vaguely. Why?''

''Well, I've been thinking about the whole situation with Beth and Peter and I think she really downplayed the way she feels about him and I know it's because you were there. I could tell. She's intimidated by you—''

''Intimidated by me?'' Edie lay back on the pillow. ''You've got to be kidding.''

''No, I'm not kidding. Look, Eed…'' A pause. ''Okay, I'm not criticizing you. You're probably not even aware of it, but it's just the way you come across.'' *Been there, done that. Tell me something I don't know.* ''It's intimidating, Eed. People are scared to tell you what they really feel.''

Edie studied a brown water spot on the ceiling. ''Vivian,'' she said. ''I've probably spoken to...five people since I got back to Little Hills and that includes Honey at the IGA. And what with ringing up the groceries and making change, she didn't get down to talking about her personal feelings—''

''See? That's what you do. Here I'm just trying to help you by pointing out that you can be a little hard to deal with sometimes and you have to be sarcastic and snippy. I'm telling you for your own good, Eed. None of us are perfect, you know. Even you.''

''Thank you, Viv.'' Edie picked up the Asia document and put her glasses back on. *The role of the journalist as a detached, objective observer,* she read, *can be compromised when personal feelings...* ''I'll try to remember that.''

''I hope you're not being sarcastic, sweetie,'' Viv said. ''I'm only telling you for your own good. You're my sister and I love you. Sometimes, I think, we don't say that enough. Oh and one more thing. I wouldn't ask you, but I'm driving myself crazy with everything I have to do... I told you about Brad, and that little trampy girlfriend, right? But don't get me started on that. Anyway, Ray went off this morning without his briefcase and he wants me to drop it off. If you could just stop by and get it when you take Mom to the IGA—she needs toilet paper, by the way—and then drive it over to the school, I'd really appreciate it. *Wasabi powder.* I swear to God.''

''JUST CAUGHT Melissa Fowler smoking outside the school,'' Ray Jenkins poked his head into Peter's office to announce with obvious satisfaction. ''Shouldn't she be in class right now?''

''Yes, she should.'' Peter remembered the bruise on

her wrist he'd noticed a few days earlier and felt a stab of guilt. He'd meant to talk to her. "Is she out there still?"

"No, I sent her inside." Ray moved farther into the office. "I've had it up to here with that little tramp," he said in a lowered voice. "Always hanging around my son. I caught them both in the garage last night—just talking, Brad said—but I wish to hell she'd leave him alone."

After Ray left, Peter walked over to the English classroom and waited outside until the bell rang. Melissa appeared shortly, sauntering along in the midst of a pack of jostling, laughing students. Her smile faded when she saw him standing there.

"Melissa." She stopped and the other kids hurtled on, one or two of them casting backward glances at her. She wore a black sleeveless shirt and, as she raised her hand to brush the hair from her face, he caught the bruise on the underside of her wrist. "How is everything?"

"Good."

He said nothing, just looked at her. After a moment, her face colored and she glanced away.

"Mr. Jenkins told you?"

"Told me what?"

"That I was smoking and…?"

"And?"

"I was late for class?"

"Were you?"

"Yeah, but I was with three other kids and he didn't say a word to them, he's just picking on me."

"Let's talk about the smoking first," Peter said.

"I'm going to quit."

"Good, then you won't need a lecture from me about all the terrible things smoking does to your body."

She shook her head. "I know all that. I just…I don't know, I just did it but I swear that's my last one and, Mr. Darling, the reason I was late was that me and Marcus…he's my boyfriend. We kind of broke up, because there's someone else I like? And I was, like, telling my friends about it and I just kind of forgot what time it was."

He nodded at her wrist. "Where did that bruise come from, Melissa?"

"Oh…" She looked down at her wrist. "We were just goofing around—"

"We?"

Her face colored. "Me and Brad, he doesn't go to school here. He wasn't trying to hurt me or anything, he just grabbed me too hard." She glanced at her wrist again. "It doesn't hurt."

Peter looked at her. "Melissa, I believed you when you said you wanted to graduate from Stephen's—"

"I do, Mr. Darling."

"Well, so far I'm not seeing very much evidence of that. The next time you're tempted to cut class, I want you to remind yourself of your goal. And if I learn that you've been late again, or that you've missed class, I will personally suspend you."

"I'm sorry, Mr. Darling."

"I don't want apologies, Melissa. I want deeds that demonstrate your commitment."

"Can I just say one thing though?"

"Go ahead."

"I think Mr. Jenkins is picking on me because he's mad that Brad likes me."

"Were *you* late for class?"

"Yes, but the others—"

"I don't care about the others. You were late?"

She nodded.

"Are there other times when you've felt Mr. Jenkins singled you out unfairly?"

"No...not really."

"No other times?"

"No, but he doesn't like me and I know why. He thinks I'm not good enough for his son."

Peter looked at her for a moment. "Melissa, Mr. Jenkins's opinion of you vis-à-vis his son is not important. You're an intelligent, capable person with a lot of potential. Except for your one rather obvious flaw, I see nothing at all wrong with you."

"What flaw?"

"Your inability to tell time, or at least your insistence on ignoring it. Work on that and I think you'll do splendidly."

After Melissa left, he paid visits to a couple of classes, intervened in a scuffle between two junior boys, confiscated a package of sunflower seeds and was starting back to his office for a two o'clock parent meeting, when he saw Edie Robinson walking toward him. As she drew closer, he felt an idiotic grin spread across his face. He tried to arrange his features into something less indicative of the fact that the sight of her had produced a wild burst of happiness that was making his heart race.

"Edie." They'd stopped outside the science classroom where, through the partially opened blinds, he could see heads bent over textbooks. Edie wore faded jeans and an equally faded yellow T-shirt. "What brings you here?"

"An errand for my sister. Ray forgot his briefcase this morning. My mother's in the car waiting for me. After that, we're going to the IGA for toilet paper."

He met her eyes for a moment.

"I lead a very busy life," she said.

"Clearly. But immensely rewarding, I should imagine."

"And challenging. Last time we went to the IGA, I bought the wrong kind of toilet paper. One-ply, which Mom says is far too thin. I had no idea."

"One learns," he said.

"One does." She pushed her hair back behind her ears. "And on top of all that, I've actually had time for some introspection."

"Good heavens," Peter said. "Amazing."

"Isn't it? After I met you in the park, I thought a lot about the remark I made to you about children being a foreign language—"

"Which you had no interest in learning." He nodded. "Yes, I do remember you saying that."

"In retrospect, I think that perhaps what I really meant was that while I do find children…well, what I'm saying is I don't know much about children, nothing really, but that doesn't mean…" Her face colored slightly. "I have no idea why I'm making such a mess of this. I just didn't want to leave you with this impression that I'm cold and unfeeling, because I'm not. Really." She bit her lip. "God, I'm embarrassing myself. You seem to bring that out in me."

Peter watched her face. Cool composure was clearly struggling to regain control. If he hadn't been aware of the curious looks from students in the science classroom, he might have put his arms around her. Instead, he removed a yellow leaf from her shoulder that had fluttered down from the gutter above the classroom.

"I didn't think for one minute that you were cold and unfeeling," he said.

"Good. How are your daughters, by the way?"

"Very well, thank you. How is your mother?"

"Probably getting very impatient," she said. "I should go."

"By the way," he said. "The journalism club I mentioned. I'd like to set up something for tomorrow after school. Around four."

She nodded. "I think I'll be through at the IGA by then."

"Terrific. We'll be meeting in the arts building. Anyone can direct you."

"See you then."

Peter started to walk away, then turned to glance over his shoulder. "And Edie," he called. "Don't forget the toilet paper. Two-ply."

CHAPTER NINE

"HEY, MOM." Edie was grinning as she climbed into the car. "Sorry to keep you waiting. I got talking to Peter. The principal." She started the ignition. "He's asked me to help set up a journalism group."

She drove out of the parking lot and started down Broadway, heading for the IGA. "I think it'll be fun."

In the rearview mirror, she peered at her reflection. Her eyes looked bright, her face slightly flushed. Peter Darling. Had his parents been thinking of Peter Pan when they named their son? She'd have to ask him. She tried to remember his daughters' names. The quiet one was Delphina. She glanced at Maude. "Mom, I want to ask you something."

"No, I've got one of those little spots up my nose again," Maude said.

"Viv said I'm intimidating," she said. "Do you think I'm intimidating?"

"I'd like to see you start dating," Maude said. "I'd like to see you settled down and married. You're getting too old to be traipsing all over the world. What about children? You think you're ever going to have children? I clipped an article from one of those magazines Dixie passes on to me. I don't care for them much myself—too much sex stuff. I don't know why people want to read about sex—as far as I'm concerned, it's a private thing between two people—but it said women of fifty are having babies these days. It's a common thing. In my days, you stopped having children much younger but—''

"Mom." It's not worth it, Edie told herself as she pulled into the IGA lot, but stubbornness made her persist. "Look at me." She switched off the ignition and turned in the seat to face Maude. "Intimidating," she said slowly. "Do you think people find me intimidating?"

"Mating?" Maude's soft pink face was tense with concentration. "Is that what you said?"

"Viv said I'm hard to talk to. And I wanted to know if—"

"You snap," Maude said.

"But when I'm not snapping…" Foot curled up under her, keys in her hand, Edie tried another approach. "Are you scared of me, Mom?"

"Scared of you?" Maude's mouth pursed. "No. Why would I be scared of you?"

"Because I'm intimidating."

"If you're saying what I think you're saying," Maude said. "You look fine, but I don't like your hair like that. Makes you look older."

Edie gave up and got out of the car. I'm not intimidating, she decided. Viv's nuts. Over on the passenger side, she helped Maude out of the car, and then held her arm as they slowly crossed the parking lot to the IGA, where the windows were advertising 8 Jumbo Rolls for $3.99. The problem, she reflected, was family perception. If you started life as bossy and obnoxious, you could evolve into Mother Teresa but to the folks at home, you'd be bossy and obnoxious until the day you died. But Viv was wrong. She wasn't intimidating—a fact she intended to demonstrate throughout her visit to Little Hills.

"I need prunes, too," Maude whispered. "Haven't gone for three days."

"Good idea, Mom," Edie said. "I'll go and find them for you." Well, obviously Peter Darling didn't find her intimidating. It was a pleasant thought.

WHILE PETER'S BRAIN officially dealt with Millie Adams and her son Robert, he found himself playing and re-playing the exchange with Edie outside the science building. *I didn't want to leave you with the impression that I was cold and unfeeling.*

"...So Robert says he completed the course," Millie Adams was saying. "But he says they're not giving him credit for it. It doesn't seem fair to me. Robert should be encouraged when he does good, not picked on."

"I'm quite sure no one is picking on him." Peter turned to the computer on his desk and tapped in Robert's name. Unlike most Luther High parents, Millie Adams was involved in her son's education. Unfortunately, Millie hadn't, so to speak, gotten religion until Robert's sophomore year, when she married a man who insisted that no wife of his was going to work. Suddenly she had more free time on her hands than she knew what to do with, and Robert, who had been skipping school with impunity—which was how he had landed at Luther to begin with—became the focus of Millie's attention. At least three times a week, Millie would call to complain, suggest or demand. And, as he listened, Peter would have to remind himself that at least she cared. "He missed two independent-learning sessions last week," he said when he'd pulled up Robert's records. "And one this week. Mr. Jenkins said he discussed the issue with you.''

"He did. I thought he said Robert could make up his credits some other way. Robert was all excited because he had almost enough credits to graduate. Now he says you've got some new rule that makes it really tough to get the credits he needs and I don't think it's fair. Robert deserves an education—"

"I completely agree, Mrs. Adams," Peter said. "That is why we no longer allow students to earn credits merely for occupying a seat."

"Turning up for class, you mean? Mr. Jenkins didn't have a problem with it."

"That may be the case," Peter said. "But I do. Now, if you'd like to discuss some ways we can help Robert actually earn credits…"

"No offense, Mr. Darling," she said. "But Mr. Jenkins has been at Luther longer than you have. If he believes it's a good thing to give kids credit for good attendance, then I don't see why you need to go around changing things."

"DADDY, come here." As Peter whispered good-night to his daughter, Kate reached up to pull his face down close to her own. "Auntie Sophia says we need a new mommy," she said softly.

"She's going back to England," Abbie said from the next bed.

"I miss Mommy," Kate said.

"I know," Peter said and felt himself struggling for words. He smoothed a lock of hair off her forehead. "Tell me a happy story about Mommy," he said. It was a game they often played. The twins had been too young when their mother died to actually remember much, but he'd told them so many stories about Deborah that both girls could recite anecdotes—usually highly embellished—with so much vivid detail, that he'd have to remind himself that their accounts were secondhand.

"Want to hear the one where she put the great big bag of dog food on her back?" Abbie asked.

"And pretended it was light as a feather?" Kate added.

"Does that one make you happy?" Peter asked.

"It makes me happy," Abbie said. "Mommy was strong."

"She was, wasn't she?" Peter said. Physically and emotionally, it was one of the qualities he'd loved most about his Deborah. He wondered if it was a similar quality, a certain toughness that drew him to Edie. A stab of disloyalty made him push the thought away. "Tell me some other happy stories," he said.

"No, you tell us some stories, Daddy," Kate said.

"Kiss me Daddy," Abbie sat up in bed. "I want a big kiss."

"No, I get the last kiss." Kate sat up. "I want a story, too. Please."

Abbie began bouncing on the bed. "Tell. Me. A. Story."

Kate shot her twin a look and began bouncing in unison. "Tell *me* a story."

"I'll tell you both a story," he said. "After you've stopped jumping and you're lying quietly." All blond curls and flashing pajama-clad limbs, they both climbed back under the covers, pulled them to their chins and watched him with unblinking saucer-wide eyes.

"Good," he regarded them solemnly. "Would you prefer the one about the blackbird who camped outside Buckingham Palace so that he could see the queen hang out her laundry? Or the butterfly who landed in the queen's rice pudding?"

"Did the queen eat the rice pudding?" Abbie wanted to know.

"No, silly," Kate said. "She ate the butterfly. Right, Daddy?"

"Well, I can't tell you, can I?" Peter said. "That would ruin the ending."

"Tell us about the blackbird," Abbie said.

"Butterfly," Kate said. "Butterfly, butterfly, butter-fly."

"Blackbird, blackbird, blackbird," Abbie pleaded

Kate began to giggle. "Butterfly. Butterfly. *Butterfly.*"

"Blackbird." Abbie hurled herself out of bed and onto Peter's back. "Blackbird," she screeched.

Later, after Natalie and Delphina were also in bed, Sophia eyed him as he collapsed into the armchair by the fireplace.

"Hard day?"

He considered. "Mixed. The assistant principal is not at all sure of me. He's a firm believer in maintaining the status quo, and I think it rather disturbs him that I'm changing things around."

"He feels threatened," Sophia warned. "Watch your back."

"Oh, he'll come around," Peter said with less confidence than he felt. He told her about the exchange with Millie Adams. "Unfortunately, many of the parents seem to feel the same way."

"Change will always produce resistance," Sophia said. "Give it time." She set aside a blouse she'd been sewing a button onto. "About the other matter…"

Peter extracted himself from the chair, moved to the couch and reached for the day's newspaper. Lately, he never found time to read it in the morning before he left for school. Flat on his back, feet propped over the end of the couch, he started to read, but he could feel Sophia's eyes on him.

"Don't ignore me, Peter. I'm quite serious about this whole thing."

"Look," he said. "You've made your point. However, I'm not about to embark upon a whirlwind courtship and marriage just to provide you with peace of mind."

"Six weeks, Peter. And then I'm gone."

He kept reading. "I'm aware of that."

"Natalie misses Deborah," Sophia said. "Has she told you that?"

"Actually, she hasn't," Peter said, stung. "But it's hardly surprising."

"Peter, I worry," Sophia said. "Natalie's getting to the age where she'll need a female figure in her life. You can't be everything to her, no matter how hard you try. Girls need their mothers."

"I know." Peter kept reading. "I think I've already explained my position."

"Is it Deborah? You feel that no one can ever replace her, so you don't even try."

Peter surveyed her with exasperated affection. Sophia was nothing if not dogged. If he'd entertained any idea at all of a quiet evening with the newspaper, Sophia clearly had a different agenda, one she wasn't about to give up.

"I don't want to replace Deborah," he said carefully. "She's the girls' mother and nothing will ever change that fact. But it doesn't mean another woman couldn't love them... Look, Sophia, we went over all this the other night."

"What's happening with the foreign correspondent?"

"Her name is Edie and she's coming to school to-morrow. I asked her to help me set up a journalism club."

"Have the girls met her?"

"Briefly."

"She's the one in the park?"

He turned to look at her. "Yes."

"Abbie doesn't like her."

"Abbie knows nothing about her. They didn't exchange a word."

Sophia shrugged. "Children are very intuitive. The others weren't keen on her, either, although Delphina doesn't mind her, or so she says. But with Delphina, one has no idea what's really going on beneath the surface. Remember, though, that this is a woman who said children are a foreign—"

"Language. I know. I saw her at school today. She said she didn't really mean it."

Sophia smiled. "Well, I suppose that's encouraging. Will I meet her? This Edie?"

Peter considered. He couldn't quite picture Edie in any scenarios that included more than just the two of them. "I don't know," he said.

"Why not?" Sophia asked. "Have her here for dinner. Perhaps I'll like her. Does she *have* to be a foreign correspondent?"

THURSDAY AFTERNOON, Edie sat in a molded plastic chair in Beth's small glassed-in office at one end of the teen mother center. Through the window, she could see Maude down at one end of a long, brightly lit room that seemed filled with the high-pitched chatter of teenage girls and the insistent wailing of two red-faced babies in a playpen. A bulletin board was crammed with baby pictures pasted onto brown-paper teddy bears. On a red paper heart at the center of each bear, names and birth dates had been printed in elaborate calligraphy. Near where Maude sat, several girls were bent over a table covered with kraft paper and colored pens.

Edie folded her arms across her chest, observing it all. Her instinct, as always, was to categorize the details, to frame a context as though this were something she was about to report on. She caught herself. *This is not an assignment. You're sitting here watching your mother play with babies. See how involved she is? It's called living in the moment. Get up off the sidelines, for God's sake. Un-detach.*

She got up and wandered in Maude's direction. Beth was occupied and Maude was cooing at a plump, happy-looking baby in blue rompers. Her back against the wall, Edie stood quietly, the watchful observer still. It was a hard habit to break. After a while, she became aware of a girl nearby shooting glances at her. Struck by the girl's clear olive skin and large dark eyes, Edie smiled.

"That's my little boy," she said. "Roger."

"He's cute," Edie said. "How old is he?"

"Six months."

"You go to school here?" Edie asked, realizing that she wasn't quite sure how the teen mother program worked.

"Yeah." The girl shrugged. "For now, anyway."

"You're ready to graduate?"

"No, Bobby, my boyfriend, doesn't want me going to school. He gets kind of mean about it."

Edie felt her eyes widen. "Your *boyfriend* doesn't want you to go to school?"

The girl grinned at Edie's indignation. "Well, he's got pretty strong ideas about how things should be."

"*He's* got strong ideas? God…" Nearly spluttering in angry disbelief, Edie shook her head. "You're what? Sixteen?"

The girl nodded, still smiling, as though torn between embarrassment at being the focus of Edie's anger and appreciation for a sympathetic audience. "See, we live with Bobby's mom and she's supporting all of us—"

"How old is Bobby?"

"Seventeen."

"He's not in school, either?"

The girl shook her head. "No, he says diplomas don't do no good, he can make more in construction. Except that he got laid off and now he can't find a job, so it's kind of tough…"

The girl's voice trailed off and she gazed over at the baby. Ordinarily not given to metaphysical thoughts, Edie felt a sudden and intense conviction that fate had caused her to drop Maude off at the teen mother center and that she was there to help this girl. Even as she had the idea, she suspected that she'd later scoff at it, but right now it was a clear command.

"Look—" she fished in her purse for a card "—my name is Edie Robinson and I have nothing to do with this center. That's my mom over there—"

"She is the sweetest little lady," the girl said. "We all just love her."

"Thank you. We do, too." Edie felt a tad hypocritical. "Anyway, I'm just here in Little Hills for a few weeks, but…I want to talk to you. I don't want you to drop out of school."

"Okay," the girl said.

"No, don't just say okay." She scribbled her mother's

number on the card and held out it out. "What's your name?"

"Jessie."

"Jessie, listen to me. Your boyfriend's an idiot. Do not let him talk you into dropping out of school. Will you promise me you'll at least call me?"

The girl nodded again.

"Say, 'I promise, Edie, I'll call you.'"

"I promise, Edie, I'll call you."

"Personally, Jessie, I wouldn't want to be in your shoes if you broke that promise." Peter had suddenly materialized at Edie's side. "I think Edie could be quite formidable."

Edie glared at Peter, disconcerted and angry. She'd been focused on Jessie, and Peter's sudden appearance had thrown her off stride. Jessie, with a shy glance at Peter, had slipped off to take care of the baby and Edie feared that any tentative bond was now most likely severed.

"She's thinking about dropping out," Edie told Peter. "Because her idiot boyfriend doesn't want her in school."

Peter nodded, his smile fading. "Unfortunately, it's not at all unusual. If she were in a larger school, she probably would just drift off. Because this is a small campus, we can pay closer attention to each student."

"So you know about Jessie?" she asked.

"I'm aware that she has a difficult home situation," he said.

"But that's a given, right? Don't most of these kids have difficult home situations? I'm asking about Jessie."

Peter's expression darkened. "Specifically?"

"Specifically, that she's sixteen." She was still angry at Jessie's situation. "She's got a four-month-old baby and a boyfriend who wants her to drop out of school so that he can knock her up again…I'm sorry." She shook her head at him. "It's not my place to grill you. The whole thing just makes me so damn angry."

He nodded once more.

"Does it make you angry?"

"'It' being…societal conditions that lead to children having children?"

"Yeah, that would be a start." Across the room, a cluster of girls was sneaking covert looks at them, and beneath the anger she felt a stab of curiosity. How many of Luther's female students nurtured secret crushes on Luther's tall, dark and handsome principal? As if on cue, Beth came over to where they stood, summery in a pale green shirtwaist abloom with pink, orange and blue wildflowers. An enameled butterfly was pinned to her left lapel.

Beth's smile embraced Edie then lingered a moment on Peter, who cleared his throat and glanced off across the room, his face faintly tinged with color.

"Edie, I'm so glad you decided to stay for a while. Your mother is having such a wonderful time," Beth said. "I think she's completely fallen for Roger."

"Kind of looks that way." Edie watched Maude, who was actually down on her knees, changing the baby's diaper. "It's nice to see her involved in something besides herself." As soon the words were out, she wanted to take them back. Beth's smile had congealed slightly; Peter was looking at her as though she'd revealed her true colors, which perhaps she had.

"I didn't mean that the way it sounded," she said. "I just meant that when she has nothing else to do, she tends to obsess about herself—her blood pressure, that sort of thing." Whether she'd redeemed herself in his eyes, she couldn't really tell.

"What your mother's doing is mutually beneficial," Peter said, after a moment. "She's helping us tremendously." He looked at Beth. "Before you arrived, Edie had just asked me whether I ever became angry—"

"At the futility," Edie interrupted, feeling the anger return as she relayed her exchange with Jessie. "I mean, this is one school, one student, but Jessie's story must be played out over and over. How could you not feel angry? And kind of helpless, too?"

"Angry," Peter said. "But not entirely helpless. I'm not particularly qualified to discuss societal problems in general. I can tell you what I think, what I believe. I can even come up with opinions on what should be done. But, realistically, my area of influence is this school. If I can keep Jessie in school, prepare her to lead a productive life, know that I've made a difference in one life, I can feel reasonably at peace with myself." He smiled at Edie and clasped her shoulder. "Anyway, I'll see you in an hour."

"Right." To her embarrassment, her face had turned scarlet; she could feel the blood pulsing under her skin. Her shoulder throbbed where his hand had touched it. "The journalism club."

PETER SAT at the back of the classroom, listening to Edie talk to the students. Watching, more than listening. She wore a slim pale green dress, and her hair was caught up in a loose knot at the back of her head. In her left hand, a pair of heavy tortoiseshell-framed glasses dangled. Every few minutes, she'd pull them on to glance at the notes on her lap, remove them a moment later, and then perch them back on her nose to peer over the top at the students. Her expression was animated, engaged. She knew the subject and clearly loved it. He looked for the same quality in his teachers, but too often didn't find it.

"...And the answers to the kinds of dilemmas and questions you face as a journalist," she was saying now, "are usually not found in textbooks. Life is more practical. You have to look to yourself, to who you are as a person, what you care about, what you think is important and what you think is the right thing to do."

She went on to talk about other things and his mind drifted. Not far, though. Edie fascinated him. He could fall in love with her. He already felt that heightened awareness, the intensity of feeling that in the past he'd confused with love. Part of it, he knew, was the fascination with her lifestyle. A sort of Othello–Desdemona role reversal. It enthralled him to imagine her flying off to distant parts, facing danger, living from moment to moment, always on to the next story. He suspected that he was romanticizing her a bit, but it didn't dim his imagination. He saw her in dark smoky bars where war-toughened journalists sat around drinking whiskey and telling tales. Last night in bed, as he lay awake thinking about her, that image had incited a stab of jealousy. One of the war-toughened journalists, ruggedly handsome in a battered safari suit, had had his arm draped around Edie's shoulder. He wondered again about the boyfriend. A serious relationship?

Peter tuned back in to see Edie tap her watch and shoot him a questioning look.

"I could keep going all night," she said. "But I realize you people probably have things to do, so I'll wrap it up by saying that the one cardinal rule in journalism is that you need to get to the heart of the story. Dig beyond the hearsay, the secondhand tales, the gossip, rumor and speculation. Don't settle for the official statements, the press conferences and guided tours. Find the truth. See things for yourself. It's the only way you can stand by your words afterward. You saw it, you heard it, you are telling the truth as far as you know."

Peter walked down to the front of the room and smiled at Edie. The students, who had clearly been hanging on her words, broke into enthusiastic applause. Edie's smile was radiant, her face flushed, as she acknowledged the applause.

"I loved that," she told Peter after the students had trickled out. "They were really captivated, I could see it in their faces." Wordlessly, as though reliving the moment, she shook her head. "What a trip."

"The way you're feeling right now is exactly what makes teaching worthwhile," he said. "Unfortunately, those moments don't happen as often as we'd like them to."

Edie, clearly still high on the experience, just smiled. "God, if that's the feeling teaching can give you, maybe I should switch careers."

Peter raised an eyebrow. "Maybe you should."

"Nah…" She shook her head. "I don't want to *talk* about reporting. I want to do it."

He smiled. "Can I entice you with a coffee and some gooey butter cake?"

She smiled back at him. "Peter, Jack the Ripper could entice me with gooey butter cake. It's after five, though. Don't you have to go home to your daughters?"

"Um…the girls adore gooey butter cake and I thought perhaps—"

"Sure, bring them," Edie said a shade too quickly.

She regarded her feet for a moment. "I do have to drive my mother home though and—"

"Pick up toilet paper at the IGA."

"Well, that's a given."

"Let's all have coffee, then," he said. "Maude, too."

She looked amused. "Is that supposed to be an incentive?"

"I find your mother quite charming."

"That's because she's not your mother."

"Anyway, I'd like to swap Ethiopia stories with you."

"You were in Ethiopia?"

"Years ago. My wife and I were in the Peace Corps."

Edie narrowed her eyes at him for a moment as though assessing the truthfulness of what he'd just said, and then she laughed aloud. "Oh, what the hell? Let me see what Mom wants to do and I'll meet you back here in ten minutes."

"Better still," Peter said, "we'll meet you both at the Olde Towne Bakery."

"COFFEE?" Maude, sitting in a wicker rocker, smiled down at the baby in her arms. "You got some yesterday, didn't you?"

"Mom." Edie crouched down on the floor in front of Maude and peered into her mother's face. "Look at me. Peter invited us to have coffee. And gooey butter cake. His daughters are going, too."

Maude's forehead creased. One hand went to her ear. "So much noise in here, babies crying and all. I had to turn my hearing aid down. Now what?"

"Coffee, Mom. Want to go have coffee?"

"I had coffee. One of the little girls got me a cup.

That one over there with the long black hair. Sixteen,'' she said in a lowered voice. "And a mother already.''

Edie took a breath before she tried again. Around the room, girls were shooting amused glances over in their direction. "Mom, look at me.''

"You need some lipstick,'' Maude said. "You look washed out.''

"Coffee,'' Edie said. "With Peter. Do you want to go?''

"No.''

Edie sat back on her heels. She'd been playing tug-of-war and her opponent had suddenly released the rope. "No?''

"Tonight's good on TV.''

"Edie.'' Beth had come over. "Go and have coffee. I'll drive your mom home.''

Edie stood. Beth looked amused, kindly and slightly harried, with an armful of tiny pastel sweaters. Beth, who had a crush on Peter. "Why don't you join us, Beth. Peter just mentioned something about Ethiopia. He was there with the Peace Corps—Addis Ababa, probably— and I think he just wants to reminisce. I was there for a while too and… Join us. His daughters are going, too.'' She felt uncomfortable and unable to stop babbling. "Gooey butter cake. The Olde Bakery does great gooey butter cake…''

Smiling, Beth was shaking her head. "Can I talk to you for a minute, Edie?''

"There's coffee over there if you want some.'' Maude nodded at the coffeemaker in the corner. "No more for me, though.''

"Okay, Mom.'' She patted Maude's hand. "I'll be right back.'' A moment later she followed Beth to her office.

"Have a seat." In her tiny cubicle, Beth moved a stack of manila folders from a chair. "It's kind of cramped in here. Peter apologized when he hired me, but the budget doesn't extend to a whole lot more. Anyway, I've been meaning to talk to you…"

"Beth. Before you say anything, I just want you to know I have no…designs on Peter. Honestly. He's obviously very attractive and seems like a good man, but—"

"Stop." Beth laughed and patted Edie's hand. "That's what I wanted to talk to you about." Her smile faded and she hesitated. "I was truly embarrassed when we all went out last week and Viv went on about Peter." She picked at a thread on her dress. "I admire Peter tremendously and…well…he is good-looking, but somehow Viv has taken all that and turned it into this romantic thing she thinks I have for him. Quite frankly, it's getting very awkward. Whenever I have to talk to him about something, and I do on a daily basis, I can't help thinking about the things Viv has said about…goodness, I can't even repeat them."

Edie sat back in her seat, assimilating what Beth had told her. "So you're not interested in Peter…romantically, I mean?" Her face felt hot suddenly, and she grinned. "Damn, why do I feel so awkward talking about this kind of stuff?"

"I know, I stumble all over myself, too," Beth said. "About Peter though, it's like…well, you know if you've got this crush on a movie star or something?"

Edie laughed. "It's been a while since I had a crush on a movie star, although…I have to admit I saw *The English Patient* three times, just to gawk at Ralph Fiennes."

"Exactly. It's not like you're ever even going to meet him, but you can still appreciate him."

"But Beth, Peter is right here. You see him every day."

Beth nodded. "I know. But he's just too... I don't know, I guess I'm a comfy old-shoes kind of person and with Peter I'd never really relax and be myself. Does that sound weird?"

"Well, not weird, but—"

"Edie, I swear, if you ever breathe a word to Peter."

"I promise." She thought for a minute. "But about Viv, though. You're saying she conjured this all up herself? Why?"

"I think Viv is unhappy, Edie. She's always busy doing a million things, but I honestly think all that activity fills some void in her life."

"But she's always talking about how happy she is. The boys and Ray. Decorating the new house..." She stopped, thinking about what she'd said. "A cover for how she really feels? Is that what you're saying?"

Beth nodded. "Look at that house, Edie. It's gorgeous, but how can she afford it on Ray's salary? And she spends like there's no tomorrow. We went to the mall together last week because she wanted to buy makeup. She spent two hundred dollars on creams for her neck and eyes and she's talking now about a face-lift. And she drinks way too much." She sighed. "I'm sorry to lay all this on you, but I don't know who else can help her. I don't think your mother's picked up on it..."

Edie shook her head. "I don't think so, either. Is Ray aware, do you think? If they're living beyond their means, he has to know that."

"Ray's an idiot," Beth said sharply. "I'm sorry, I

don't usually talk about people like that and I know he's your brother-in-law, but he can be an insensitive clod.''

"Wow." Edie grinned despite herself. "I'd never imagine hearing something like that from you. I mean, I blurt out whatever is on my mind, but you seem…I don't know…more restrained and—"

"Tactful?" Beth said, laughing. "I guess I usually am, but Ray's been treading on thin ice with me lately. Between the two of us, of course.''

"Of course." Edie glanced up at the wall clock. "I told Peter I'd meet him in ten minutes and it's already twenty past. Listen, thank you, Beth. I'm not exactly sure how I'm going to handle this, but I'm glad you told me.''

Beth stood. "Viv seems like a competent, take-charge sort of person," she said, "but underneath it all, I think she's got some real issues." She walked Edie out of the office. "Don't think about it until tomorrow. Go have coffee with Peter. And enjoy.''

Edie looked at her.

"I think he's attracted to you," Beth said, smiling. "I'm quite intuitive about that sort of thing.''

CHAPTER TEN

"I'LL HAVE TWO of the almond thingies, one of those chocolate squares and a gooey butter cake," Peter told the assistant behind the counter at the Olde Towne Bakery. "Actually, stick in a napoleon…no, wait. What's that?"

"An éclair."

"I'll have two of those and…is that marzipan, by any chance?"

"Almond paste. Same thing, I think."

"Is it?" Peter wasn't sure himself. "Well, stick one of those in, too. No, no." She'd started to put them in a box. "We'll eat them here."

"Here?" The assistant's eyes widened. "You're going to eat all of these here?"

"Well, we're going to give it a try," Peter said. As he carried the tray across the room to the table where Edie sat, he felt almost giddy. This was a breakthrough. Although she'd needed some convincing to have coffee, she had come. He would take things very slowly, he decided. Perhaps not even a good-night kiss, although the prospect of kissing her in the next hour or so was one he parted with reluctantly. As he set the tray down, she looked at him, mouth agape.

"Are we expecting company?"

"There's more," he said. "I'll be back."

"Peter," she said when he'd sat down again. "You're not seriously planning to eat all of this tonight?"

"I'm not," he said. "We are." He couldn't quite read the look she gave him and on the chance that it might be disapproval, he said, "I intend to take some back to the girls. What they don't eat, I'll take in to school tomorrow."

She looked at him for a moment. "Okay, fess up. What's the real reason you didn't bring your daughters?"

"It's exactly what I told you. My sister had rented a video they've all been clamoring to see—well, all except for Delphina, who much prefers books. And Sophia had promised them they could make their own ice cream sundaes. This was before I got home. So I arrived and made an alternative proposal and, even though it included gooey butter cake, I couldn't sway them."

Edie narrowed her eyes. "They think I'm a witch."

"I don't think you're a witch. And the girls hardly know you."

"Neither do you."

He smiled. "But I'm learning a little more every day."

She smiled back at him, a moment passed and then she glanced down at the cakes. "I stopped eating this sort of thing when I was about fourteen," she said, cutting into a napoleon.

"Why?"

She laughed. "*Why?* Only a guy would ask a question like that. A guy who probably doesn't have a fat cell in his body and never had zits."

"Zits? Pimples, you mean? I can assure you I had plenty of them. Horrible looking lad, I was. My mother used to cover my head with a bag when she had to take me out in public."

"Liar."

"Have some of the marzipan thing." He cut into one of the cakes with the back of his fork. "And tell me whether you prefer it to the napoleon. It's actually a character test."

She gave him a long look. "I'm not sure I'm in the mood to have my character tested."

"It's painless." He cut into both cakes and leaned across the table to put a piece in her mouth. "This one?" He watched as she ate it. "Or—" he fed her another piece "—this one?"

"The first one," she said.

"Marzipan," he said. "My favorite, too, after gooey butter cake, which is in a class by itself."

"So what's the character test?"

"You like what I like, which means you're discerning, exceptionally intelligent, and kind to animals and small children."

"All that from a piece of cake, huh?"

"Astounding, isn't it?"

"I'm astounded," she said.

"So am I."

"The last part of it is untrue, though," she said. "The small children bit."

Peter said nothing. She was paying rapt attention to her coffee now, gazing into it as though it had turned from coffee to a novel from which she couldn't remove her nose. He demolished the marzipan cake and stuck his fork into the gooey butter cake.

"It's not that I'm unkind," she amended. "Just not particularly maternal."

"Some women aren't," he said, thinking about Sophia's remark. He refrained from taking issue, which he very much wanted to do, and waited to see what else she might say.

"The thing is," she said, still addressing her coffee, "children are a tremendous responsibility. Once you have them, they're a lifetime commitment." She looked up at him now. "I was late getting here because Beth wanted to talk to me about my sister. Viv's having…personal problems. I had no idea and I have even less idea about what I can do to help."

"You're not close, then?"

"I suppose not, because I didn't even recognize there was a problem." She mashed a crumb with her finger. "I *want* to help. She's my sister. At the same time, though, I feel as though I'm assuming another layer of responsibility. It's the same thing with my mother. I'm not entirely sure that giving up her house is what she really *wants* and it's leaving me with this niggling doubt that I can't ignore. And part of me just wants the freedom to walk away from it all…"

"And you could."

"I could, I know. In fact, it hurt my feelings when my mom said she didn't know why I'd come back. I'm sure she wasn't trying to hurt me. 'No one expects anything of you,' she said. I couldn't get the words out of my head. It just made me feel so damn lonely."

"It's hard to have things both ways, Edie. Needing people and caring about them, and vice versa, very much limits one's freedom to just walk away from it all."

"I know. Intellectually, I know. Emotionally, I'm stamping my foot because I want it both ways. So." Chin cupped in her hand, she regarded him. "I bet you never really had zits."

"Neither did you, I'm sure."

"I've always been perfect," she said.

"You have exquisite eyes," he said.

"Exquisite. Wow."

"You're blushing."

"Because you're staring at me." She broke off another piece of cake. "And 'exquisite' kind of threw me. It's not a word I hear much, at least not applied to myself."

"Sorry. I didn't mean to embarrass you."

"It wasn't a complaint. I was just explaining…"

They were, he realized, leaning closer toward one another than they'd been when they first sat down. He leaned back in the booth, drank some coffee, then set his cup down. "Tell me how accurate this is," he said after a while. He told her about his craggy safari-suited war-correspondent fantasy. "Is that what it's like—hotel bars and whiskey and cigar smoke?"

She laughed. "Not exactly."

"That first day when you spoke at school, I remember you saying that your friends were mostly other journalists."

"They are."

He picked at a piece of cake, seeing again the smoky bar and the guy with his arm around Edie's shoulders. He returned the uneaten cakes to the box and stood. "This boyfriend of yours?" he said as he followed Edie outside. "Another journalist?"

"Yeah…"

"Are you in love with him?"

"I never was."

Somehow the disclosure didn't surprise him. He resisted the temptation to question her further.

"I don't want to leave you," he said when they were

back outside on the dark street. "May I walk with you to your mother's?"

Edie laughed. And then she stood on tiptoe to kiss his cheek. "You are so sweetly formal, Peter. It's very endearing. I feel as though I should fan myself and have the vapors."

"I can assure you," he said as he took her elbow and they walked up Monroe, "that beneath this civilized exterior, I'm a raging uncouth beast, full of uncontrollable lust and completely insatiable."

"Is that supposed to unnerve me, or entice me?"

"I wouldn't mind if it did both, actually. You'd be enticed but so unnerved, you'd succumb to the vapors and then I'd have to revive you."

"Ah," she said.

"Would you like to go away with me for the weekend?" he asked as they reached Maude's house.

She smiled. "I think not, but if you'd like you can come in for a while."

"It's a start," he said.

AND NOW he stood in the living room, amidst all the knickknacks and the lumpy armchairs with their knitted afghans and sprung seats. Maude had been sitting at the window with Tinkerbell in her lap and Panda and Poochie at her feet—watching for them, Edie guessed, although Maude vigorously denied it.

"I've got more to do with my life than sit around waiting for my daughter to come home. How are you, Peter? You like music? Gramophone records." Tinkerbell leaped to the floor, as Maude eased herself up from the armchair, took his hand and led him over to the old record cabinet. "Know how old that is? Edith, make Peter some coffee."

"We just had coffee, Mom. I'll make some for you if you don't think it will keep you awake all night." Maude, impossibly tiny beside Peter, was flitting around the room now, thrusting framed pictures at him. Edie caught Peter's eye and he winked, clearly enjoying himself. I want the freedom to walk away, she'd told him.

"Look at all these records." Maude flung open the cabinet door to show Peter the shelves of old vinyl albums inside. "What about a glass of port? You smell something burning?"

Edie sniffed. "Do you have something in the oven?"

"Chicken potpie in the oven," Maude said. "Should be just about done. Here, Peter, play this one. I'll have the pie with some of that potato salad from yesterday, Edith. Bring it all in on the green tray."

Edie glanced at her watch. "Isn't it kind of late for you to be eating, Mom?"

"No, not the coleslaw. Don't like coleslaw," she told Peter. "Never have. Bring it in on a tray, Edith. The green one."

In the kitchen, the oven timer was chiming. Edie took the pie out of the oven and set it on a tray. She took a knife and fork from the drawer and tore off a piece of paper towel. From the living room, she heard a crackly old World War II song that she remembered hearing in childhood. "I don't eat coleslaw, never have," Maude was telling Peter as Edie set the tray down on her mother's lap.

"She doesn't like the green peppers," Edie said, sotto voce.

"Don't like the green peppers," Maude said.

Edie winked at Peter. "Do I know my mom, or what?"

"My husband used to collect them," Maude said.

"Gramophone records," Edie murmured to Peter, who had lifted an album out of its cover. "Not green peppers."

"Hundreds of them," Maude said. "I told Vivian to take them, but she's not interested. Ray bought one of those...*deedeedee* things."

"DVDs." Edie sat on the floor next to Peter. "And Edie doesn't want them because she doesn't have any room in her apartment."

"And Edie doesn't want them," Maude said. "No room in her apartment, she said."

Edie felt Peter clasp her ankle. Still sorting through albums, he was grinning. After he took his hand away, she could still feel his fingers. She wanted to just sit there and look at him. Peter Darling. If she were writing an article, she mused, how would she describe him? Languidly elegant, perhaps. Or would it be elegantly languid? As she watched him he pulled himself up from the floor and dropped onto the couch beside Maude.

"Maude." He brought his mouth to her ear. "'The White Cliffs of Dover'? Have you got that record?"

Maude's face lit up. "Got it with Vera Lynn singing. 'There'll be bluebirds over the white cliffs of Dover, tomorrow, just you wait and see...'"

"'There'll be love and laughter,'" Peter sang along with her. "'And peace ever after—'"

"'Tomorrow, when the world is free...'" Maude smiled, clearly tickled by the duet. "What else?"

"'Red Sails in the Sunset'?"

"Yep." She nodded triumphantly. "'Red sails in the sunset, dum da dadeedee...oh carry my loved one home safely to me.' Used to dance to that one at the USO. Lots of happy memories. I had a lovely yellow taffeta dress. I was wearing it the night I met Edie's father. You know 'I'll Be With You in Apple Blossom Time'?''

"'I'll be with you in apple blossom time,''' he crooned into Maude's ear. "'I'll be with you to change your name to mine.'''

Edie watched his mouth. She could drive herself crazy.

"'Blue birds will sing,''' Maude warbled. "'Church bells will chime…'''

"'In apple blossom time,''' they harmonized.

"Good heavens, 'Lili Marlene.''' Peter was back at the record cabinet. "This is like a walk into the past. The night my parents were married was the worst bombing of the war. They were married at her father's house in London. My mother told me the story so many times. At the reception after the wedding, everyone was singing and dancing and having such a wonderful time that when the air raid sirens went off, everyone just ignored them. And then one of the guests glanced out of the window and called out that London was in flames. My mother said it was the most terrifyingly beautiful thing she had ever seen. The dark night and the red flames…"

They all sat there for a while, as though in the spell of his story. Finally Maude pulled herself to her feet.

"Well if you won't get the port, I will." She toddled off into the kitchen.

"Come here." Peter, back on the carpet, crooked his finger at Edie.

Wordlessly, her heart thundering, she sat down beside him. He took her face in his hands and kissed her. Very soft and very slow. She put her arms around him and they kissed until she heard Maude's voice calling from the kitchen.

"Hold on, Mom," she responded.

"Edie." Peter's face was dazed. "Edie, Edie, Edie. I'm quite besotted with you."

She laughed, raising her head from his chest to look at him. "*Besotted*. And you say it as though you've just announced that you're tired or hungry."

He laughed too, pulled her onto his lap and kissed her again. She leaned into him, her fingers in his hair, mouth open to his tongue. Her body twisted pretzel-like around him. She couldn't seem to get close enough. And when she pulled away to look at him between kisses, she imagined him coming home to her after a hard day at school. *Candlelight, dinner in the oven. The kids in bed.* The kids would have to be in bed.

"Mmm, Peter," she whispered between kisses. "I'm trying to stay cool and objective, but…damn."

"Indeed." He pulled away to look at her. "I've often been disappointed to discover that reality doesn't quite live up to one's fantasies. In this case, however, it exceeded them."

"Edie," Maude yelled. "Where are the…oh, never mind. I've found them."

"Okay," Edie yelled back. She eased off Peter's lap and onto the seat beside him. His mouth, she imagined, looked bruised. He would go into school tomorrow and other teachers would see his still-swollen lips and speculate on romantic entanglements. The thought of her mouth bruising Peter's excited her so much that she kissed him again.

"I've never kissed a headmaster before," she said.

"You still haven't," he said. "I'm a high-school principal."

"Shh. I prefer the idea of you as a headmaster. It's much more romantic. Besides, you look and sound like a headmaster."

He appeared to be amused. "And your notion of what a headmaster should look and sound like is derived from…?"

"Movies, of course." She grinned at him. "Are all the girls in love with you?"

"Yes, Edie. They arrive at school in their gym slips and blazers, brandishing their hockey sticks and chattering about their jolly-good end-of-term hols."

"Are you saying that I'm romanticizing you?"

"Just a bit."

"I get that, too, since I've been home. Viv's idea of my life has no relation to reality."

"I should imagine her version is a little more on the spot, though. You do fly off to far-flung places on the globe, do things and take risks that aren't in most of our frames of reference. By contrast, my days are spent sorting out fights and motivating parents who can't see the need for education because that's what welfare's for, so why should they drag themselves out of bed to get Sonny off to school? Throw in a few disgruntled teachers who wish to God I'd strangle myself with a butterfly net and then it's off home to burn dinner and see my daughters up to bed."

"Yeah, but would you do anything else?"

"Absolutely not. Would you?"

"No." She shook her head, but saw again the small black question mark she'd seen ever since that day at the hospital in Kabul. "Well, do you want the honest-to-God truth, or the 'Of course I'd never do anything else, journalism is my life' version?"

"The first."

"The honest-to-God truth is that sometimes I don't know if I want to do this for the rest of my life. It's exciting and challenging and all that sort of thing…but it can get pretty lonely. The boyfriend I mentioned is a freelance journalist. Very exciting, very dynamic, almost completely without scruples. Which,'' she added, ''I've only realized in retrospect. He was married. I honestly had no idea. I knew he was commitment-phobic, but then, so are a lot of men. It all came out after he was captured in Iraq. He's freed now. Not that I was really concerned. Nothing could hold Ben captive for long.''

''Edith,'' Maude called again. ''Come and give me a hand.''

''Coming.'' With a glance at Peter, she jumped up and found Maude in the kitchen pouring something into three small glasses set out on a tray.

''Port,'' Maude said. Her face was pink, her hair pinned up at the sides with gold barrettes. She looked pretty, Edie thought. Something almost girlish about her.

''Since when do you drink port?'' she asked.

''Special occasion. I've got some cheese in the fridge, if you haven't used it all. Put some of that on a plate. And there're some crackers in the top shelf of the cupboard. I could open a can of ham—''

''Mom, it's late. I'm not even hungry.''

''Peter might be.'' Hands on her hips, she regarded Edie for a moment. ''It's not often that I get a handsome gentleman caller, so if I want to go all out, then I certainly think I have the right to do so.'' She brought her face closer to Edie. ''Go and put on some lipstick,'' she said in a stage whisper. ''You look washed out.''

In the living room, Peter sprang up to take the tray from Maude. Edie dropped onto one end of the sofa. There was an intriguing dynamic going on, she thought. Maude and Peter were both so clearly enchanted with one another that, odd as the thought was, given their ages, she might have felt like a third wheel. That she didn't, of course, was because of this simmering thing between herself and Peter that was making her nervy and sensitized and hot. *Down, girl.*

"So—" she picked up one of the glasses "—are we going to have a toast, Mom?"

Her face puckered in concentration, Maude lifted a glass. "A toast to music and dancing and feeling young again." She clinked her glass against Peter's. "You're good for me, you know that?"

Peter smiled from the floor. "Thank you, Maude. It's entirely mutual."

"All right, you two," Maude looked from Peter to Edie. "You've got to clink, too."

"To making my mother feel young again." Edie leaned forward to clink Peter's glass. "Thank you," she said.

"To amber eyes," he said, looking directly into hers. "And intriguing women."

"Have a piece of cheese, Peter." Maude presided over the tray Peter had set on the coffee table. "Take some, ham too." She sipped her port, settled back on the sofa and sighed happily. "This is nice. Put another record on, Edie. See if you can find, 'I'll Be Seeing You.'"

"Wow, I remember that song." Edie set her glass down and returned to the album stacks. "Mom used to play it all the time," she told Peter. "And it always made me feel like crying. Something something…'I'll be seeing you, in all the old familiar places…'"

"'In that small cafe,' Peter sang. "'The park across the way.'"

"Across the bay," Edie said.

He touched her nose. "It's way."

"Bay. Betcha." She started searching through another

stack. "'I'll be seeing *yooooooooo* in all the old familiar *plaaaces*, that this heart of mine *embraaaaces* all day *throooooooogh*.'" She flung her arms up. "And then the violins get louder and her voice has this throbbing sound as though she's about to bawl her eyes out. 'In that small *cafaaaaaaay*…the park across the bay, the chestnut tree, a wishing well, a small hotel, a carousel.'"

"Steeple bell," Peter said. "The children's carousel comes in the middle somewhere, right before chestnut tree, I think."

Edie glanced over at Maude. "Who's right, Mom?"

"I wouldn't mind." Maude held out her glass. "There's another bottle in the cupboard."

Her head full of the song, Edie went into the kitchen, returned with the port and filled their glasses again. Maude was tapping her feet and singing "I'll Be With You in Apple Blossom Time." She smiled as Edie filled her glass.

"Have a piece of cheese, Peter." Maude presided over the tray Peter had set on the coffee table. "Take some, ham too." She sipped some port, settled back on the sofa and sighed happily. "This is nice, Edie. You should come home more often."

Impulsively, Edie leaned down and kissed Maude's cheek. "Yeah, you're right, Mom, I should." Despite everything, this was home; its roots deep, tendrils of memories reaching out over the years. This musty old living room where both she and Viv had posed for pictures on the arms of prom dates, their names long forgotten; the dusty-rose brocade curtains that she dimly remembered Maude had bought years ago from a catalog, the plastic daffodils and silk roses blooming improbably together in a brass pot. And Maude, tapping her feet to the music.

All the moments, Edie thought, all the hours, all the years she'd lived her life away from this place, but this was the picture she saw when she thought of home. It had been that way forever and would go on forever. But it wouldn't. Tears, fierce and unexpected, stung the back of her throat and she wrapped her arms around her mother, resting her head on Maude's shoulder. "I love you, Mom."

"Nothing more to drink for you," Maude said. "Peter, don't give her any more wine. She's getting maudlin."

"Obviously." Stung, Edie tried to shrug it off. The declaration was prompted less by feelings for Maude, she decided, than nostalgia for a time she knew nothing about firsthand but that always got to her, anyway. The brave fighting soldiers, the faithful sweethearts, the longing and the yearning. Sentimental, tear-jerk stuff. Maybe the next time Maude made her want to slap her forehead in frustration, she should just play "The White Cliffs of Dover." And drink a glass or two of port.

"So, Mr. Deejay." Edie dropped down on the floor beside Peter again. "D'you find it?"

"Not yet, but I will. 'A small hotel,' he murmured. "'A steeple bell.'"

"Carousel."

"Steeple bell." He reached for his glass, smiling. "Shall we make a bet?"

"What?"

"If it's steeple bell, I'm allowed to kiss you."

"And if it's carousel?"

"You're allowed to kiss me."

She laughed. "Such a deal."

"Ah-ha," he said.

"You found it?"

"I found it."

Edie watched as he carefully lifted the arm of the record changer, removed the record that had been playing and returned it to the album cover. He has a long, thin back, she thought distractedly. The music started— lush, syrupy orchestrals made for slow dancing.

"Get up and dance, you two," Maude said from the couch. Tinkerbell had climbed into her lap again. The other two were at her feet. "Waste of good music, no one dancing."

He held out his arms and Edie leaned against his chest, swaying with the music.

"Ah, look at that," Maude said. "Edie likes you, Peter. I think you might finally be the one."

"Jeez, Mom," Edie muttered. "Isn't it time for you to go to bed?"

"There's nothing wrong with my head," Maude said. "Just ignore me."

So they did. With Peter's arms around her, Edie's chin resting on his shoulder, they danced dreamily to the scratchy crackling music.

"'I'll find you in the morning sun,'" Peter crooned softly. "'And when the night is new, I'll be looking at the moon, but I'll be seeing you.'" He kissed her then, and when they finally parted, Maude had gone to bed.

"Carousel," Peter said.

"Don't gloat," Edie replied.

"When do I get my reward?"

Edie lifted her face to him. "What are you waiting for."

CHAPTER ELEVEN

"...A CHILDREN'S PROGRAM at the planetarium in Forest Park," Sophia was explaining when she called Peter at school the following morning. "Natalie and Delphina will be fine, but it might run a little past the twins's bedtime. Still, I think they'd all enjoy it."

"I should imagine they would," Peter said with a glance at the appointment book open on his desk. "I have a few things this afternoon, but nothing to stop me from being home in time. Perhaps we could have pizza. The girls enjoy that little place on King's Highway..."

"I am taking them to that little place on King's Highway," Sophia said. "*I'm* taking them, Peter." A pause. "You're not going."

Peter leaned back in his chair. "And why is that, Sophia?"

"Because the girls spend far too much time with you as it is."

"They're with you all day," he reminded her. "And quite a few evenings too."

A pause. "Well, I'll have a friend with me," Sophia said. "And you going along would make things awkward."

"What friend?"

"David."

"David? David next door?" he asked, thinking of the sixtyish neighbor with whom he occasionally chatted about roses. "How on earth could my going along make things awkward?"

Sophia sighed. "Honestly, Peter, sometimes you can be so thick. I'm trying to arrange for you to have another unencumbered evening."

Peter scratched his head. "Unencumbered?" And then the penny dropped. "Ah, Project Wife."

"Naturally. Project Wife," Sophia said. "If you're to do a little ardent wooing, which you'll have to do before she meets the girls, you'll need a free evening or two. Perhaps, ultimately, a weekend—"

"If I need your help in organizing my romantic affairs, Sophia, I'll let you know. For now, I'm quite capable of managing on my own."

"Don't bluster, Peter. I understand these things. Now, tell me, is it still the foreign correspondent? It is, I have an intuitive sense. Pity. I'm sure there must be a nice teacher… I really wish you would think this whole thing through carefully."

"GOOD MORNING to you, too." Edie sat on the stairs smiling dreamily, Peter's voice like a caress in her ear. "I thought about you all night, too," she said.

"Shall we kiss and dance a little more tonight?"

"Tonight?"

"Tonight. My sister disinvited me from a trip with the girls to the planetarium and told me to…go out and carouse. I managed to get two tickets tonight to a concert at Powell Hall. Mahler. Do you like Mahler?"

She thought for a moment. "I would really, really like to tell you that I love Mahler and particularly enjoy, I don't know, Opus 57 in C-sharp or something, but I've got to say that I wouldn't recognize Mahler from Mozart."

"But would you like to go, anyway?"

"When do we dance?"

He laughed. "After the concert. I'm not sure it would be appropriate during…"

"Will you sing and whisper things in my ear?"

"Oh, Edie," he murmured. "Gladly.

"In that case then, I'll go."

"Good. We'll be hearing Mahler's Eighth. Quite baroque. The First would be a better introduction to his work. It actually sprang from the lieder cycle, a beautiful work that arose out of a love affair with a soprano. Unfortunately, it didn't quite work out. The love affair, I mean."

"Oh," Edie said.

"I actually play it for the girls. The twins are a little young yet, but Natalie quite enjoys it."

"God, that makes me feel musically illiterate. I'm probably better with my mom's World War II stuff. Vera Lynn and 'I'll Be Seeing You' is about as out there as I get, musically."

"Mmm. Well, if you enjoy this, and I think you will, I'll make you a copy of the First and you can work your way through the rest."

"The rest? How many are there?"

"Let's just start with the first few."

Edie smiled and, as Peter went on to explain the symphony's first movement in a level of detail that made her eyes glaze over, the journalist part of her brain began cataloging the details she was learning about him, referencing them under a file she decided to dub, Things That Set Peter Darling Apart From Most Men I Know. The butterflies, of course. Very sweet tooth, particularly likes gooey butter cake. Kind to elderly women. Actually listens attentively to the endless rambling of a particular elderly woman. Loves to dance to World War II songs. Knows the words to a surprisingly large number of World War II songs. Incredibly sexy and tender. Great kisser. *And four young daughters.*

"…And the song cycle is intimately related to the symphony thematically," Peter was saying now, "which offers some idea of what Mahler was thinking when he wrote it."

"Good," Edie said. "At least someone does, because I don't have the foggiest idea what you're talking about."

"Really?" Peter sounded surprised. "I thought I explained it rather simply. Natalie understood."

"That could be because Natalie is much more intelligent than I am, but it's probably because she was actually listening."

"And you weren't?"

"No. I was thinking about kissing you."

He laughed. "I can see I'm going to have to work very hard at broadening your horizons."

"Please do," Edie said. "I love having my horizons broadened."

"Do you? I wouldn't have taken you for that kind of girl."

She leaned back against the stairs, phone cord wrapped around her hand, replaying the moment he'd first kissed her. "Just goes to show you. By the way, was a Mahler concert what your sister had in mind when she told you to go and carouse?"

"Not really. My sister is actually very keen for me to remarry. And extremely opinionated about the type of woman she considers suitable. Sophia wouldn't approve of carousing. Anyway, I'll come by around six. We'll have dinner first."

EDIE HUNG UP and walked into the kitchen in a daze, which Maude, like the sun bursting through an early-morning mist, immediately dispersed.

"Was that Peter?" Maude sat at the table, a filmy blue scarf tied turbanlike around her head, eating a bowl of prunes. "I like Peter. You like Peter? I'm eating these because I haven't gone for two days. I told Viv and she said eat some prunes, so that's why I wanted to get some at the IGA the other day. What time did he leave last night? I thought, well, I'll just go up and give those two some privacy." She motioned for Edie to come closer. "He's not still here?" she whispered.

Edie measured coffee into the pot. It was like walking into a wall of sound. Maude, she was beginning to realize, didn't require any response, which didn't really matter because she wouldn't hear, anyway.

"He's sleeping?" Maude asked. "Doesn't he have to be at school?"

Edie turned to look at her mother. "Mom, how could Peter still be here if I was just talking to him on the phone?"

"Did you?" Maude smiled. "That's good. Viv called. She wants you to call her."

"Okay." Edie shook a box of dry cat food into three little blue plastic bowls. She had to decide how to approach her sister about the things Beth had said yesterday. Lunch maybe. They'd go to lunch and talk. Or maybe a drink somewhere—although if Viv was, as Beth claimed, drinking too much, maybe not. As if on cue, the phone rang. Edie snatched it up on the first ring, sure it was Viv.

"May I speak to Edie Robinson?" a girl's voice asked.

"Speaking." Edie smiled. "Is this Jessie?"

"Yeah. It's okay for me to call?"

"Absolutely," Edie said. "Hold on a minute." She held her hand over the receiver. "It's for me, Mom."

"Don't tie up the line," Maude said as she shuffled out of the kitchen.

"Sorry," Edie told Jessie. "What's up?"

"I just…well it's my boyfriend, he's giving me a real bad time and everything and I can't talk to his mom because she never thinks he does anything wrong. And anyway, you said for me to call you, so I did."

"A bad time, how?" Edie wedged the phone between her ear and shoulder and began picking up the kitchen as she listened to Jessie unload: Bobby didn't help around the house, Jessie told her, he was always off somewhere playing pool with his friends or something, he talked mean to her, he never changed the baby's diapers. Listening, Edie found herself wondering why there wasn't some kind of law against sixteen-year-old children procreating? Jessie made her old, world-weary and uncharacteristically at a loss for a solution.

"Well I'm glad you called," Edie said, wishing she could come up with a more constructive way to help the girl. "Could I meet you somewhere?"

"Are you going to be at the teen mother center this afternoon?"

"I wasn't planning to, but I could be," Edie said. "Are you okay right now, though? You're not in any…danger or anything?"

"No. Bobby's gone to Kansas City to see his brother. He'll be back tomorrow."

"Okay, I'll meet you at the center at three."

Edie hung up and heard Maude calling for her from upstairs.

"Coming." She ran up the stairs and found Maude in

the bathroom sitting on the toilet with the lid down, a towel wrapped around her head. The front of her mother's robe was soaked and her teeth were chattering. "What's going on?"

"I was putting a rinse on my hair." Maude's chin was quivering. "But I bent my head over the sink and had a dizzy spell. I called out to you, but you were on the phone and I got all panicky. I thought, ooh, what if Edith goes out and doesn't come back for hours and I fall and crack my head and bleed to death? 'Course, it would solve your problem—"

"Mom, for God's sake." In one swoop, she'd replaced the sopping towel with a dry one from the rack, wrapped it around her mother's head and led Maude into the bedroom. "Why couldn't you have just asked me to help? And what the hell do you need a rinse for anyway?"

"Get my green robe from the closet." Maude had started unbuttoning the one she wore. "No, not that one. The one with the buttons—"

"What's wrong with this one?" Edie pulled a chenille robe from among half a dozen lined up on hangers in her mother's jumbled closet, which she couldn't look at without the uncomfortable thought that one day she and Viv would have to empty it out.

"I don't like that one," Maude said. "The color's not good on me."

Edie turned from the closet to look at her mother.

"Maybe it's not important to you," said Maude, who had obviously caught the look on Edie's face. "To you, I'm just an old woman waiting to die. But it's important to me. Peter said I should always wear green because it brings out the color of my eyes. He told me that at school. Green is his favorite color, he said."

Edie stared at Maude, stumped for words.

"Oh, I know what you're thinking," Maude said. "Silly old fool—"

"Don't tell me what I'm thinking." Edie picked through the blouses, robes and assorted housedresses until she came to the green robe, then she handed it to her mother. "And the rinse?"

"Vince?" Maude bent her head to fasten the robe. "That's the man you're seeing? Does Peter know? D'you eat breakfast yet? Those prunes weren't enough. I thought maybe you could make me another one of those omelets. No green peppers though. They repeat on me. I've never liked green peppers."

Ten minutes later as they shared an omelet at the kitchen table, Edie brought up the day's agenda. "These are the things I have to do…" she started.

"I thought so, too," Maude said. "I told her she could join a gym. That would help her lose weight."

Edie put down her fork and twirled her finger at her ear. "Hearing aid?"

"Don't need it," Maude said. "I can hear what you're saying." She got up from the table and started for the front door. "I've got some seeds I want to plant. They'll dry out if I don't get them in."

Edie sighed and grabbed Maude's arm again. "Mom, there are a dozen other things we need to do that are more important than planting seeds in the garden." She guided Maude back into the chair. "Listen to me, okay?"

Maude eyed her for a moment. "I want to stay here."

Edie sat down. "Here in this house?"

"I've been thinking about it. This is my home. I've always been happy here. I like my own chair to watch TV. I like sleeping in my own bed. That place you and

Vivian took me to see, lot of old people sitting around waiting to die. That's not for me. I'll stay here.''

"Then *you* tell Viv," Edie said.

JUST AFTER NOON, Peter left his office and strolled over to the far end of the campus, where a dozen or so students were carefully digging green starter plants into long, neat rows. Tom Carpenter, the science teacher, waved as Peter approached.

"We're putting in potatoes, carrots and beets," Tom called. "Plant in September, plow under in June." He rose to his feet, wiped his hands along the sides of his faded jeans. "I meant to stop in and tell you. The program's already going great guns. We've got a deal working with the gal who runs the restaurant management course. They're going to take the lettuce and peas we harvested last week."

"That's good to hear." Peter felt his mood take an upswing. The landscaping program, along with half a dozen other programs he'd implemented, was a radical change from the previous administration's more traditional approach. Millie Adams's comment a few days ago had only confirmed what he already suspected. A handful of parents and certain members of the faculty would be only too happy to see him fail. Change, he'd found, was inevitably met with alarm by those wedded to the status quo.

Like Ray Jenkins, for example, standing nearby, jingling the change in his pockets and looking amused as he listened to Tom. Now the assistant principal was slowly shaking his head.

"Ain't gonna work, Pete," he said. "Trust me, I know these kids. I used to have all these highfalutin ideas, but I'm telling you. Get 'em in, get 'em out. It's all you can do.''

"...installed all the automatic sprinklers," Tom continued as though Ray hadn't spoken. "I've already been contacted by a couple of landscaping outfits looking for part-time employees. I have a couple of kids I'd recommend without hesitation."

Peter chatted to Tom for a few more minutes, spoke to a couple of students and then headed back to the administration building five minutes early for a 3:00 p.m. staff-development meeting. When he stuck his head around the conference room door, he saw that Beth Herman had already arrived.

"Hi, Peter." She was over by the coffee machine, cutting a yellow cake into small squares. "Have some pineapple-upside-down cake. I made it for the meeting because everyone's always complaining that we don't have cookies anymore."

Peter helped himself to a small square of cake. Budget cutbacks had put an end to a lot of frills, including the cookies once served at every staff meeting. Ray Jenkins had predicted outrage if not out-and-out rebellion. "It's a morale thing, Pete," Ray had said. "See, maybe it's different where you come from, but the teachers here want to know they're appreciated." Peter had eliminated the cookies, anyway.

"Do you spend all of your spare time whipping up cakes and pies?" Peter asked Beth.

Beth smiled and her face went pink. "Oh..." She licked cake off her finger. "Not really. I do other things too. I have two cats. Chairman Meow and Katmandu."

Peter laughed. "Very good. I used to have a cat. Roxanne. Amazingly cranky animal. Wanted everything just so."

"So we're both cat people," Beth said. "That's nice."

Peter rubbed his jaw. He didn't particularly think of himself as a cat person. In fact, he'd rather disliked Roxanne. And apparently it had been mutual. A friend had eventually assumed custody and whenever Peter visited, Roxanne seemed not to know him at all. The girls liked cats, though. Delphina adored them. He saw a picket fence and the requisite rose-covered cottage and Beth standing at the front door, smiling as she watched the girls frolic on the verdant green lawn with a litter of kittens. Pretty picture. Problem was, he couldn't quite put himself in there beside Beth. Hardly surprising. Edie had blinded him.

EDIE AND JESSIE, with the baby in a backpack carrier, walked from the teen mother center over to the Burger Barn, around the corner from the school. Jessie, after some prodding from Edie, had confessed to skipping lunch because she'd left her money at home. While Jessie found a booth, Edie ordered burgers, fries and sodas. When she carried them over to the booth, Jessie was spooning pureed carrots into the baby's mouth.

He grinned when he saw Edie, a wide, gummy, carrot-smeared grin.

"I know," she said, smiling back at him. "You want a cheeseburger. I don't blame you, but you have to wait until you're a little bit older."

"Do you have kids?" Jessie asked.

"Nope."

"But you still could. You're not old."

Edie grinned. Not old. Not young; just not old. A depressing thought if she were to dwell on it. She ate a

French fry, sipped some diet soda. "I can't imagine it somehow."

"Bobby wants us to have another baby," Jessie said.

"Jessie." Edie shook her head.

"I know. I don't really want to. But he can be so sweet sometimes. He says he wants us to go to Las Vegas and get married. He's a good daddy. Except sometimes he feeds him bits of meat. I get so mad, I tell him Roger could choke, but Bobby just gets mad and says he doesn't want no mama's boy."

Elbows on the table, chin propped in her hands, Edie stared at Jessie.

"I know," Jessie said, reading the look on Edie's face. "Bobby's sometimes like a kid himself."

"He is, Jessie. You both are." Edie tore open a package of ketchup and squeezed it over her fries. Jessie had finished feeding the baby and was rapidly devouring her cheeseburger. The place was crowded with kids from the high school, the noise level almost deafening. Jessie seemed unconcerned. She'd dug a plastic toy from the backpack and was holding it above the baby's face. He'd reach for it, and she would lift it higher, smiling at his efforts. Edie ate another fry.

"Why do you stay with Bobby?"

Jessie's smile faded. "I love him."

"I thought I was in love when I was sixteen," Edie said. "He ended up marrying my sister and they lived happily ever after. They were much better suited anyway."

"So do you still talk to your sister?"

"Oh sure. Jessie, we were kids, all of us. It's ancient history. So much has happened in my life since then." *I'm still lonely as hell and fighting closeness tooth and nail.* "I have a great life. The point I'm trying to make, though, is that you're so young. You've got your whole life ahead of you. Think of all the things you could do. You can't really want to stay in this situation.''

"He can be so sweet when he wants to—"

"When *he* wants to." Edie sipped some soda and told herself to back off. "What do *you* want?" she asked the girl.

"I just want things to be good for Roger. I want a nice home. Bobby says we'll have all that one day. He's going to get a job in construction and we're going to build a house with a big backyard."

"Okay." Edie leaned back against the booth and looked directly at Jessie. "Let's say that happens. You go home tonight, Bobby tells you he's got a job. He makes a ton of money, you build a house, have a couple more kids, maybe. Then, I don't know, four or five years from now, Bobby decides he doesn't want to be married anymore. Or you decide you want out. What then?"

Jessie frowned. "See, there's never been anyone else for me or him. It's like we just understand each other…"

"So you understand why he wants you to drop out of school? That's what you told me last week," she added when Jessie shook her head. "I can't remember exactly what you said, but something about how he didn't see any point to school."

"He doesn't."

"You think that's really why he wants you to drop out?"

"I don't know. Maybe."

"No, that's not why. Education gives you power and Bobby doesn't want you to have power. If you have power, it threatens his control. He wants you powerless and under his control."

Jessie looked at the baby, pink faced and long lashed, asleep in her arms. "I guess I should get going."

"Why did you call me, anyway, Jessie?"

The girl smiled, clearly embarrassed. "I know, you must think I'm this big flake, calling you like it's some big emergency…"

"Was it?"

"Bobby's so hard to figure out. One day he's real mean and the next day he tells me he's sorry. He's always buying me flowers and telling me he loves me. I guess I really want to believe him. I love Bobby and I want Roger to have a daddy."

Edie looked from Jessie and the sleeping baby to the ketchup-smeared remnants of their lunch. She felt old and weary and jaded. This girl could be her daughter and the sleeping baby, her grandson. God, there was a thought to make you feel ancient. She wanted to help them both, though, but how? She was, she realized, completely out of her league. Jessie had hoisted the baby up on her back and was starting for the door. Edie took two twenties and a ten—all the money she had—from her billfold. When they were outside, she stuffed the bills in the pocket of Jessie's jean jacket.

"You don't have to stay, Jessie. You have control."

"Thanks, Edie." Jessie wrapped her in a quick hug. "You're really sweet."

"No, I'm not," Edie said. "But I do care. Call me, okay? And stay in school."

On an impulse, she walked over to the administration building and stuck her head around Peter's office door.

"Mr. Darling's in a staff meeting," a secretary called out. "Can I give him a message?"

Edie smiled. "I'll just leave a note on his desk."

"Can't wait for tonight," she scrawled on a yellow Post-it note. Unoriginal, but exactly the way she felt.

HALF AN HOUR LATER, she was in Viv's kitchen, watching her sister pipe intricate swirls of whipped egg yolk into hollowed-out whites. One tray already completed sat in the fridge, each egg a miniature work of art topped with tiny blossoms of red caviar and slivers of green chives. Viv had shown her the eggs and the carved-watermelon basket, the pinwheel salmon sandwiches and the puff-pastry shells waiting to be filled with a cream-cheese concoction. Edie had just shaken her head, lost for words.

"I know, I know." Vivian's smile was rueful. "I should stop knocking myself out, but we're getting very involved in the community lately—Ray's actually considering a run for city council. And of course, I'm on the Friends of the Library board and the hospital auxiliary and God knows what else, so we just decided we'd have a cocktail party and bring all these people together. I'm wondering, though, whether I should alternate the red caviar with black. Would that be more interesting, do you think?"

"I don't know, Viv." It's just food, she wanted to say. Half the people who devour a deviled egg in two quick bites won't even notice the fine touches. And hardly anyone will give a damn about the way the chives are cut just so. "It seems like a lot of work, though. Couldn't you just compromise a little? Throw in some chips and dip? Some of those little hot dogs you mix with mustard and grape jelly?"

Viv gave her a look.

Edie grinned. "I used to like those. I thought everyone served those at parties."

"Maybe your kind of parties." Viv stood back to survey a finished egg. "What's Mom doing? How's the packing going? When I have a minute, we need to work out a schedule. We'll need everything out of the house before we can list it. The Maple Grove people called me this morning. They're thrilled that Mom's going there. What do you think?" She held out an egg for Edie to inspect. "A tad top-heavy? No, I think it's fine."

Edie pulled a stool up to the counter, reflecting as she did that Viv shared Maude's wall-of-sound verbal style, one topic blending into another, on and on, until Edie could feel her eyes glaze and her head begin to nod. She was starting to feel thankful that she didn't, as far as she knew, share this particular trait, when she remembered Peter telling her that he thought her a lot like Maude.

"Have you even started clearing out Mom's closets?" Viv asked. "I'll be really mad if you go off and leave it all up to me."

"Viv, I think you need to talk to Mom." Edie braced herself. She hadn't intended to bring up the subject. "She doesn't want to go to Maple Grove. She told me this morning. I told her to tell you."

Viv set down the knife she'd being using and sighed. "I honestly don't have time to go over this again, Edie. We've gone over it a dozen times and I can't seem to convince you—"

"Vivian, it's not me you need to convince. Mom doesn't want to leave her house. She's made it quite clear."

"As I said, I don't have time for this. I'm planning a cocktail party for at least fifty people. Look, Edie. Please go, okay. I don't want to hurt your feelings, but I can't focus on what I need to do with you sitting there."

CHAPTER TWELVE

PETER WAS HOLDING HER HAND. Edie watched the orchestra
conductor point his baton at various players, his left arm
making deep scooping movements. She heard a high thin
note blossom through the auditorium—a flute, maybe, or
it could be a clarinet for all she knew. Peter would know.
His shoulder and arm, in a navy blazer, were touching
hers. If she leaned fractionally closer, she could feel his
bone structure. Up on the stage, the conductor had
worked himself into a frenzy, crouching, leaping, shooting his arms everywhere.

Just before the music started, he'd leaned over to
whisper in her ear. "The very first time I heard Mahler,"
he'd said, "I honestly felt a shiver run down my spine.
Just the pure magic of the orchestra's sound. Eight oc-
taves of harmony…" She'd felt his breath on her ear
and felt a shiver run down her own spine that had nothing at all to do with Mahler.

Trumpets dominated now, and an assembled choir in
burgundy gowns was belting forth. Peter's fingers moved
in her palm and she actually squirmed in her seat.

God. She tried to pay attention. "The first act starts
in deepest night," Peter had explained as the orchestra
warmed up. "And then the fanfare comes in, and the
day starts to wake up." Her program lay open on her
lap, and she glanced down at it. Too dark to read, but
not too dark to see Peter's white shirt cuff extending

below his blazer, the back of his hand and his fingers clasped around hers. Or his thighs covered in gray flannel…well, maybe it wasn't gray flannel, probably too hot for gray flannel, but headmasters wore gray flannel and she liked thinking of Peter as a headmaster.

And then something caused the audience to break into wild applause and Peter removed his hand from hers and joined in, vigorously clapping and smiling. She followed suit. It was like watching a football game and having no idea why everyone in the stands was hooting and stamping.

"Magnificent," he whispered. "The naiveté of the beginning makes the sorrow seem so much more intense."

"Mmm." The music had started up again. A lone soloist singing, arms flung out to the audience. Edie stifled a yawn. She wanted Peter to hold her hand again. She'd give him ten seconds. If he didn't reach for her hand again, she'd take the initiative. The soprano, if that's what she was, had completely lost it now, clasping her bosom and staggering around the stage. Maybe this was where the love affair ended unsuccessfully. Another yawn threatened and Edie tightened her jaw to block it. Peter glanced sideways and with a sweet little smile caught her hand.

Edie squeezed her knees together and tried to remember what panties she was wearing. She needed a new supply. Hers were all dingy and boring. She'd never really been the lacy-underwear type. What kind of underwear would Peter wear? She couldn't decide. Perhaps she'd find out tonight. No, too soon. Anyway, if she slept with him, where would they go? If Maude was already asleep, she wouldn't hear them creep up the stairs, but it might feel kind of weird. What if Maude woke in the middle of the night, toddled into the room and found her youngest daughter and Peter *in flagrante delicto?*

Another outburst of applause, but this time Peter didn't join in. "The violins were all over the place," he whispered. Edie nodded sagely, relieved she hadn't rewarded such inferior playing.

Okay, so if they couldn't go to Maude's, they certainly couldn't go to his house. Not with a sister and four little girls, one of whom enjoyed Mahler. Edie was skeptical about that claim. If she drew the child aside, she was almost certain she'd learn that little Natalia—

Was that her name? No, Natalie—little Natalie had only been trying to please Daddy.

Daddy. Edie shifted in her seat. She was holding hands with Natalie's daddy. Working out the logistics of sleeping with Natalie's daddy. Frantic to rip the gray flannel trousers off Natalie's daddy.

"MAGNIFICENT PERFORMANCE," Peter said when they were seated on the couch back at Maude's, sipping more of the port. "The second movement is…almost bucolic. If I close my eyes I can see peasants pairing up with the local musicians to create this music to dance it." He turned to look at Edie. "You know, it just occurred to me, it's rather like Beethoven's *Pastoral Symphony*. The third movement before the storm when—"

Edie, who had been sitting quietly, was suddenly now convulsed with laughter, rolling around on the couch clutching her middle.

Peter watched her, bemused. Then the peals of laughter became contagious and he started laughing, too, but with no real idea why. Maude had gone to bed, and he wondered whether they might be keeping her awake. Not likely, he realized a moment later. Edie kept laughing, at one point extending a leg to kick her sandal across the room.

Finally, she subsided. Groaning, she swiped at her eyes. "God, Peter. I think I love you. You are so sweet and earnest and solemn about this... Kiss me, okay? Just kiss me."

He did. She'd gone to the concert looking formidably elegant in a simple black dress, her hair arranged in a complicated knot at the back of her neck. By the time he finished kissing her, she lay almost horizontal across his lap, dress up around her thighs, hair tumbling about her shoulders as she smiled up at him. I think I love you, too, he wanted to say. The realization terrified him.

"I shall have to ask around to see whether that's a common reaction to Mahler's First," he said.

She sighed. "Oh, Peter."

He bent his head down toward her. "What?"

"Nothing, just oh, Peter."

"And the joke was?"

"What was I laughing at?"

"Uh-huh."

"Mmm." With her finger, she traced his mouth. "Pent-up tension, I think. The music was so grand and solemn and we're all dressed up like these proper, respectable people—"

"I am a proper, respectable person," he said. "Aren't you?"

"It's debatable," she said. "Plus, I seem to recall a remark you made outside the Olde Towne Bakery." She watched his face. "Something about a raging uncouth beast full of uncontrollable lust..."

He grinned. "Oh, right."

"So..." Still watching him, she loosened his tie, then unfastened the button beneath his collar. "If I keep doing this..." She undid another button, "Would I eventually release the beast?"

"Too late." He lunged for her neck, pinning her down against the couch with his upper body. "Shall I ravish you here, or carry you up to your bed chamber?"

"Neither." She slid out from under him, sat up and smoothed her hair. "At least, not tonight. Maude tends to wake up and I'm not sure her heart could stand it. I have to confess, though, that I sat through the entire concert so incredibly turned on by you that I couldn't see straight and—"

Peter put his arm around her shoulders, pulled her close. "You weren't hanging on to every note of the music, then?"

"Sorry to disappoint you, but no. I spent a great deal of time trying to decide where we would go if we decided to sleep together. Maude's was out and then I thought of your house but you have the girls there and..."

Peter waited. Upstairs, he heard the creak of floorboards and then a door close. Edie leaned into his arm.

"The thing is, I've never been involved with a man who has children. Well, not the sole responsibility of children. The complexities of it all suddenly hit me...trying to find a place to be together, imagining your daughters' reactions if they found me at your kitchen table the next morning. It just felt, I don't know, strange and incredibly difficult, and I kept coming up with all these different scenarios and..." She turned her head to look at him. "What?"

"Nothing."

"No, there is. I can feel it. Have I offended you?"

"Not at all." He shook his head, but an almost imperceptible change of mood had taken place, a wisp of a cloud across the moon. Maude's cuckoo clock announced midnight. Time to go.

"Hey…" Edie shifted on the couch to face him. "I've done or said something and I don't think it's just that I laughed at Mahler."

"It's very complicated, Edie." He picked up his port, set it down again. "I haven't quite sorted it out in my own mind. Perhaps it's about keeping my daughters quite separate from my…"

Edie was watching him intently. "Romantic entanglements?"

He smiled. "Want to entangle?"

"Very much. But Peter…" She caught his hand, frowning down at it. "If you were in a serious relationship, you'd eventually have to bring the girls into it, right?"

"Of course."

"Has that ever happened? Since your wife…"

"No." He tried to come up with a way to describe Deborah that didn't sound maudlin and sentimental. *She was my soulmate,* he wanted to say, *I thought we'd be together for a lifetime.* But Deborah was dead, and Edie, vibrantly alive, was sitting beside him, and he couldn't seem to find a way to explain his feelings without feeling disloyal to Deborah or appearing to discount what he felt for Edie.

One of Maude's knitted blankets had slipped down from the back of the couch and settled behind her back. She reached around and drew it across her knee, her face troubled. "I guess a relationship with a journalist who swoops into town and then swoops back out," she said slowly, "is hardly likely to evolve into a serious one?"

"Edie." He took her hand. "What is this all about? You could hardly have made it more clear that you're not after a serious relationship. My sister would be furious to hear me say this, but your determination to avoid entanglement is one of the things I find so attractive about you.''

Her eyes still intent on his face, she nodded, as though coming to some kind of decision. ''You're absolutely right. Kiss me good-night and let's forget this whole conversation.''

He stood up and leaned down, supporting himself by gripping the arm of the couch. He rested his forehead against hers. ''I can't separate myself from being the girls' father,'' he said softly. ''They're part of who I am. But I like you very much. In fact, I think you're wonderful.''

AFTER PETER LEFT, Edie carried the glasses they'd used into the kitchen and stood staring into the sink. After a moment, she heard Tinkerbell, out on a nocturnal prowl, scratching at the screen door. As she let him in, she glanced up the path and saw Panda and Poochie trotting toward the light. They were both black and she had difficulty telling them apart. One of them had a white paw, but she could never remember whether that was Panda or Poochie.

She yawned and thought about going up to bed, but the evening with Peter had left her restless and sensitized. The cats jostled for attention, sidling against her legs, twitching their tails. Tinkerbell batted one of the black cats on the nose. Edie pulled out a chair and sat down, drawing her knees up on the seat, watching the cats play on the yellowed linoleum floor. If she were a different kind of person, she would pick them up and coo over them. Feed them treats. Peter would want that kind of woman to meet his girls.

Ten minutes later, she lay on the bed, staring at the ceiling and thinking that if the phone was by the bed and not out in the damn hallway, she would call Fred. She got up, carried the phone to the stairs and called him, anyway. For the last month, he'd been between assignments and living at his home in Los Angeles, the home his wife, Annie, was always complaining that he never spent enough time in.

Annie answered and they chatted. Fred had already gone to bed, she said. "No, it's only a little after ten here," she cut off Edie's apology. "Don't worry about it. I never go to bed until one or two. Fred doesn't usually, but he's slowing down. Don't tell him I said it though or he'll divorce me. Want me to have him call you?"

"If you would." Edie picked at her thumbnail. "Annie…this is probably going to sound like a weird question, but have you ever been sorry you married Fred? With him being gone all the time and everything?"

Annie laughed. "What's happening? You've met someone and he's talking marriage and babies?"

"No, no, nothing like that. God, no. Please, spare me. My sister went that route and it's definitely not for me…"

"Got you," Annie said. "Okay, so you want to know have I ever been sorry I married a guy who wasn't home when any of our three kids were born? Who's bored to death after two days when he is here? Who's missed more Thanksgivings than I can count?" A pause. "No, because I love the jerk. But I tell you, it's no walk in the park."

"Have you ever tried to get him to do something that involves less traveling? A stateside job?"

"Ha. We banned that question the first year we were

married. Couldn't discuss it without me ending up in tears and Fred slamming out the door. What I know now is that even if I'd got my way and he'd stayed at home, he wouldn't be happy. And if he's not happy, he makes my life a misery, so it's better that he does something he loves.''

"I guess," Edie said, not entirely convinced.

"It's true," Annie said. "Most people aren't lucky enough to be in love with what they do. Fred is. You are. You can't have that kind of love without cheating on someone else. I come second to Fred's work, and so do the kids. We all know it. We've just accepted it."

"You've got a hangover, haven't you?" Maude asked the next morning. "You and Peter drank all my port. You shouldn't drink like that, it's not good for you. Turn your nose into a strawberry if you're not careful."

"I'll remember that, Mom. And I had one glass of port last night." Did Maude lecture Viv on drinking? "I feel great," she lied. She felt miserable and confused and lost, somehow. She stood at Maude's pantry door, alphabetizing little red and white tins of spices. She hadn't meant to. She'd gone to the pantry to look for cinnamon and then started thinking about Peter. Before she realized what she was doing, she'd organized cumin, cinnamon and cloves on one shelf and had started looking for A's.

Maude appeared at the pantry door, shook the can of allspice and stuck it back on the shelf, right in the middle of the newly organized C's.

Edie stuck it back in the A's next to a bottle of almond essence and shot Maude a defiant look. "You should really toss it, Mom."

"Empty?" Maude grabbed the container again and

shook it, spattering the front of her pink housecoat with allspice. "It's not empty. There's plenty left."

"Okay, but take a sniff." Edie snatched the spice away and shoved it under her mother's nose. "See? No smell. You've had it so long, the stuff is useless."

"Smells fine to me." Maude grabbed the tin and replaced it on the shelf. "Don't go changing my kitchen to suit yourself. It's been this way for more years than you've been around and I like it just fine the way it is. I just wish I knew what happened to all the eggs."

"For God's sake, Mom, we've gone over this twice this morning already. I'll go to the store and buy you some damn eggs."

"Don't swear. And don't raise your voice at me. I'm still your mother. If you can't talk to me without shouting and swearing, you can leave."

Edie drew a long breath. Maybe that was what she should do. It was only at home that she ever felt weird and confused. Maude was still in the pantry, breathing over Edie's shoulder and rearranging the spices to her liking.

Claustrophobic, Edie went into the kitchen and made coffee. She'd just poured a mugful, when Viv called.

"What's wrong?" Viv asked.

"Nothing." She was supposed to be asking Viv what was wrong.

"Edith," Maude called from the pantry. "What did you do with the box of oatmeal? I can't find it. Where's the oatmeal? *Edith*."

"Hold on," Edie said into the phone. "I didn't touch the oatmeal, Mom. It's right where you left it. She thinks I've moved the oatmeal," she told Viv.

"Edith," Maude called again.

"Grrrrh." Edie slapped her forehead. "Viv, can I call you back?"

"Found it," Maude crowed. "Different shelf. You must have moved it."

Edie groaned into the phone. "Take me away from this, please."

"See! Now you know what I go through. You'll leave, I won't."

"It's just…I swear, I try to be patient, but she goes over the same thing a dozen times. She can't hear anything I say, so I have to raise my voice, and then she gets upset because she thinks I'm shouting at her."

"Yes, well, keep in mind she's old," Viv said. "You need to try and be a little more patient with her."

"I do try. I'm just frustr—"

"Ray is so furious at Peter Darling," Viv broke in, having clearly lost interest in discussing their mother. "And I don't blame him. I mean, the man is totally unrealistic. Remember that little tramp, Melissa?"

"Brad's girlfriend?"

"No, she is not his girlfriend, she's a little… Well, anyway, Ray's caught her in so many things, but every time he tries to discipline her, Peter steps in and over-rules him. Now Peter's got her signed up for some Mickey Mouse course—"

"It's a journalism club, Viv. I told you about the program. I'm working with some of the students."

"Oh well, if *you're* working on it, Edie," Viv said, "it can't be Mickey Mouse."

Edie felt her teeth clench. She opened her mouth to speak, closed it again. "You know what, Viv?" she finally said. "Why don't you go straight to hell?"

She slammed the receiver down so hard the vibration ran up her arm. Her legs shook and her face felt drained of blood. She picked up the coffee mug she'd been using and carried it to the sink. One of the taps was dripping. She counted the drops. One. Two. Three. Behind her, she could hear Maude moving about the kitchen.

"I'm going to make meat loaf," Maude said. "Maybe Peter would like to come to dinner. I suppose you used up all the eggs. Don't know how I'm supposed to make a meat loaf with no eggs. Didn't you think before you used the last egg? Now you'll have to take me to the IGA and I bet they don't have them on sale this week. What's this in the garbage? Garlic salt? You threw it away? Tsk-tsk-tsk. Waste, I tell you…"

Edie buried her face in her hands and pressed her fingers hard against her eyes. The phone rang. She didn't move. It rang three more times and Maude answered it.

"Viv wants to talk to you."

"Tell her I'm dead."

"She's going to bed," Maude said into the phone. "…I don't know. Tired, I suppose. Beth's what? Hit her? Oh, sweater. I'll ask her when she gets up."

Tears seeped through Edie's fingers. She gulped air and sobbed.

"Edith." Maude had come up beside her. "What is it, honey?"

Edie shook her head, but Maude was pulling at her arm now, forcing her hands down from her face. She allowed Maude to lead her to the table. Maude told her to sit down and she did. Eyes and nose streaming, she looked across the table at her mother.

"Always did bottle things up." Maude's hands were on the table, clutched around a tissue. Shoulders hunched, she shook her head at Edie. "I can see you now, about fourteen you were. Acting like nothing was wrong, then I walk into the kitchen one day. Standing just about where you are right now. I could see your shoulders just shaking and shaking. You remember that?''

Her head in her hands, elbows propped on the table, Edie nodded. The tears flowed unquenched, running down her face, dripping off her chin and through her fingers, trickling down her arm to wet the cuffs of her shirt. She swiped at her eyes, at her nose, and at her eyes again, and they just kept filling.

''You mean when I killed Jim Morrison?''

Maude regarded her from across the table. ''That rabbit you had with the long ears? I'd tell you and tell you that he had to have food and water, but you'd go off to school and I'd go check and sure enough, the bowls were empty, so off I'd go and fill them—either me or Vivian. She loved that rabbit, too. Hate to think what the poor thing would have done if we hadn't been there…''

Edie stared at Maude through a blur of tears. ''He died, Mom.''

''‘Course he did. He was old. Had to be ten years old when Dixie gave him to us, and then you must have had him…I don't know, five years or more. Nothing lives forever.''

''But his water bowl was dry.''

''You'd left for school that morning. Forgot to give him water, of course. I remember filling his water and food bowls and thinking to myself, that girl needs to be taught a lesson. So later on when I went out there and saw he'd passed away, I just emptied out the bowls.''

For a moment, Edie couldn't speak. ''All this time…'' she finally managed to say. ''I thought he died because of me. *And you let me think that.*''

''He would have died,'' Maude said, ''if he'd had to rely on you.'' She got up from the table and walked unsteadily around to where Edie sat. Then she bent and wrapped her daughter in an awkward embrace. "You are who you are, honey," she said, pressing her mouth against the top of Edie's head. "We all are."

Edie stared wordlessly at Maude as her mother returned to her seat across the table.

"There's no one that's perfect," Maude said. "Not even your sister, who's so eaten up with envy that she can't even see straight. Can't see why though. The way I reckon, Vivian's got everything any woman in her right mind would want. Good husband, sons, big fancy house. What does she have to envy you about?"

"PETER WAS RAISED in England," Maude told Edie as they drove to the high school. Maude's purse was clasped in her lap and she stared straight ahead, addressing the windshield. "His mother and father were English."

"That would kind of figure." Edie shot Maude a quick smile. Since the concert, Peter had left several messages. More than once, she'd picked up the phone to call and explain…but explain what? "I think I might be in love with you, but…I don't think I'm what you need." No, that smacked of martyrdom—and who was she to tell him what he needed? "I'm too selfish and set in my ways and I'd be a terrible mother to your daughters." Closer to the truth, but she didn't want to think that about herself, no matter how accurate the assessment. Finally, she'd decided that the whole thing with Peter would be best nipped in the bud. Now she just had to find a way to tell him.

Weird how bombs and rockets hardly fazed her, but she was practically having a panic attack at the thought of talking to him. God, she missed him. Missed that walking-on-air dreaminess whenever she thought about him. What she felt now was a resigned acceptance. You are who you are, Maude had said. And it was true. She was not the kind of warm fuzzy person who would make a good mother for Peter's children. Better to accept that than to remake herself into someone fake and insincere who would end up making everyone unhappy.

The Nova had no air-conditioning and she drove with one hand on the wheel, an arm resting along the frame of the open window. Yesterday, the temperature had hovered pleasantly in the mid sixties; today it had shot up into the nineties. A thunderstorm was forecast for later in the day and the air was so hot and humid that she imagined herself slowly melting into a sticky, lethargic blob. If there was a positive side to it all, she reflected, it was that the heavy suffocating air created a sort of gray, weary indifference to pretty much everything—including the blowup with Viv, Maude's revelation about the rabbit and the realization that she'd carried guilt all these years for something she hadn't done.

Although, as Maude had pointed out, the rabbit would have died if someone else hadn't stepped in, so maybe the guilt wasn't entirely unfounded. She poked a finger down the back of her dress, where a trickle of sweat was starting to itch.

"This heat doesn't bother you?" She glanced at Maude who looked amazingly chipper in a lemon-yellow pantsuit. "Heat," she repeated in a loud voice when Maude gave her a vague look.

"I'm meeting him at three," Maude said.

Edie turned the fan to high. After the journalism club, she would go and make peace with Viv. Not an apology; she'd done nothing to warrant that. Just a sisterly talk to sort things out, smooth hurt feelings. And tonight, maybe, she'd call Peter.

She yawned. Intense emotion was amazingly draining—a good reason for cultivating, in her professional life at least, emotional detachment and noninvolvement. Involvement was full of traps of all kinds.

In a jeep with four other reporters on a road in central Bosnia, she'd come across a woman hit by sniper fire. They were out in the middle of nowhere. The woman was bleeding badly and her family was begging them to take her to the nearest field hospital. They'd ended up lifting her into the jeep and taking her in for treatment.

Three days later a similar press vehicle was attacked, and one of the reporters was injured so severely that he later lost his leg. The second incident was retaliation against her own group who, by assisting the woman, had helped the opposing side. "You help the other side, then we treat you as the enemy," one of the attackers had said.

The incident had shaken her for days. By helping this woman, she and her colleagues had indirectly caused another reporter to lose his leg. "We don't operate in a vacuum," Ben had reminded her. Everything has its consequences. Including, she realized now, kissing Peter.

"I told him about your father," Maude was saying now. "Peter's sweet on you. All we do is talk about you."

Edie felt color creep into her face. She didn't want to know.

"I told him how your father went out one night to buy cow's milk because you wouldn't drink my milk. Vivian had no trouble with my milk, I told him, but not Edie. She squalled and puked—"

"Jeez, Mom, I'm sure he was fascinated."

"Couldn't keep it down, running out of both ends. I told him how your father finally had to walk down to the IGA and buy some cow's milk, and the way that car came out of nowhere and just mowed him down. Didn't kill him that time, I said, but then, wouldn't you know, it happened again. Then I told him how you nearly killed your sister..."

Edie slapped her forehead. "Goddamn it, Mom. Why d'you tell him stuff like that?"

"There you go, slapping your head again," Maude said. "You're going to give yourself a brain tumor. That's what I told Peter. Edith has no patience with me, I said, always slapping her head and swearing. He's a good listener. It wasn't easy raising two girls without a father, I told him, and Vivian with her asthma attacks, but it's like I always said, if Edie hadn't wanted that bike so bad, I wouldn't be a widow today...and then she hides Vivian's inhaler..."

I am going crazy, Edie thought. By the time I leave this house, I will be gibbering like a monkey, and men in white coats will put me in a straitjacket. As they carry me off, the last words I'll hear will be my mother saying, "She kept slapping her head. Slapped herself silly. I tried to warn her, but that's Edith for you, she never listens."

As she pulled into the Luther High parking lot, she decided that if she saw Peter, which she most likely would, she would be cool, calm, professional...and detached to the max.

CHAPTER THIRTEEN

"TWO TEACHERS have family emergencies. One has the flu and one has laryngitis," Betty Jean cheerily told Peter. "No substitutes yet, but I'll keep trying. You have a parent meeting at two. It wasn't scheduled, but the mother says she has to talk to you today. I penciled in a meeting with that probation officer who rescheduled last week. It's tomorrow at eleven, which might be cutting it kind of close, but I'll buzz you. The fire marshal is also coming by tomorrow at three and the photocopier is on the blink again…"

Peter nodded. "I suppose I haven't had a call from a Ms. Robinson?"

"Ms. Robinson? No. Hold on…" She picked up a ringing phone. "Your sister," she said with a smile at Peter.

"Tell her I'm in a meeting."

"I'm sorry, Sophia, but…just a minute." She held her hand over the mouthpiece. "Your sister says she knows very well you're not in a meeting."

Peter massaged the back of his neck and sighed. "I'll take it in my office."

"Abbie has a stomachache," Sophia said. "Kate might be coming down with something. Possibly they both have whatever's going around. Natalie would like to go to England next summer and Delphina is wondering about her butterfly wings."

Peter, at his desk now, propped his head in his hands. "Sophia," he said. "I am a high-school principal. I have an endless number of matters major and minor all clamoring for my attention. I leave for work every morning confident that the girls are in your capable hands. This allows me the freedom to concentrate on all these major and minor matters…" He drew a breath. "Why are you ringing me at work with the sort of things you routinely handle every day?"

"Yes, I see your point," Sophia said. "Of course, if the girls had a mother at home…"

"I'm not discussing this with you right now," Peter said. "We'll talk about it tonight."

"No, we won't. You'll be busy with the girls and then you'll tell me you're too tired. Look, Peter, I want you to take this a little more seriously. I'm worried at the thought of my nieces being cared for by a stranger. You have to be very careful about the nanny you select." Her voice broke. "The girls *need* a mother, a fact you seem determined to ignore. This foreign correspondent…she's still in the picture, I suppose?"

WITH AN HOUR TO KILL before the journalism club, Edie decided to stop in at the teen mother center, hoping she might find Jessie, whom she hadn't heard from since their lunch the week before. She found her in Beth's little glassed-in cubicle, head drooping, dabbing at her eyes. Beth sat across from the girl, their knees almost touching. Beth glanced up, saw Edie and motioned her inside.

Jessie smiled tearfully at Edie and stood to embrace her in a long hug that brought Edie to the edge of tears herself. "Hi…" She pulled back to look at Jessie. "I've been wondering about you. Things aren't going so well?''

Jessie shook her head and her face dissolved. ''Bobby's being real mean.''

An understatement, it seemed. Bobby had become increasingly abusive, physically and emotionally, and Jessie was concerned for her own safety as well as the baby's. Beth had suggested a battered women's shelter, but Jessie seemed unconvinced and, Edie thought, scared to death.

Boxes of pamphlets on child rearing and breast-feeding were stacked on the only available chair. Edie removed them and sat down. At her feet were more boxes: formula, disposable diapers. From the room outside the cubicle, she heard a baby wail.

Beth leaned close to Jessie, her face concerned, voice soft.

''It would be the safest thing for you and Roger. You need to get away from Bobby…his home. At the shelter, you'll be safe from him. They can help you find a job and housing and get you back on your feet.''

Edie watched Jessie. The bracelet she wore had a heart-shaped charm that glinted in the sunlight from the window. She seemed to be watching the play of light and for a few moments, she said nothing. Then a tear splashed on her lap.

''I loved Bobby.'' She looked from Beth to Edie. ''I tried so hard to make it work.''

Edie felt her throat close. She pulled a tissue from her purse, handed it to Jessie, then pulled out another one for herself. Beth was up on her feet now, hugging Jessie and patting her back.

''You're doing the right thing, Jessie.'' Beth's voice

was low and soothing. "I've been worried about you. You've walked into a few too many doors lately."

"He can be so sweet," Jessie said. "When he's not being mean."

"Sweetness doesn't excuse him for hitting you," Beth said. "You and Roger both need to be in a safe place. Even if Bobby never touched Roger, it isn't good for a child to grow up seeing his mother pushed around."

"But he'll be growing up without a father," Jessie said.

"That's better than seeing his mother beat up." Beth had moved to the file cabinet and was taking out papers and handing them to Jessie. After Beth finished, Jessie gave Edie a quick hug, thanked her for everything and walked out of the office.

Edie swallowed, not trusting herself to speak. "She's not convinced, is she?"

"I can't tell," Beth said. "I hope so, but she's still emotionally connected to her boyfriend. It's often hard to make the break."

"What happens if she does decide to go to the shelter?"

"Someone will pick her up—probably at a coffee shop, somewhere where kids aren't likely to see Jessie and tell Bobby. She'll be driven out to the center, they'll give her seventy-two hours to get settled and then she'll enroll in a nearby high school."

Edie nodded, absorbing the information. "Where is the center? Maybe I could go and see her, take her some things. She probably won't get many visitors."

"She won't get *any* visitors. That's the whole point," Beth said. "She's there for her own protection. If anyone knew where she was, it would defeat the whole system. This way, the boyfriend can't get to her."

"God, it seems so...lonely." She thought of Jessie sitting across from her as they had eaten lunch "It's so sad. Why the hell can't her mother care enough to see that her daughter needs help?"

Beth smiled sadly. "Oh Edie, who knows? Any number of reasons. Maybe Jessie's mother never received much in the way of mothering herself. Some of these kids have stories that would break your heart."

Jessie was still on Edie's mind a few hours later when she walked into her mother's house and found Peter out in the backyard with Maude. She froze, rooted to the spot. Maude had been diapering a baby when Edie left the teen mother center. Beth would drive her home, she'd said. Peter hadn't attended the journalism group— a relief but, she had to admit, a disappointment, too.

Now he and Maude were both bent over, inspecting something on a bush Edie couldn't name if her life depended on it. Whatever it was, they were so engrossed that neither of them heard her approach. It was early evening, not quite dark, and the air felt warm and smelled sweet. Edie glanced around and saw that the source of the perfume was a red rosebush a few feet away, covered in bloom. Down at the end of the brick pathway that bisected what used to be the lawn, Peter was showing Maude something on the palm of his hand. Maude was smiling up at him, rakish in a wide-straw brimmed hat and a green cotton dress.

Peter looked good—so good that Edie found herself reviewing her conversation with Fred's wife. She recalled the bit about those who were lucky to be in love with what they did and how they couldn't do it without cheating on someone else. A cool and detached smile pasted across her face, she strolled up to where Peter stood. He nodded cordially—quite cool and detached

himself, she noted—and held out his open palm to show
her a small butterfly.

"Pieris rapae," he said. "Or cabbage white."

Edie eyed the butterfly in Peter's hand. White with
two black spots on the tip of its wings. Pretty, but what
butterfly wasn't pretty? Peter had long, slender fingers.
The blue cuff of his oxford-cloth shirt had frayed. A wife
would have noticed—well, a good, stay-at-home, de-
voted wife. Her own damn heart was fluttering like the
butterfly's wings. When she looked up at Peter, his eyes
were an incredible gray green. Had she noticed their
color before?

"Rare?" she asked.

"Pardon?"

"Pierre whatever his name is. Is he rare?"

"Pieris and it's a she."

She gave him a skeptical look.

"The male has one black spot."

"I'll take your word for it."

He smiled. "Hello, Edie."

"Hi, Peter." *And please stop smiling at me like that
or I might send Maude into cardiac arrest by throwing
myself on your body.* "What are you doing here?"

"Peter stopped by the teen mother center and I invited
him to dinner," Maude toddled over to announce. "I'm
making stuffed bell peppers. And look." She motioned
for Edie to follow her over to a small section of newly
turned dirt. "We put in zinnias and dahlias. Peter got
the bulbs for me."

"That was very kind of you," Edie said. "But
shouldn't you be at home with your daughters?"

"My sister had other ideas," he said enigmatically.

"So." She folded her arms across her chest and

glanced around at the weed-strewn garden. "A little run and relaxing yard work, huh?"

"When I dropped by the center," he said, "Maude mentioned that she's been concerned lately about the state of her backyard. Since I rather like doing a bit of gardening myself, I offered to come by and have a look at it…"

"Peter…" Maude called out to him from the toolshed. "Come and help me get this bike out of here. Edie can clean it up. Used to be hers when she was about your oldest daughter's age."

"I'm bringing the girls over tomorrow afternoon," Peter said in response to Edie's questioning look. "With all of us working, we'll have the garden cleared out in no time."

She looked at him, searching his face for a hidden motive, and found nothing but an impersonal friendliness. *He was out-detaching her.* She felt a little disconcerted—by Peter's presence, mostly, but also by Maude's sudden involvement with his daughters. What was that all about?

"The grandparents on both sides are dead," Peter said as though he'd read her thoughts. "Natalie just happened to mention the other day that she wished she still had a grandma." He smiled. "I think she'd been watching a show on TV, one of those sentimental, idealized things that have no relation to reality…but Natalie's a child."

Maude had started up the path to the kitchen steps and Edie watched her retreating back. "So it was your idea?"

"To bring them here? No, it was your mother's. She said she misses having small children around. Now that her grandsons are in their teens, she apparently doesn't see them all that often. That led into her asking me about the girls." He stooped to pick up a trowel, stuck the blade down into the dirt. "Anyway, I'd like to get some of this overgrowth cleared away before dinner."

And then he turned and began hacking away at a clump of weeds. *I've been dismissed.* Her face hot, Edie walked up the path to the kitchen. Maude was on the phone, apparently with Viv.

"Well, I've been waiting for the boys to clear it," Maude was saying. "Three months I've been waiting, but they don't need to bother now because Peter's doing it. His little girls are coming over tomorrow…what? His little girls. I got that old bike of Edith's…what? No, she's right here."

Edie had started clearing the clutter of onion skins and spilled rice left from Maude's dinner preparation, her mind still working on Peter. She did not want to get into a discussion with Viv, but before she could escape, Maude had handed her the phone.

"No idea," she said, already anticipating the question. "I had nothing to do with it."

"I find that kind of hard to believe," Viv said.

"Damn. You're so smart, Viv. You saw right through me. You know how I love small children. I can't think of anything I'd rather do than spend an evening with four giggling girls eating Mom's stuffed green peppers."

"Why is Mom making green peppers? She knows they give her heartburn. Didn't you remind her?"

"I told you, Viv, I had nothing to do with it. Maybe she thinks Peter likes them."

"Peter. God, I am so sick of hearing his name."

Edie swiped a dishcloth across the counter. "Is that it, then?"

"What's that supposed to mean?"

"Whatever you want it to mean, Viv."

"Obviously, the real reason he's there is because of you."

"Maybe. Want me to go and ask him?"

"Very funny. You just think you're so damn clever, don't you? What exactly is going on with you and Peter, anyway?"

"Nothing, actually."

"That's not what Mom says."

"Well, then, don't ask *me*," Edie snapped.

"He's got four children, Edie."

"Thank you, Viv. I hadn't realized it, but now that you've told me, I guess I'll have to return the engagement ring he gave me. Wow, what a relief. Saved just in the nick of time. No way I could marry a man with four children."

Edie heard the simultaneous sounds of the phone being slammed down and the screen door behind her slamming. When she turned around, Peter was standing in the doorway. How much of the conversation he'd overheard, she had no idea. His face gave away nothing.

"So," she said brightly. "Ready for some of Mom's famous green peppers?"

IF THERE WAS ONE FOOD he absolutely loathed, Peter mused, it was stuffed peppers. They were always flaccid, sickly green and filled with something unidentifiable. He detested everything about them—smell, texture and taste. Edie had placed three huge peppers on his plate; he'd managed to get through one and was contemplating various disposal scenarios for the other two. Yelling "fire" was a possibility. Pity Maude kept cats rather than dogs, who at least could be relied upon to quickly dispatch anything surreptitiously slipped beneath the table. A cat would eye the pepper, which was roughly the

size of a cat's head, sniff disdainfully and walk away.
Cats had good sense. To make matters worse, he wasn't
at all hungry.

"Another pepper, Peter?" Edie asked.

"No thank you, this is more than enough," he said
truthfully. In retrospect, accepting Maude's invitation to
dinner hadn't been a good idea. Although he was quite
fond of her and willing to give her a hand in the garden,
his real motivation for being there sat across the table
from him. He knew it and he felt certain that Edie knew
it too. "You're not eating much," Maude observed with
a glance at the two untouched peppers.

"Savoring them," he said. "They're very tasty
though. Delicious."

Maude smiled back at him, but vaguely, as though
she hadn't understood. "I'll make fish next time you
come," she said.

"Lovely." Peter worked at his peppers. Tension hovered like a fourth presence in the room. He glanced up
and caught Edie's eye for a moment before she looked
away. The twins had a story they liked him to read about
a large bird that flew around with an even larger basket
in its beak. It would swoop down and whisk children off
to various adventures. Right now, he wished the bird
would come and whisk him out of this kitchen.

"So, Peter," Edie said in a conversational tone. "You
never did tell me about Ethiopia."

He gave her a blank look. His brain felt mired in
muck.

"I don't use broth," Maude said. "Makes the peppers
fall apart. My sister used to use chicken broth, never did
like her stuffed peppers."

"You said you were in Ethiopia," Edie prompted.

"Yes, right." He marshaled his thoughts, which were

running along the lines of trying to determine exactly what it was about Edie that drew him. Perhaps if he could break down her appeal, he could resist it. "The Peace Corps. Addis Ababa. My wife and I spent two years there."

"Teaching?"

He nodded. They'd lived in a hillside house with blue wooden shutters and doors. At night they'd graded papers by the light of a lantern. A shepherd lived in the house next door. At night, they could hear the thin notes of his bamboo flute.

"Your wife was a teacher, too?"

"A very good teacher."

"My daughter Vivian was going to be a teacher," Maude told him. "Went to college for three years. But she married Ray and decided she wanted to stay home and raise her boys. Ray's a good man. Used to be Edith's boyfriend. Did you know that, Peter?"

"Mom." Edie shot Maude a warning look.

"What?" Maude stared right back at her daughter. "It's no secret. She wore Ray's ring on a chain around her neck," she told Peter. "First boy that ever looked at you, wasn't he?"

Edie threw her fork down. "For God's sake, Mom. Why are you dragging this stuff up? I'm sure Peter doesn't give a damn and I certainly don't. I was fourteen."

"You don't need to shout, Edith. I can hear without you shouting. She's always shouting at me," Maude addressed Peter. "Vivian never shouts like that. I don't know what's wrong with Edith, never had any patience."

"In case you haven't picked it up," Edie said, "Vivian's perfect. I'm not."

"Eat your dinner," Maude said. "You too, Peter. Vivian tried hard at school. But she had asthma, so she was sick a lot."

"Health problems slowed her progress," Edie said sotto voce.

"Health problems slowed her progress," Maude said. "That's what it always said on her report cards. Remember that, Edith?"

"It's etched on my brain," Edie said.

"Your girls fight all the time?" Maude asked Peter. "Edith and Vivian fought like cats and dogs, never did get along. Edith was a difficult child, though. She usually started it. I remember one time—"

"Okay, that's it." Edie jumped up from the table. "I'm sorry, I've had it. Good night, Peter. Enjoy your green peppers."

CHAPTER FOURTEEN

AN HOUR OR SO LATER she saw Peter caught in the glow of the streetlight, coming down the hill as she headed back up. Briefly, she considered turning around, running from whatever it was he had to say to her, from Maude and Viv and Little Hills and the whole damn serpentine tangle of family relationships. Instead, she shoved her hands in the pockets of the jean jacket she'd pulled on as she stormed out and kept walking toward him.

"If you'd rather be alone," he said, "just say so."

"No." Shoulders hunched, she looked directly at him but couldn't summon the detachment she'd felt earlier when they were out in the backyard. The anger was gone but she felt too drained to even try to appear cool. "Stay. I think I've run off enough steam that I'm pretty sure I won't explode all over the place."

"Good. Want to talk?"

"*Ugghh.*" She drew her hands to her face, exhaled into them. "I don't know." She dropped her hands, stuck them back in her pockets and looked up at him. "Can you help me understand how it is that I can go about my life feeling pretty good about myself, feeling like a decent, compassionate person...until the minute I get home?"

He considered. "I'll try. Shall we keep walking?"

"I've walked enough. I need a beer. Maybe two. And

peanuts in shells I can toss on the floor. And a dingy bar with high stools and a pool table.''

He laughed. ''Sounds like the Rat's Nest down by the docks.''

She narrowed her eyes at him. ''You know about the Rat's Nest?''

''I have a dark side,'' he said.

They said little to each other during the ten minute walk to the Rat's Nest. Inside the dimly lit bar, Peter helped her off with her jacket, and they sat on a pair of stools over by a window. Neon signs reflected pools of color on the dark sidewalk outside. Peter ordered two beers and set one in front of Edie.

''So is this a haunt of yours?'' he asked after they were sitting on high stools with their beers and a bowl of peanuts on the table between them.

''Long time ago.'' She bit into a peanut, tossed the shell to the floor. ''These days, nothing in Little Hills is a haunt. Thank God.''

''Does this happen every time you come home?'' he asked.

''To one degree or another. I start off with all these good intentions—I won't be sarcastic, I won't let Viv needle me, I won't yell at my mother...'' She grinned. ''Well, that one is unrealistic, but you know what I mean. I start off so well and it always ends up like this.''

Peter drank some beer. ''And it's all your fault, of course?''

She shrugged. ''Maybe, deep down I think it is. It's almost a family joke now that I killed my father, but as a kid I'd heard that damn story about how he only got hit by the bus because I wanted a bike... I'd heard it so many times, that I think on some level I really believed it.''

"Your mother mentioned it."

"I know. She thinks it's so cute when she trots these little stories out and maybe it is, if you haven't heard them all a thousand times." She cracked a couple of peanuts together, dug out the nuts. "And I swear to God, in every story she tells, Viv is the innocent victim of my maliciousness. When Viv and Ray got married, I'd just been sent overseas—my first foreign assignment. Even though things had been kind of strained between us, I booked a flight to come back. Then one of the senior correspondents dropped dead of a heart attack and there was no one else to fill in for him, so I canceled my trip. Viv accused me of sulking."

"Do you think Viv's envious of you?"

"My mother thinks so. Although Maude can't understand why Viv would envy me since Viv has a husband and children and I don't."

"That's your mother's generation, though. Women weren't fulfilled until they were married and pregnant. My mother used to nag my sister, Sophia, about the same thing. She left Sophia with a huge burden of guilt for not providing grandchildren."

"Your sister's never wanted children?"

"So she says. In fact, we were just talking about it the other day." He stirred the peanuts in the bowl and took a handful. "In relation to you, actually."

"Do I want to know?"

"Do you?"

"I don't know. I think the whole thing with Mom tonight only confirms how much I want to put vast distances between myself and Little Hills. The longer I'm here, the more…entangled I feel."

"That's a no, I take it?"

She laughed. "Yeah…I think so."

He regarded her for a moment and smiled. "Actually, Sophia said she's never wanted children. Not all women are maternal, she says. And I should probably go." He glanced at his watch. "I've got an early meeting tomorrow."

Edie drained her beer and they walked out of the Rat's Nest and back up the hill to Maude's. The porch light was on, but the living-room drapes had been pulled and the front of the house was in darkness. Peter reached for his keys and frowned at them for a moment. For a split second, she thought he might kiss her. She wanted him to as much as she hoped he wouldn't try.

"As long as your family has the power to hurt you— and, clearly, they do," he said finally, "you might think about whether your determination to be anywhere but Little Hills is, in fact, a form of running away."

She hadn't been expecting that. Her immediate inclination was to hit back with a sarcastic response. But she saw concern in his face and perhaps a touch of trepidation. Maybe he'd also expected her to strike back. "Thank you," she said finally. "I'll give that some thought."

"Good night, Edie." He leaned forward to kiss her cheek. "I still think you're wonderful."

AFTER HE LEFT he drove back home, kissed his sleeping daughters, undressed and went to bed. He switched off the bedside light, closed his eyes and tried to sleep. His brain had other ideas. It lighted on Edie and essentially refused to budge. Edie, Edie, Edie. In his head, he sounded like Cary Grant. Judy, Judy, Judy. What was that movie? Did Cary win Judy after all? He couldn't remember. Maybe he'd never even seen the movie. He couldn't remember that, either. He punched the pillow, turned onto his stomach. Edie, Edie, Edie. He turned onto his back, stuck the pillow over his head. Edie, Edie, Edie. Edie, Edie, Edie, Edie, Edie. God, this was absurd. He sat up. Edie, Edie, Edie.

He finally gave up, went downstairs and lay on the couch, where a tedious journal article eventually did the trick. Sophia found him asleep there the next morning.

"An enjoyable evening?" she inquired.

Peter sat up, bleary-eyed and groggy. "Fine."

"Do anything fun?"

"I had dinner," he said. "With someone's elderly mother."

"I see." Sophia folded a sweater one of the girls had tossed on a chair. "And did this someone join you?"

"Yes."

"The someone being this foreign correspondent?"

"Yes. Edie. That's her name." He stretched and yawned. "And now, if you'll excuse me, I need to get the girls up." A moment later, halfway up the stairs, he decided that he might as well get it over with, and he ran back down to tell her that he would be taking his daughters to Maude's that afternoon.

"Just a thought," Sophia said later as he was getting ready to leave for school. "If there's no future with this foreign correspondent—"

"Edie." He stuffed papers into his briefcase. His brain, still yammering on about Edie, was starting to irritate him. Until later this afternoon, when he picked up the girls to go to Maude's, he wanted to think about nothing but school matters. Down on his hands and knees, he peered under the couch for the journal he'd dozed off reading last night.

"Peter."

"Sorry." He retrieved the journal, stood and brushed carpet fluff from his pants. "You were saying…"

"*Asking.* Specifically, why, if there's no future with this woman, are you involving the girls?"

Peter felt a surge of impatience. It was difficult enough to sort out his own feelings for Edie, much less provide Sophia with an ongoing narrative. "Sophia, the girls are going, primarily, to help weed an elderly woman's garden. Maude is looking forward to meeting them and I think they'll like her very much. She'll be a grandmother of sorts."

She folded her arms across her chest. Her expression suggested he'd just tried to sell her a dubious bill of goods. "And Edie?"

He grabbed his briefcase. "What about Edie? Oh, you're wondering whether she'll be there? I honestly haven't the foggiest idea."

"No OFFENSE, Peter, but you look…tired," Beth Herman said when she stopped by his office with a tin of gingerbread. "Is something wrong? How are the girls? I've almost finished Delphina's wings, by the way." She smiled. "They're darling. I think she'll be thrilled."

"I'm sure she will, Beth," he said. Beth, it occurred to him—not for the first time—was one of those sweetly sympathetic listeners who seemed put on earth to become confidantes. "You're very kind. And the girls are fine. We're all fine." *Other than the fact that I'm besotted with a completely inappropriate woman.* On the verge of soliciting Beth's advice, he decided that a heart-to-heart with a teacher about the agonies of unrequited love would be inappropriate and unseemly, no matter how sympathetic the listener.

After Beth left, he stopped by Betty Jean's desk.

"It's possible that Edie Robinson might call." He scratched the back of his neck. "She's advising me on a journalism group. If she should call, please—"

"Put her through immediately." Betty Jean smiled. "You already told me."

"Did I?"

"You did."

"And if I'm not in my office—"

"I'll find you. Take your cell phone."

He looked at her blankly. "Cell phone. Oh right. Good idea."

Betty Jean gazed at him so searchingly that he glanced down at himself, worried for a moment that he'd left his fly undone. No. All zipped up. *Edie, Edie.* His brain was at it again. He ran his hand across his face. *Edie.*

"Are you okay, Mr. Darling? You're not coming down with that flu that's going around?"

"No, no, fine." The phone on her desk rang and he waited for her to announce that it was Edie. He had willed Edie to call and tell him she thought he was wonderful, too, that she was tired of being a foreign correspondent and had been joking when she'd made the foreign-language remark about children. I love children, he was willing her to say. The other secretary had picked up the phone. He waited. It did not appear to be Edie. "I don't care who else has blue hair," the secretary was saying. "I don't care if the Pope has blue hair. You are not dying your hair blue. And don't call me at work with this stuff." She slammed down the phone.

It wasn't Edie.

"I'm going to make a new pot of coffee." Betty Jean was out from behind her desk. "You look like you could use some, Mr. Darling."

The intercom buzzed. "She didn't give me her

name," Betty Jean said. "But I think this may be the call you've been waiting for. I'll put her through."

He picked up the phone. "Edie?"

"Vivian." She laughed. "Our voices sound just the same, huh? I hear that all the time. Or I used to, when Edie was around more."

She said something else, but for a moment Peter was so disconcerted that the caller wasn't Edie that he missed it. "Sorry. You said…"

"I said I'm having a little surprise birthday party for Beth Herman. I'd have asked Ray to put the word out, but I was scared it might get back to Beth that way. Sunday night. I know it's short notice but…" She sighed. "I'm naturally trying to do a million and one things and that seemed to be the only date that worked."

"Right." Peter made a note on his calendar. "May I bring my daughters?"

Vivian hesitated. "Oh wow, now I'm in a spot. It's not going to be that kind of party. Now the boys are older, my house isn't exactly child-friendly…"

Peter tuned out the rest of her explanation. He didn't really care, except to wonder if Edie's antichildren bias was genetic.

"I'm just trying to get a rough idea of how many will be there," Vivian was saying now. "And, I wondered if you would be bringing a date?"

"No," he said. "But I'm not entirely sure I can be there, Vivian. Can I let you know in a day or two?" Edie would be there. Wouldn't she? He wanted to confirm that, but asking might seem a bit heavy-handed. But she'd surely be there and the thought lightened his mood. "Actually, put me down for probably. No, definitely…make that definitely."

He hung up the phone and beamed at Jennifer. "Sorry about that."

"Hey, don't worry about it. Everything okay?"

"Everything's fine," he said. "Now where were we? 'Conflict resolution,' he read from his notes. "'Anger management, peer and family relationships.' Let's talk a little bit about that…"

THE DAY AFTER THE BEER with Peter—and the second time he'd told her she was wonderful—Edie drove Maude to the Kut 'n' Kurl for her weekly shampoo and set, and decided on the spur of the moment that her own hair could do with a little attention.

She sat in the chair, a black cape wrapped around her shoulders, and tried to avert her eyes from the face that stared back at her. No matter whether the place was a high-end salon or the local clip joint, she always hated the way she looked in beauty-shop mirrors. It was one of the reasons she'd started pulling her hair back into a smooth and trouble-free knot that didn't require constant visits to keep in shape.

"So what are we looking at here?" Becky, her name in black on a pink plastic badge, lifted strands of hair. "Wow, it's been a while, huh?" She looked at Edie in the mirror. "Your hair's real dry and your ends look like a dog's been chewing them."

"Doesn't sound like good news." Edie said. "What would you suggest?"

"I'd say cut it all off."

"Yeah?"

"Longer hair when you're older…I'm not saying you're old, I just mean—"

Becky, who might be twenty-three, was blushing so furiously at the imagined insult that Edie wanted to put the girl out of her misery. "Don't worry about it, okay?" Edie said. "Tell you what, go ahead and cut it. I'm overdue for a change."

"Wow," Viv said when she dropped by later that afternoon to find her mother and sister both newly coiffed. "Look at you two. What's the deal, you both have hot dates?"

Maude, at the stove, patted her sparkling white hair. "Peter's bringing the girls over. We're all going to work in the yard. I'm making a pineapple-upside-down cake. Haven't made one for years. Edie? D'you use up all the eggs?"

"There's a whole carton in the fridge, Mom." Edie got up to find them and glanced at Viv, who had just poured coffee into a dark green mug, every movement so elaborately casual that she must be gearing up for an assault. Edie braced herself. The last time they'd talked, Viv had hung up on her. The time before, she'd hung up on Viv. She'd tried to follow up on Beth's concerns, but Viv had been too busy. Ditto the issue of Maude's still unresolved long-term living arrangements. The time was, amazingly, flying by. Another fight with Viv would help nobody. "Look." She showed Maude the carton of eggs. "Plenty."

"Edie." Vivian set her coffee mug down and lifted Tinkerbell from the counter where he was lapping daintily at some spilled cream. "God, that is so disgusting. Out." She threw open the back door and nudged the cat out with her foot. "Cats."

"Actually, I'm growing quite fond of them," Edie said. "They're really quite entertaining."

"You're nuts." She sat down. "Listen, Edie, I know nothing I say to you is going to make a difference. When has it ever? But you're starting up all these things, then you'll leave everyone else to pick up the pieces. It really isn't fair.''

"By things, you mean…Mom's volunteer work.''

"Well, that's one, but there—''

"Okay, but let's deal with that first.'' She glanced at Maude, who was pouring batter into a pan. She thought about bringing her into the discussion, then decided against it. One, she didn't have the patience to deal with Maude *and* Viv and, two, since Maude loved working at the teen mother center, this was really Viv's problem. "What do you object to about her spending a couple of hours a week at the center?''

"Don't say it like that, Edie. You make me sound like some kind of monster. It's not that I mind Mom going to the school. I'm sure it's good for her to get out. It's just that it's one more responsibility for me. You'll leave and I'll have to drive her—''

"Beth has already offered to drive her. She doesn't mind at all.''

"When Mom goes to Maple Grove, it'll be too far. And then guess who—''

"Viv, we need to talk about Maple Grove. Ask her.'' She nodded at Maude, now carefully setting a cake pan in the oven. "She doesn't want to go.''

"Shh.'' Vivian frowned in Maude's direction. "Let's not get into that now.''

"We need to. I want the issue resolved before I go.''

"Why? I can take care of it, Edie. I could have taken care of it without you. You wanted to come here and we're all tickled you did, of course, but it's not like…well, you know what I mean.''

Edie, looking at her sister across the table, was struck by the sudden suspicion that she might understand exactly what Vivian meant. Various scenarios were running through her mind and she didn't like any of them. Looking over at Maude, she knew one thing with absolute certainty. Maude would not leave this house against her will, if it meant Edie stayed here to guarantee it.

"Anyway," she said. "What about all these other loose ends?"

"Oh…" Viv shrugged. "Let's drop them, okay? I don't want us to end up mad at each other. Anyway, I have a little news. I'm having a surprise birthday party for Beth next Sunday night." She sat back in her chair, drank some coffee and set the mug down. "I've already started calling people. I left it too late to send out invitations. You know me. Busy, busy, busy." She smiled. "Peter's coming."

"Good." Edie nodded, affecting a nonchalance as phony as Viv's casual tone. "Who else?"

"Oh…all kinds of people. But Edie, he sounded thrilled when I told him the party was for Beth. I know you disagree with me, but I really, really think he likes Beth. When I asked him if he'd be bringing a date, he said, 'No, I'll be alone.'"

Edie shrugged, the significance lost on her. "So?"

"Well, Edie. I don't think he'd be coming alone if he wasn't secretly in love with Beth."

"BUT *WHY* DO WE HAVE TO DO this, Daddy?" Kate asked as Peter drove slowly along Monroe looking for a parking spot near Maude's house. "It doesn't sound like fun."

"Not fun." Abbie kicked the back of his seat. "I'm thirsty."

Natalie in the passenger seat turned to give them a

warning look. ''Behave,'' she said. ''You're being brats.''

Peter glanced in the rearview mirror. Delphina sat between the warring twins, her nose in a book, seemingly oblivious. He wanted Edie to be there, to open the front door and smile, and yet he didn't. Edie would completely change the dynamics. He'd be watching her, observing any interaction with his daughters. The situation would be tense; it couldn't be otherwise. With Maude alone, he could relax and enjoy the afternoon with his daughters. And yet, he thought as he pulled into a spot two doors down from Maude's and parked, if Edie wasn't there he'd be disappointed—he couldn't help himself.

They all piled out of the car. Natalie held Abbie's hand. He took Kate's. Delphina brought her book along. Maude's house was a large two-story clapboard with peeling paint and a neglected front garden. As they trooped up three wooden steps and onto the wraparound front porch, he pictured Maude raising two daughters there and reflected on all the memories such a house must hold. It had to be a difficult decision to leave, he thought, recalling the conversation that day at the burger place. He could still see the angry flicker in Edie's eyes, the equally fierce burn in Maude's.

He rang. They all waited. He rang again.

''No one's home,'' Abbie said.

''Let's go,'' Kate said.

''Are you sure this is the right house, Daddy?'' Natalie asked.

He rang again. Moments passed and then he heard the sound of running footsteps, down the stairs and along the hall. Edie threw open the door, a polite smile barely

covering an expression of angry impatience. She'd cut
her hair. It quite changed her appearance.

"Sorry to keep you waiting," she said. "I was working upstairs. I thought Mom would answer the door.
Hi." She tugged at the seat of her denim shorts,
scratched the back of her calf with the toe of her bare
foot, ran her fingers through her newly shorn hair and
surveyed the girls. "Let me see if I remember your
names." She held her chin. "Nope. Forgot them all.
Now you'll have to tell me all over again."

As he watched his daughters shyly introduce themselves, Peter felt the familiar wash of pride and fath-
omless love that had on occasion moved him almost to
tears. Abbie and Kate, the fair-haired holy terrors in pink
shorts and sneakers. Delphina, dark-eyed and solemn
like her mother. And Natalie who, he sadly recognized,
needed more freedom to just be a child. They were his
life, his universe. How could anyone not love them? He
glanced at Edie, who had asked Natalie a question, remembering that Natalie had thought her haughty. He
tried to see Edie through a child's eyes. Haughty? Definitely less so now, but then he'd never seen her that
way in the first place.

"Daddy said we have to pull up weeds," Abbie said.
"But I don't want to."

"*Abbie.*" Natalie shook her head. "We're helping
Mrs. Robinson. It's nice to help people, right, Daddy?"

"Absolutely," Peter looked at Edie. "Where is
Maude?"

"The last I saw of her, she was squeezing lemons for
lemonade. She whipped herself into quite a frenzy of
activity for your visit." Hands on her hips, Edie looked
at the girls. "Do you like pineapple-upside-down cake?"

The twins looked uncertainly at Peter. "I'm not sure they've ever had it," he said.

"Oh." Edie thought for a moment. "Do you like pineapple?"

They both nodded.

"Do you like cake?"

"Yesss," they both chorused.

"Well, I'm pretty certain you'll like this. How about brownies?"

"Yesss," the twins said, clearly entertained now. "Auntie Sophia makes brownies," Kate said. "And she melts chocolate on them."

"Hmm," Edie said. "Seems like overkill, but hey, what do I know?"

"Delphina. How about you? Do you like brownies?"

Delphina nodded.

"With or without melted chocolate?"

Delphina blushed. "Melted chocolate's all right."

"Really? Not too…sweet? Well then," she said when Delphina shook her head, "I might have to try it that way myself. Ah…" She'd spotted Maude approaching from the kitchen. "And here's my mother now." She made an elaborate bow. "Lovely to meet you again, girls. Good to see you too, Peter. And now I have work to do."

And then she was gone and he was following Maude through the kitchen into the backyard, which he'd somehow forgotten was such a jungle. Enough so that he had to stop thinking about Edie in order to concentrate on the work at hand.

"Good heavens." He scratched his scalp, already starting to sweat. "You could lose an army in here." In fact, the twins had already disappeared into the tall grasses, whooping and exclaiming. "This is… When was the last time anyone cleared your garden?"

Maude cackled. "Pretty bad, isn't it? My husband used to keep it up, but he's been gone for years. Viv tries, but I stopped her because she kept cutting back the roses too far. Shouldn't take too long, though, all of us working together. Don't know where Edie is, said she had some work to do or something."

He looked at Maude. "Well, I suppose we have to start somewhere." As he started working, he heard, from an open upstairs window, a telephone ring.

As Maude hustled Peter and the girls into the backyard, Edie ran back upstairs and into her room, closing the door behind her just for good measure. It would have taken very little for her to be·persuaded to join in the weeding party. Pretty amazing given that she didn't interact well with children—although Peter's girls were all very pretty and seemed well behaved—and wasn't wild about gardening. What did that say about the way Peter had grabbed her heart?

But she didn't want Peter grabbing her heart. The whole thing was too complex, too fraught with obvious difficulties. Those, not so obvious now, would become glaringly apparent if she allowed this relationship to run its course.

The phone rang. Edie picked up one of the three cordless phones that, over Maude's protest that her old black phone was good enough for her, Edie had bought and plugged in about the house. It was Beth.

Edie stood at the window, back far enough that Peter couldn't see her watching. Maude in a straw hat and holding a plate of brownies was animated about something. Edie grinned. From the bedroom, she couldn't hear what was being said, but her mother's mouth hadn't stopped moving for the past ten minutes. The younger girls were tearing around the yard, and the older two appeared to be making daisy chains. Peter, the only one actually working, was hacking away at a chest-high clump of something, while Maude looked on.

"...and I'm sorry to bother you at home," Beth was saying. "But I know you talk to Jessie and I wondered if you'd heard from her lately."

"Not since you told her about the battered women's shelter. What was that, a couple of days ago? Why?"

"Because I don't think she went to the shelter. One of her friends told me she saw her with Bobby last night at the Burger Barn and they were fighting. She hasn't been at school and she hasn't been bringing Roger. I'm a little concerned."

"I am, too." Edie moved away from the window and sat on the bed. "You've called her home, I guess."

"The number's disconnected."

"I could go by her house," Edie said. "Just to see if she's at home."

"I don't think that would be a good idea," Beth said. "These situations can get pretty volatile and I'm not sure you should involve yourself."

"I don't mind at all," Edie said. "Just give me her address. I won't stir up trouble, if that's what you're thinking."

Beth laughed. "No, that wasn't what I was thinking at all. Listen, if she should call, just let me know. This sort of thing happens all the time. The only reason I'm involving you at all is that you're a friend of Jessie's."

"I hope she thinks so, too," Edie said, pleased to hear Beth describe her that way. "It would make me feel good." Downstairs, she could hear Maude calling her name. "Hold on, Beth." She carried the phone out to the top of the stairs. "I'm up here, Mom."

"Come and have some brownies before they're all gone," Maude shouted.

"I will," she yelled back and returned to the bedroom. "Peter and his daughters are over," she told Beth. "They're helping my mom clear the yard. Or Peter is. Everyone else seems to be chowing down on brownies."

"Peter's such a sweet guy," Beth said wistfully. "How many guys would offer to do something like that?"

"No others that I know," Edie said. "Plus, he's available. You love children and they apparently need a mother. It's a match made in heaven."

Beth laughed. "Oh Edie, you're sounding like your sister." She sighed. "No, Peter's one of those men I'm content to love from afar. I'm happy with that."

Edie returned to the window. Peter had taken off his shirt. "Speaking of loving from afar, right now I'm watching him from my upstairs bedroom window. Be still my heart, he's now bare to the waist."

"Oh, be still *my* heart," Beth said, still laughing. "Does he have a nice chest?"

"Very nice."

"Edie, you're a journalist. I'm sure you can do much better than that. Let me have the details. I want to live vicariously. Hair, no hair? Muscles? Tan? Please don't tell me he's flabby and pale with a potbelly—although perhaps if he was less than perfect, I wouldn't feel quite so intimidated by him. Who wants to feel intimated as you're being lowered to the bed? God, Edie. I won't be able to look at Peter at school tomorrow. Pretend I didn't say that."

"Consider it done," Edie said. "Although, I have to

tell you he looks pretty damn good. Just enough chest hair to be sexy, no flab that I can see. Right now, he's turning to show my mom something he's pulled up… Let's see. Great back, long and lean. Ooh, he just crouched down, I see the top of his butt and…'' She grinned. ''God, Beth, I'm getting kind of hot myself.''

''*Butt* doesn't seem an appropriate word to use on Peter,'' Beth said. ''How about *derriere?* I think that's more suitable, don't you?''

''I have no problem with *butt*, myself,'' Edie said.

''Go down and ravage him,'' Beth said. ''I think you'd both enjoy it.''

''I'm not sure his daughters and my mother would.''

''Listen to us,'' Beth said. ''Two mature women and we sounds like the girls at the center. Seriously, though, Edie, are you…attracted to Peter?''

Edie felt the smile fade from her face. ''Seriously attracted. More than just that, in fact, and it's scaring the hell out of me. I think he's wonderful.'' *I still think you're wonderful, Edie,* he'd said. ''Kind, caring, compassionate. Intelligent, involved with what he does.'' She moved over to the bed, lay down on her back. ''I haven't said this aloud to anyone, Beth, and I'd appreciate it if you didn't mention it to Viv or—''

''Of course not,'' Beth said. ''It sounds as though you're in love with him.''

''I think I might be.'' Tears stung the back of her nose and she didn't try to fight them. ''I've dreamed of meeting a man like Peter. I just didn't dream of him coming with four small children.''

''Does he know how you feel?''

Edie sighed. ''I doubt it. My cool, aloof persona is quite a practiced act. Although he may. I don't know. He took me to a concert—''

"Mahler?"

"He's invited you, too."

"No, no. He plays Mahler in his office."

"Beth." Edie switched the phone to her other ear. "Did he have to explain that it was Mahler, or did you actually recognize it?"

"I know nothing about classical music," Beth said. "I went in one day when it was playing and I noticed this little refrain that sounded for all the world like Frère Jacques. You know, that little song we all sing as children? He went into a very detailed explanation of how the First Symphony is like a walk in the woods and, I swear, after five minutes he'd completely lost me…"

Smiling as she listened to Beth, and thinking of Peter's complete absorption in the music at the concert that night, Edie felt engulfed by a wave of tenderness so intense it wracked her insides. "I don't know what to do, Beth."

"Are you asking me for advice?"

"Do you have some?"

"I have some observations."

"And?"

"You strike me as extremely capable and confident, Edie. Fearless, really. Peter has four small children, something you hadn't bargained for. And I would imagine your job is also a huge consideration. But if you love him, these aren't insoluble problems. We set our own terms, Edie, that make problems insoluble."

CHAPTER FIFTEEN

AS HE AND THE GIRLS worked in Maude's yard—he considerably more than the girls, who after thirty minutes or so had accepted Maude's invitation to dig out the old toys and bicycles still stored in the toolshed—Peter also worked through a spectrum of emotions regarding Edie. Disappointment during the first hour when she didn't come down, then anger. No matter what her feelings about children, or about him for that matter, it struck him as rude and unfriendly that she'd just absented herself. If nothing else, she could have helped out.

Anger gradually gave way to resignation. Edie hadn't extended the invitation, Maude had. And Edie had made no secret of her lack of maternal instinct. When Sophia called him unrealistic, she was probably right. Edie, the jet-setting foreign correspondent, intrigued and excited him. But he also wanted the type of woman who would want to make a home for his girls. And the two images seemed incompatible.

Since he was deep in thought, Edie's voice over his shoulder startled him.

"Aha." She handed him a beer. "Caught you napping. Where is everyone?"

"The last I saw of the twins," he said, "Kate was riding off on a tricycle with Abbie screaming blue murder. Your mother went after them. Natalie's watching TV and Delphina is reading."

He picked up a clump of what he'd thought was a weed, but on closer inspection was possibly an extremely overgrown geranium. "What do you think?" He held it out to her. "*Geranium officialis*, or…"

"I haven't the slightest idea. Come on, take a break."

He swiped his hand across his forehead and carried the beer to the shade of the back steps. Edie followed him, opened her beer and sat down beside him. "There's still plenty to be done," he said. "You're more than welcome to pitch in."

"Do you think I'm horrible and antisocial for sequestering myself?"

"I'm not sure how I feel about that," he said. "I've already worked through the horrible and antisocial bit. Now I've just decided that you are who you are."

Edie laughed. "God, that sounds terrible. 'You are horrible and antisocial, Edie, but you can't help it. You are who you are.'"

"I didn't mean it that way." Peter drained half his beer. Edie disconcerted him to the point that he found himself wishing she'd go back upstairs.

"Did my mother drive you crazy?"

"Well, she's certainly quite a talker, but overall the experience has been quite pleasant. And she's obviously enjoying having us all here."

Edie shot him a long look.

"What?"

"I'm wondering if I should call you St. Peter. It's hotter than hell and humid to boot, and you've just spent the better part of an afternoon hacking away at an overgrown jungle while an old woman you barely know yammers away, and you describe it as 'quite pleasant.'"

"It was."

"I don't get you. I can't believe that there weren't a

dozen other things you could have been doing instead. So what gives? She doesn't have a huge fortune, I promise you.''

Peter got up and started gathering the tools that lay scattered around. Hot, tired and irritated by her arch cynicism, and even more by his unfathomable attraction to her, he wanted just to finish the work in the backyard, gather the girls and leave.

''That was, of course, my motivation,'' he said, picking up a rake. ''It seemed such a brilliant plan too— convince her to make me the beneficiary of her palatial estate, then quickly finish her off by ensuring she gets sunstroke.''

Edie, still on the steps drinking beer, laughed. ''Very funny.''

He handed her a long wooden-handled rake. ''If you gave me a hand, we could probably finish this off today. I'm sure your mother would appreciate it.''

''At the risk of confirming your probable belief that I'm completely without redemption, I have to tell you that earning my mother's appreciation is not a really high motivating factor.''

''Please yourself then.'' He turned away, feeling close to taking her by the shoulders and shaking her. ''Quite honestly, I couldn't care less.''

A moment later, she tugged the rake out of his hands. ''Give me that damn thing. I might be all the awful things my family claims I am, but I'm not lazy.''

Peter eyed her a moment but said nothing, and for the next forty-five minutes or so they worked in silence, broken only by occasional grunts from Edie followed by muttered announcements that she needed her head examined. Occasionally, he'd glance over at her, red-faced and determined, and have to stop himself from throwing down his shovel and taking her by the shoulders, but no longer out of irritation. Again, he resisted. When they were through, he collected the girls, who all hugged Maude but looked shyly at Edie, said goodbye and left.

"I like Grandma Maude," Natalie said as they drove away.

Peter glanced at her. "*Grandma* Maude?"

"She said that's what she wants us to call her. She said she likes having children around because it makes her feel young again."

"She put my butterfly poem on the fridge," Delphina said from the back seat.

Peter stopped himself from asking Delphina whether she'd shown the poem to Edie. He wanted not to think about Edie. But Edie was like a song he couldn't get out of his head; an endlessly repeated refrain. He could still feel her in his arms as they'd danced to her mother's scratchy gramophone records.

"I'll be looking at the moon, and I'll be seeing you."

"HE'S SWEET ON YOU," Maude announced that night as they sat in front of the TV watching *Frasier.* "It's a rerun," she complained for the third time. "Don't know why they have to show them over and over. It's not like those actors are overworked, all the money they make. He kept looking up at the window. I told him you were up there. She's working, I told him. Edie's always busy. Look at that, I'll tell you what happens, Frasier brings a girl home—"

"Mom, if you've seen this program, put something else on. I don't care." She'd played and replayed the conversation with Peter, and with each repetition she got angrier and more frustrated with herself. What the hell was wrong with her? Talking to Beth, she'd imagined walking outside to where Peter was working. Her arms around him, she would tell him that, frightening and amazing as it was to hear herself say it, she loved him. And if he felt the same way…

But then what had she done instead? Given him her idiotic, jokey-sarcastic shtick. And the more she dug in, the more difficult it became to stop. And then the girls had hugged Maude but not her. Well, why would they want to hug her, for God's sake? If *she* were eight years old, she wouldn't hug her adult self.

"Look, now Daphne's going to tell Niles she's going out," Maude said.

Edie stood. "I'm going to bed, Mom."

Maude glanced at her. "I'll have some, if you're going to make it."

Hours later, Edie had given up on sleep altogether and was reading when the phone rang just after two in the morning.

"May I speak to Edie?" a young voice asked, so softly Edie could barely hear it. "It's kind of an emergency."

"This is Edie," she said, then recognized the voice. "Jessie? What's wrong?"

"Bobby and me got into this big fight. He was drinking beer and he started getting real mean. I waited until he went to sleep…passed out, and then I packed up some things and got Roger dressed and walked down to the liquor store."

"That's where you are now?"

"Yeah. It's not such a good place—"

"Give me the address. I'll be there as fast as I can drive. And Jessie, stay by the phone. If anyone even looks at you cross-eyed, call 911."

"SOME ANIMALS don't change much as they grow up," Peter was explaining to the twins as they stopped to look at one of the exhibits that wound through the tropical conservatory of the Butterfly House. He crouched to the twins' eye level. "Humans, for example. Although grown-ups might have...more wrinkles and gray hair—"

"You have gray hair, right there." Abbie pointed to his left temple. "And on the other side too."

"And you have wrinkles by your eyes," Kate said.

"And on your forehead," Abbie observed.

"The point is," Peter said, moving on, "that despite all that, grown-ups look very much like children. Bigger children," he said when they both appeared doubtful. "A head, two arms, two legs."

"Belly buttons," Kate said.

Abbie giggled. "Pee-pees."

"But butterflies," he said in a louder, more emphatic voice intended to prevent things from getting out of hand, "go through four very distinct stages and they only look like a butterfly in the very last stage."

"Peter." Sophia had appeared with the two older girls. "There's an interactive thingy over there that the twins might like. Toilet-paper tubes and lollipop sticks and whatnot. There are children over there making butterflies out of colored paper."

"I want to make a butterfly," Abbie said.

"Abbie, there are *real* butterflies all around you," Peter said. And there were. Above and all around them, thousands of butterflies drifted in free flight, alighting on vibrant tropical foliage. Earlier, even the twins had stood still long enough to watch a butterfly magically emerge from its chrysalis. "A butterfly was born right in front of my eyes," Delphina had said, awestruck. But now the miracle of birth had lost its novelty and the consensus was for making paper butterflies. He shot Sophia a look of resignation and watched, bemused, as they all trooped off to a bank of paper-covered trestle tables.

"Pity your friend couldn't have joined us," Sophia said. "The one who gave you the tickets? A teacher, isn't she?"

"Right." Peter heard a familiar note in his sister's voice. She had, he suspected, conspired to get him alone for an update on Project Wife. Beth had flown into Sophia's radar after making Delphina's butterfly wings, and then again when he'd mentioned the tickets to the exhibit. Although he'd expected Beth to go, she'd claimed a last-minute appointment and suggested he take a friend. Immediately, he'd thought of Edie. As he'd said goodbye to her at Maude's last night, he'd thought again of inviting her, and then the girls had hugged Maude. If Edie had made some gesture, perhaps, but she hadn't. *Children are like a foreign language to me.*

"So I thought to myself," Sophia was saying, "even though he already has four wives and a mouthful of gold teeth, I might as well marry him—"

"What?" Peter gaped at his sister. "What on earth are you talking about?"

"Just checking to see if you are actually among us," Sophia said. "I had the feeling that perhaps you were floating up there with the butterflies. Mentally, anyway."

"I see," Peter said.

"Would you like my opinion?"

Peter grinned. "On what? And do I have any choice?"

"You know perfectly well on what. And no, you have no choice. Unless, of course, you want to make a public

spectacle of yourself by running through this exhibit
with your hands over your ears.''

"Go on, then.''

"You're clearly besotted with this foreign correspondent.''

"Edie.''

"Edie, sorry. Is that actually her name?''

"Actually, it's Edith, but she detests the name.''

"Can't say that I blame her,'' Sophia said. "Very old-
fashioned and frumpy. Smacks of maiden aunts and den-
tures. But, as I was saying, I think you've come down
with a very bad case of unrequited love. Perhaps she's
suitable and perhaps she's not. But if it's the former, I
think you need to start addressing the obstacles that
stand between the two of you and a blessed union. I will
want to meet her, of course.''

"LOOK, I know you need an answer,'' Edie said when
the newspaper's executive editor called to tell her she
had the bureau chief job and asked if she could be in
Hong Kong in two weeks, sooner if possible. "I'm in
the middle of a dozen things that need to be wrapped
up at home and...I really need time to think things
through.''

After she hung up, she sat on the stairs for a moment,
holding her head. This had never happened before. She'd
never had any difficulty leaving. Quite the opposite. The
last week of her visits had always dragged interminably.

"No one expects anything from you,'' Maude had
said on that first day back. But suddenly it didn't seem
that way at all. Jessie clearly needed her. She'd picked
up Jessie and the baby from outside the liquor store
and brought them back to Maude's until they figured
out some other arrangements. Now Jessie was upstairs

asleep, Roger in an improvised crib beside her. It had been after three by the time they got home; she'd woken around seven but decided to let Jessie sleep. Maude, not at all bothered by the prospect of a young houseguest and a baby, said they could stay as long as they wanted. Maude had left after breakfast for a shopping trip to St. Louis with Dixie and her daughter—a trip Edie hadn't first okayed with Viv.

That thought raised the Maple Grove specter and the inevitable showdown with Vivian. And then there was the journalism class. She'd given two of them now and was beginning to enjoy them immensely. And finally there was Peter. His daughter Delphina's poem, stuck on the fridge with a butterfly magnet, was inscribed, "To my new grandma, Maude."

From up in the bedroom, she heard the baby murmur. She crept upstairs, peered around the open door and saw a small flailing fist. Jessie stirred and reached out to pat the baby.

Jessie murmured as Edie bent to lift Roger from the crib.

"It's okay," Edie whispered. "Go back to sleep. I'll take care of Buster here." He was warm and damp and wailing indignantly as she carried him downstairs and she smiled down into his pink little face. "I'm not very good at taking care of anyone but myself," she told him. "Ask the cats. They have to remind me to feed them."

In the living room, she unwrapped the baby from his damp blankets and set him down on the couch. "Don't pee on the upholstery," she said, "or my mom will kill me." She unfastened his diaper, grimaced at the acrid ammonia smell. Roger regarded her through round brown eyes. "I forgot the clean diaper," she told him. "Stay there, okay? I'll be back in a flash." The baby cooed and wriggled his legs and Edie decided not to risk him falling off the couch. She scooped him up again, ran up the stairs, grabbed the diaper bag and carried him back to the couch.

Panting from the exertion, she pulled a disposable diaper from the bag, held it up trying to decide which way went what, then used the plastic tabs to snap it around him.

"The last time I changed a baby's diaper, I was in high school," she told him. "That was a *loooong* time ago." She heard a movement in the doorway, and Roger gurgled and waved his legs wildly. "Sounds like Mommy, huh? Breakfast?" she asked with a glance at Jessie.

"Can I help?" Jessie asked.

"Nope. Just hold the baby and talk to me."

In the kitchen, Jessie set Roger down in an infant seat on the table and Edie checked the contents of the refrigerator. "I'm not the world's greatest cook, mostly because I have no one but myself to cook for and I'm not too fussy."

"What about your mother?" Jessie asked. "Do you make stuff for her?"

Edie set four eggs on the counter and rolled her eyes. "I've tried to, but she complains so much it kind of takes all the fun out of it."

"You don't get along with her?" Jessie asked.

"It's not so much that we don't get along. It's more that we don't really like each other too much."

Jessie looked aghast. "You don't like your mom?"

"Well..." Edie grinned at Jessie's shocked expression. "It's hard to explain. I love her and in her own way I'm sure she loves me, but...we have a lot of history between us and we tend to set each other off. Although," she surprised herself by saying, "I think it's getting better."

Jessie said nothing.

"What about your mother?" Edie asked as she cracked eggs into a bowl. Immediately, she felt like an idiot. If Jessie had a good relationship with her mother, she wouldn't be taking refuge in the home of a stranger. She glanced over her shoulder at Jessie, who was spooning pureed apple into the baby's mouth. "Is she in the picture at all?"

"She lives in New Jersey. She's a cocktail waitress, but me and her boyfriend don't get along."

"Do you see her?"

"Not since before Roger was born. But she's okay. She's just got a lot of other stuff going on in her life."

Edie heated butter, then whipped the eggs a moment before she dumped them into the pan, wondering as she did whether Jessie's mother had any idea at all of the *stuff* going on in her daughter's life. She was still thinking about it when Viv called to remind her that Beth's surprise party was tonight and there were a million things still to be done and she could really use some help if Edie wasn't too busy with "the little journalism thing and everything." Roger's loud shriek stopped Viv in midsentence.

"What was that?"

"Roger."

"Who's Roger?"

Edie smiled at Jessie. "Roger's a very cute little boy who's getting very angry because Jessie—that's his mother—is trying to feed him carrots and I have the feeling he doesn't like them very much."

Vivian sighed. "You know what, Edie? I don't even want to know."

CHAPTER SIXTEEN

"I DON'T HAVE TIME to get into an argument about this," Viv said later after she'd insisted on a full accounting of how and why Jessie and Roger were now houseguests in Maude's home. "But I honestly think you're nuts. No, not nuts, just completely irresponsible and—"

"Actually, that was a good idea about not getting into an argument," Edie said. "So let's not." She had, as requested, arrived early to help Viv with the party. For most of the afternoon, they'd chopped and stirred and assembled platters of food that now rested on trays in the refrigerator. The guests had all arrived, the guest of honor duly surprised. Now, as far as Edie could see, there was little else to do but join in the festivities.

"I should probably go do something about myself," Viv partially emerged from the refrigerator to remark over her shoulder to Edie. "I don't even have lipstick on. Here…" She handed Edie a platter of deviled eggs. "Can you go hand those out and mingle?"

"No problem. Go fix yourself up."

"I look bad?" Vivian's hand shot up to her hair. "I didn't have time to stop at the beauty shop—"

"Viv. You look fine. I just meant that if you wanted to…gild the lily, I've got things under control."

Vivian, ever on the scent of sarcasm, frowned. "I'm not sure what you mean but, oh well, I don't have time to think about that now. I hope to God Ray's setting the bar up, I told him red and white wine and…oh shoot, I think the meatballs are scorching. Go.'' She flapped her hands at Edie. "I'll take care of this. Make sure Mom's parked somewhere with a plate of food, though. She'll get cranky otherwise."

"Got it." Platter in hand, Edie worked her way through the crowd and noticed Maude on a couch talking to Peter. The sight halted her in her tracks. She hadn't seen or heard from him since they'd cleared the garden, but last night she'd had an erotic dream about him involving butterfly nets and little in the way of clothing— a vivid dream that could make it hard to look at him directly. Peter would keep Maude fed, although the prospect of what Maude might be telling Peter was potentially embarrassing. *"Look, Peter,"* she imagined *Maude saying. "I don't want to see her end up an old maid and if you don't marry her, no one will. Sure she snaps, but she's not all bad. She does feed the cats."*

She circled the room a couple of times, until the platter was nearly empty, then saw Beth talking to a tall reedy guy with receding red hair. He had his hand on Beth's arm and they were both laughing as though they'd just shared a good joke. A teacher from Luther, she guessed. Viv said she'd invited the entire staff. Except for Peter, Ray and Beth, Edie knew none of them.

"Deviled eggs. Going, going…'' She offered the platter. Beth's companion took the last one, then held it up to Beth's mouth. "Gone," Edie said.

"Edie, this is my friend Sam O'Neil," Beth said after taking a tiny bite. "Edie Robinson, famous foreign correspondent and—"

"Please," Edie said, embarrassed, although Sam hardly seemed able to take his eyes off Beth. "Do you two teach together?"

They both smiled and exchanged glances. Beth shook her head. "Your sister, Edie, I swear. How she managed it, I have no idea, but she somehow found my address book and invited people I haven't heard from in years. Sam was one of them."

"We met a long time ago in a bookstore in Clayton," Sam said, still looking at Beth. "Fifteen, sixteen years ago?"

"God, I can't believe it's been that long." Beth held a glass of white wine in one hand and her cheeks were flushed. "It was Christmastime," she told Edie, "and we were both looking at the calendar selection."

"They were kind of picked over," Sam said, "and I was trying to decide between *New Yorker* cartoons and some abstract-art thing. I happened to look over to see Beth flipping through a calendar and she had this little smile on her face. I glanced at the calendar and it was babies."

"Babies?" Edie asked, smiling at Beth.

"Babies." Sam said. "It was cute. They were sitting in huge flowerpots, bursting out of eggshells, that sort of thing. She was so engrossed in the calendar, she didn't even notice me."

"So what happened?" Edie asked, charmed by the story and their obvious delight in one another. "You tapped her on the shoulder and said—"

"Could you help me pick out a calendar for my mother?" Sam laughed. "Yep, pretty corny, huh?"

"Well, I was going to guess secretary," Edie said. "And then what?"

"Oh, you know Beth." He winked at Edie. "She's so damn sweet and trusting. We picked out a calendar and chatted about this and that and then I asked her if she'd like to have a drink somewhere. I envisioned a bar, but we ended up drinking tea at the kind of place my mother would love. I was hooked from day one.''

"I was, too," Beth said softly. Head ducked slightly, she addressed her wineglass. "But I just couldn't believe you felt the same way and so we kind of drifted apart. And then I heard Sam was engaged…"

"On the rebound from you," Sam said, "I never stopped—"

"Well, gotta go do my hostess duties." Edie interrupted, sensing somehow that it was time for her exit. "Nice meeting you, Sam.

Back in the kitchen, she found Viv removing a cookie tray of something golden brown and savory from the oven. "God, whatever that is smells fantastic," she said.

"Miniature quiches," Viv said. "Spinach and cheese. I hope I haven't cooked them too long." She set them on the counter, glanced around the kitchen. "All right, let's see…pimento and cheddar pinwheels… God, maybe that's too much cheese. I could do a shrimp—"

"Viv." Edie slammed shut the freezer door that Vivian had just opened. "Who are you trying to impress? People aren't here for the food. They're here because of Beth. Who, by the way, seems pretty blissed-out."

Viv looked interested. "She's talking to Peter?"

"No. She's talking to an old flame."

"Oh…" Viv shrugged. "Sam O'Neil. He's just an old friend."

"I think he's a lot more than just an old friend." She glanced into the living room where, at the edge of the crowd, Sam had his arms locked around Beth's waist. "In fact, even as we speak, he's laying a pretty hot lip-lock on her."

Viv opened the freezer and brought out a bag of frozen shrimp. "Beth's in love with Peter. She's just trying to make him jealous.'' At the sink, she ran the shrimp under a stream of hot water. ''Beth and Sam go back a long way and I'm sure he's very sweet. But look at Sam and then look at Peter. I mean, Peter's flat-out gorgeous.''

Edie grinned. ''Hey, Viv. Who's really in love with Peter? Beth or you?''

''Oh, for God's sake, Edie.'' Viv smacked the still-frozen shrimp against the side of the sink. ''I'm happily married.''

''THERE'S EDITH,'' Maude told Peter. ''Hope she brings whatever she's carrying over here…unless it's that spicy stuff. If Edie made it, it'll be spicy. Probably have green peppers in it, too.''

''Shall I go and find out?'' Peter asked, but Maude shook her head, pointing to the full plate on her lap. They were sitting on a couch at one end of a vast room, elegantly done up with crystal chandeliers and off-white furnishings. Over the granite fireplace, a gilt-framed mirror reflected the casually dressed crowd who stood elbow to elbow, sipping wine from long-stemmed glasses. Had he not known this was the home of his assistant principal, he would have guessed that it was owned by a wealthy and successful heart surgeon, perhaps, or someone who had made a killing on the stock market. Since Ray's wife wasn't employed, Peter speculated idly on how he could afford such a house, but decided that he didn't care enough to question Maude, an obvious source of information. Maybe Ray sold cosmetics door to door, he decided.

''…and it's not that I haven't tried spicy food. You ask my daughters. Never have liked it and it's not because I haven't tried. Edith says I've just made up my mind and that's that, but I've tried, I really have.''

"I'm sure you have." Peter stored away this bit of information, amusing himself as he imagined a dialogue with Edie, who he could see now, laughing as she held out a tray to one of the English teachers. She looked…radiant, he thought. A cream-colored shift just brushed her knees. Freckled knees, he imagined, although from this distance, he couldn't confirm. Maude was still talking about spicy food.

"…with Edith, the hotter the better, she always says." Maude sniffed. "'Course, with Edith, it's all bravado. If the food burned her lips off, she'd never own up to it. Always got to prove herself. Been that way since she was a baby. First words she ever said were, 'Me do it.'"

"Why do you call her Edith and not Edie?" he asked.

Maude set down a small sandwich, delicately wiped her fingers and twiddled with her hearing aid. "Edith?"

"Everyone else calls her Edie—"

"It's Edith Pauline, but she hates the name Edith. Never forgiven me for it."

"Did you name her after someone in the family?" Peter asked.

Maude grinned slyly. "Nope. And you'll never guess in a million years."

"Tell me then."

"Edith Piaf," Maude said. "Ever heard of her?"

"Yes." Peter retrieved from his memory the only song he'd ever heard Edith Piaf sing. "La Vie En Rose."

"Didn't think so. You're too young to know Edith Piaf."

"Maude." Peter turned on the couch to bring his voice to her ear. "My mother listened to Edith Piaf," he said, making the words slow and distinct. "There was one song that always made her weep. I can't remember the name of it, though." He would have to see if Sophia remembered. A song about two lovers who committed suicide in a flat over a café. Very morose.

"Edith looked like a little plucked bird," Maude cackled. "So that's when her father said about Edith Piaf being known as the Little Sparrow, and so we called her Edith. Vivian was the pretty one, though, so we decided to name her for Vivian Leigh. My husband died when Edith was six," she said. "Terrible shock."

"I can quite imagine," Peter said, thinking about Deborah.

"Day before Edith's birthday. She'd been wanting a new bike. Not just any new bike, of course. Edith had to have a certain kind of bike, can't even remember what it was anymore, nothing would do but she had to have this bike. Drove everyone to distraction, going on and on about this bike. Well, there was nothing Richard wouldn't do for Edith, he loved both the girls of course, but Edith was always special. Anyway, out he goes late that night, parks the car across from the bike shop, runs across the street and gets hit by a bus. Dead on the spot."

Although Peter had heard this story from Maude before, he commiserated again. "How awful."

"*Awful*'s not the word. He was a good man, Richard. Loved his girls, especially Edith. Shouldn't say it, I know, but I've always thought, but for Edith's tantrums he'd be alive today. Ugh…phew." She spluttered into a napkin, then eyed the contents with disgust. "*Cucumber*. Cucumber repeats on me. Cucumber and green pepper, can't eat green pepper at all. There's Edie again. What's she got now?"

"MINIATURE QUICHE." After Maude had daintily set two on her plate, complaining as she did that she'd just bitten into a cucumber, Edie held out the platter to Peter, then quickly withdrew it. "Uh...I'm not sure. Isn't there something about real men not eating quiche?"

Peter reached for and disposed of the small pastry in two bites. "If you're concerned in that regard," he said in a pitch clearly not intended to reach Maude's ears, "I'd be more than happy to put your mind at rest."

Edie felt herself blush. She seldom blushed, but last night's dream with the butterfly net still lingered. And after his last cool goodbye, she felt almost exultant to see him looking at her in a way that said whatever was simmering between them was still mutual. He sat on the couch next to Maude, smiling up at her, every school-girl's fevered idea of the dark and tragically romantic headmaster. He was elegantly rumpled in his dark summer-weight blazer over a white cotton shirt—unironed, because there was no little wife back in the dark and lonely cottage in which he was valiantly trying to raise his four motherless daughters... Perhaps she should give up journalism and write fiction. She flashed him a friendly smile.

"Thanks for the offer," she said, referring to the quiche demonstration, "but since I'm neither concerned, nor particularly interested, I'll just decline."

"Regretfully?"

"Ah." Smiling still. "That would be telling."

"Edith ever tell you about the time I found the mouse in the dishwasher?" Maude asked Peter. "You should have seen me. I was in such a state."

"Mom..." Edie looked at Peter, who was listening to Maude as attentively as if she were revealing the secrets to the universe. She suspected, although his expression was quite solemn, that he was trying hard not to laugh. His head turned in three-quarters profile to her, allowing her to catalog various details unobserved. Well-shaped ears. Lobes. Some men had no lobes. She liked lobes. A dark curl of hair just above his shirt collar. In movies, wives were always straightening husband's collars, getting them just right as they sent their men off to that important meeting. Peter had no one to straighten his collar.

"...and I opened the door and the mouse jumped into that thing where you put the detergent," Maude said. "That yellow stuff that you bought me once, Edith. I told you to buy the generic brand, cheaper and works just as well." She looked at Peter. "Never listens, my daughter."

"Is that true?" Peter asked.

"Depends on who's talking," Edie said. "Have another quiche."

"Edith's scared to death of mice," Maude said. "One ran over her foot once and she screamed and wet her pants. Right there on the kitchen floor."

"Thank you, Mom. I'm sure Peter's fascinated."

"Completely," Peter said.

"I might just shove a quiche down your throat," Edie told him.

"She was wearing suede shoes and the stain never came out."

"Mom, for God's sake." Edie glanced at Peter. "You don't have to sit here all evening, you know. Go and mingle. I can stay and entertain my mother."

"Ah, but your mother is entertaining me," Peter said.

"Then you have a serious deficit in your life. Develop some interests."

"And then another time," Maude said, "Edith was laughing so hard she had an accident."

"That was Vivian, Mom."

"It was you, Edith. You were watching TV. I was in the kitchen and I could hear you laughing your head off. Hysterical, she was," Maude said with a glance at Peter. "When she got up, there was a wet spot on—"

"Peter, would you like to hear about my toilet training? I learned at a very early age and, despite a few mishaps along the way, I'm proud to say I was out of diapers by…but I'll let my mother regale you with the details."

"I'd rather hear them from you," Peter said.

"Only if you share yours with me."

"Gladly," Peter said. "I was an appalling baby. Wet the bed until I was five."

"We have so much in common," Edie said.

"Don't we?" Peter said.

Edie folded her arms, trying to appear nonchalant despite the warmth churning through her. "This is absolutely the weirdest conversation I've ever had with anyone."

"I think we should continue it outside," Peter said. "I could use some fresh air."

"THAT IS SO UNORIGINAL," Edie said. "I'm disappointed that you couldn't come up with something more imaginative."

He nodded, whispered something to Maude, then rose from the couch, took Edie's arm and led her out into the cool dark air, where Viv and Ray's enormous swimming pool glowed in the light of a full moon. Still holding her arm, he glanced around as though deciding on a direction. Then he led her around a couple of trees to the wooden porch at the side of the house, up a couple of steps and down onto an old covered swing, which creaked as Peter sat down beside her.

She turned to look at him. "What did you tell her?"

"That I was crazed with lust for her daughter and that I intended to take her—the daughter—out into the back garden and have my way with her."

"Really? And what did she say?"

"'Good idea.'"

"Might have been a better idea to check with the daughter first." She watched his face, her heart racing so hard she could taste the tingle of adrenaline on her tongue. His arm had been resting along the back of the swing and he dropped it around her shoulders, drew her close and kissed her. And then she caught his face between her hands and they kissed again. When they finally pulled apart, she laid her cheek against his chest. "I can feel your heart beating," she murmured.

"Good." He stroked her hair. "For a moment I thought it had stopped."

"Mine, too."

"What are your plans for this weekend?" he asked.

She smiled. "You get weekends off?"

"Yes, well, my sister is all for furthering my social life. There's a bed-and-breakfast in an old wooden hotel on the Mississippi," he said. "Balconies, feather beds, fireplaces in all the rooms. I've heard about it from friends," he added.

"Of course," she said.

"Chocolates on the pillows. Big fluffy white robes."

"This weekend?" She pretended to consider. "Sorry, I think I'll be cleaning out the toolshed."

"Pity," he said. "Would you happen to know another woman who might be interested?"

"Let me think hard about that and if I don't come up with somebody…I'll try and make time to go myself."

He drew her closer, kissed the side of her neck. "Try very hard, will you?"

She drew away slightly. "Bear with me here, okay? It would be a whole lot easier to be flip and sarcastic right now, but I'm not going to fall back on that, because I'm very serious about this." She thought for a minute. She didn't want to be flip, but she didn't want to be maudlin and sentimental, either. "*I* don't feel casual about…us, Peter. I can't imagine making love to you and just blithely going on my way. Quite frankly, I feel that way right now and all we've done is make out on my sister's porch swing…"

Peter wrapped his arms around her and kissed her. "I've felt that way since the first day I met you."

CHAPTER SEVENTEEN

SOMEONE SHOULD BOTTLE this feeling and make a lot of money, Edie thought as she lay on the couch early the next morning, replaying scenes from the night before. The surge of desire that had shot through her when she'd looked over at Peter, sitting with Maude, his head inclined slightly toward her. She smiled. Had he *really* been listening as attentively as he'd seemed to be doing? Maybe he'd really been thinking about kissing her, Edith Pauline Robinson. Her smile widened. Which he had, very nicely, thank you.

Again and again. And tomorrow, in a Victorian inn on the river, he would make love to her. *God, life was good.*

She yawned and stretched. Later, she was going over to Viv's to help her clean up the post-party mess, but she felt no great urge to get up and start the day. Her hands pillowed behind her head, she listened to the sounds of the house around her. The occasional creak from upstairs as Maude, still sleeping, moved on her bed. From her own room, which she'd given over to Jessie and the baby, a thin wail, and then the soft murmur of Jessie's voice and silence again. Bird sounds filtering in from outside. Peter would probably be able to identify them. "Hmm. It sounds rather like a..." She could hear his English accent, see the way his head would tilt as he listened. "Possibly the gray sprackled popinjay."

And she, of course, wouldn't know it from Adam…or a gray sprackled popinjay. She closed her eyes, dozed for a while, woke and thought some more about Peter, then drifted off again. When she woke to the sound of the phone ringing, it was, she saw with a glance at her watch on the floor beside the couch, nearly ten. Groggy, she rubbed her eyes and grabbed the phone on the fourth ring.

"Good morning," a perky voice chirped. "Mrs. Robinson?"

"Ms. Robinson," Edie replied. Did she *sound* like Maude?

"Deanna Becker from Maple Grove. Dee. Would Mrs. Robinson be up and about?"

Edie could hear Maude clomping around upstairs, but she didn't like the woman's chirpily officious tone. She could picture her, plump in pink polyester, iron-gray curls lacquered firmly in place. "My mother's still sleeping," she said. "May I give her a message?"

Deanna hesitated. "We were just wondering—" She coughed delicately "—if there might be financial problems."

"Financial problems." Edie frowned into the phone. "I'm sorry, you've lost me."

"No buyers for your mother's house?" she prompted.

"My mother's house isn't up for sale," Edie said.

"You took it off the market?"

"It was never on the market. I really have no idea what you're talking about."

"When your mother first toured Maple Grove last month, we explained to her and…" Some papers were rustled. "Her daughter, Mrs. Jenkins…that would be your sister?"

"It would," Edie said tersely. She could hear Maude

coming down the stairs and she wanted to get to the bottom of this before her mother appeared in the kitchen.

"Lovely person," Deanna Becker said. "Clearly loves her mother, so nice to see that. We find that adult children lack patience with their elderly—"

"Look, could we get to the point here?" Edie snapped. "My mother and sister came out to Maple Park—"

"Maple Grove," Deanna corrected. "For the grove of maples on the property. Your mother and sister both felt very, very comfortable here." She laughed. "Mrs. Robinson would have moved in on the spot, but, as we explained, there were various financial considerations to be met. Your sister assured me that this would present no problem, that her mother's house was already on the market and once it sold—"

"When was that, exactly?" Edie asked.

"Just a moment and I'll tell you. Let me see, June fourteenth."

Edie did a quick calculation. Two weeks to the day before she'd called Viv to say she was coming home for a visit. "Wow, Edie." Viv had sounded flustered. "That's great. The thing is, it might not be the best time. Mom's about to move to a retirement place…right, I know. We've tried to talk her out of it, but she's got her mind made up. Anyway, things are kind of frantic right now…not that we all won't be thrilled to see you, though."

"We do want Mrs. Robinson to join our Maple Grove family," Deanna Becker was saying now. "But there are those pesky financial—"

"Mrs. Robinson won't be joining your Maple Grove family," Edie said and hung up.

PETER HAD CALLED Melissa Fowler into his office to find out why she hadn't attended Edie's last two journalism groups. He'd reminded her of what she'd said about being inspired and was about to launch into a discussion on the need for self-discipline and goal setting when her face crumpled and she dissolved into tears. Head bowed, legs twisted like pretzels, her shoulders shaking, she told him, in a voice so low he had to strain to hear it, that she was pregnant.

"I don't want to have an abortion," she sobbed. "But...well, Brad, says I have to."

"Brad." Peter sifted through his mental file cabinet. "Brad." He shook his head. "I thought..."

"I was seeing Marcus," she explained, answering his unasked question. "But we broke up. Me and Brad started hanging around together this summer. At first we were just good friends, but then...well, it just turned into something else and then he said he didn't want me to see Marcus anymore and I didn't." The tears started afresh. "Now Brad says it's not his baby, but it is. I swear to God, Mr. Darling. Me and Marcus didn't—"

"Yes, well." Peter leaned across the desk to hand her a tissue from the box he kept solely for this purpose. Something was niggling at the back of his mind. Brad. Who else had mentioned the name Brad? He couldn't recall. Through his open door, he saw Ray Jenkins glance inside as he walked by. Melissa had broken into a new gale of sobs. Peter stood and walked around to where she sat. Ray, retracing his steps, took another glance inside and Peter pushed the door closed. "Melissa." He sat down on the chair beside her. "I want you to go over and talk to Ms. Herman in the teen mother center. Whatever you decide to do should be your decision, but she can help you work through some of the things you'll need to consider.''

She nodded miserably, dabbing at her nose. ''I thought Brad wanted to get married…''

''How old is Brad?''

''Seventeen?''

''He's not a student at Luther?'' Peter asked, still trying to remember where he'd heard the name.

Melissa shook her head. ''He goes to Stephen's.''

''Ah…'' Peter suddenly remembered where he'd heard the name. It was all falling into place now. Brad, he recalled with a sense of foreboding, was Ray Jenkins's son.

''MY LIFE IS OVER.'' Vivian lay on her back on the California king-sized bed in her massive and darkened bedroom, sobbing into her hands. ''I might just as well take an overdose of sleeping pills and…'' She removed her hands to glance at Edie, sitting on the edge of the bed. ''Where's Mom?''

''I told you twice already. She and Jessie took Roger for a walk.'' Edie handed her sister another tissue. A small hill of crumpled tissues had leaked a damp spot on the shot-silk spread around Viv's shoulder. ''Mom likes to push his stroller.''

Vivian sat up. ''See.'' She blew her nose. ''That's what this little tramp Melissa wants. A cute little *toy*… Fine, but she's not going to trap my son.''

''But Viv, what if it is Brad's baby?''

Vivian shook her head. ''I know my sons, Edie. You don't have kids, so you wouldn't understand. Neither of my boys would be that irresponsible. Brad is on the debate team. He's got a scholarship. He comes from a good home.'' She blew her nose again. ''I mean, Ray's always talking about the kids at Luther. This Melissa, she's just a little tramp. She's seen this house, how nice it is—''

"Viv." Edie pulled another tissue from the box. "You're starting to make me angry again. You can't afford this *nice* house. You took a second mortgage on Mom's house to pay for this *nice* house. You persuaded Mom to give you power of attorney and you were about to force her into a home—''

"No." Vivian caught Edie's arm, looked blurry-eyed into her face. "No. Everything else is true. We shouldn't have overextended ourselves. I should have talked to you first. But I swear to God, Edie, Mom *wanted* to go to Maple Grove. She wouldn't stop talking about it all the way home."

"Maybe she thought it's what *you* wanted, Viv. Maybe she thought she was too much trouble for *you*."

With a weary sigh, Vivian lay back down. "Edie…" She lifted a palm to her forehead. "Please don't tell me what Mom thinks," she said in a voice barely above a whisper. "While you're leading your glamorous life—''

"Vivian," Edie said in the soft, patient voice her sister had used. "If you say one more thing about my glamorous life, you will no longer need sleeping pills because I will reach over and throttle you."

"You hate me, don't you?"

"No, I don't hate you," Edie said. "I'm trying to understand what you did, but—''

"But how could you understand?" Vivian sat up again. "When Mom finally dies…" She shook her head. "I don't mean that. I want her to live to a hundred, but when she does…go and that house is sold, any money you get will just be a drop in the bucket—''

"Because you've already mortgaged it to the hilt,''

Edie said. "Is that what you mean?" It wasn't, she knew that, but couldn't resist.

"No, Edie." Vivian covered her face with her hands and breathed another weary sigh. "I meant that you didn't need the money and we did. If you'd come home after Mom moved into Maple Grove and we'd sold the house then, I honestly don't think you'd have known the difference."

"So I'm just curious. You've blown most of the money on this house. How were you planning to pay for Mom going to Maple Grove?"

"We didn't *blow* it, Edie. We have a beautiful home... Besides, we didn't use all the money and Ray's been looking into a loan." She reached for another tissue. "And we did think that you would help. After all, she's your mother, too."

Edie looked at her sister. She had no idea how many hours had passed since she'd confronted Vivian with the whole thing; three or four at least. But they could sit there talking for the rest of their lives and Vivian would remain unshaken in her conviction that, despite everything, she had earned the right to do what she'd done. Vivian had been the dutiful daughter, caring for Maude while Edie led *her glamorous life*. Vivian was endlessly patient with Maude, while Edie snapped. Vivian knew Maude, while Edie didn't.

And Edie could see now that Maude had been right. Vivian was eaten up with envy. Her own glamorous life might exist largely in Vivian's imagination, but it was enough to justify mortgaging Maude's house. And now Vivian's heart was breaking because one of her golden sons had probably impregnated his little tramp of a girl-friend.

While Edie was dreamily contemplating a romantic

weekend with Peter Darling. She scooped up the pile of sodden tissues, carried them into the bathroom and tossed them in the trash. "Listen, Viv. I'm talked out. Are you going to be okay?"

"I guess." Vivian swung her legs over the bed. "Ray will be home soon and we're going to sit down and talk to Brad." She wrapped her arms around Edie and hugged her close. "I'm sorry, Eed. Please don't hate me, okay?"

Edie pulled away to look at her sister. "Stop it. You're my sister. Of course I don't hate you. And no more talk about sleeping pills, okay? We'll all pull through this, I promise."

"I know. I guess I was being a little melodramatic. I don't even have any sleeping pills." She swiped at her nose. "You're stronger than me, Eed. You know that? You've always been. But then you didn't have asthma."

"True," Edie agreed as they walked down the stairs.

"I mean, maybe if Mom hadn't—I don't know, fussed over me the way she did—I'd be like you. Anyway…" They were at the front door now. "Edie, could I just say one little thing? I feel kind of weird about bringing it up—"

"Go ahead." Edie glanced at her watch. Lace underwear was on her list of things to pick up before tomorrow…and maybe some exotic perfume. Usually, she never indulged in either, but she'd earned it. Vivian was looking at her as though she had something to say but wasn't sure how to say it. "What?"

"Oh, forget it." Vivian shrugged. "I guess it's not important."

"Vivian. Tell me, for God's sake."

"Well, it's about last night. I kind of feel like you let me down a little. I mean, I wouldn't say this, but—"

"But you did, so go ahead and finish. How exactly did I let you down?"

"Well, the way you took off and left me in the middle of everything. I had crab quesadillas in the oven and I had to leave them and go pass out hors d'oeuvres because I couldn't find you anywhere."

God give me patience. Edie took a breath. "Viv, I thought you'd finished with the food. Remember? I took the quiches out and told you to come out and have fun. People already had more than enough to eat."

"Well, Eed…" Viv glanced at her feet. "Maybe in your opinion, but my friends aren't quite as…bohemian as yours—"

Edie laughed "Bohemian?"

"Well, you know what I mean. My friends are settled… Established people. They have certain expectations."

"And I'm sure you exceeded them. Good food, lots of it. I think everyone had a great time." She thought about Peter. "I know I did."

"Mom told me you went outside with Peter," Viv said, her voice casual. "Since I needed help in the kitchen, I went out to look for you." She straightened the rug with the toe of her shoe. "You were so wrapped up together, I couldn't tell where he left off and you started."

"And?" Arms folded across her chest now, she held her sister's eyes. "What's your problem?"

"Well, for God's sake, Edie. It's kind of embarrassing. Ray's the assistant principal and here's his sister-in-law kissing the principal."

"So what? Peter's single, I'm single. I can't see that

it's anyone's business but ours. Listen, if that's it, I need to go.''

"That's probably a good idea, Eed." Viv smiled sadly. "We're sisters, but I don't think I'll ever really understand you.''

CHAPTER EIGHTEEN

PETER WORE an unbuttoned shirt and a bath towel wrapped around his waist. In one hand, he held a brown paper bag of Thai food that had just been delivered to their room from a nearby restaurant. Edie sat on the bed, propped up by pillows and wearing nothing but a pearl necklace. He'd insisted, last night, as he divested her of her linen pants, silk shirt and newly purchased lace underwear, that the pearls remain. Since arriving at the inn, they had spent the entire time either in bed or in the claw-footed bathtub that was too short for either of them, but especially Peter, whose feet hung over the edge. It didn't matter much.

They'd been in the bathtub, immersed in bubbles, when the food arrived.

Edie watched as Peter set the food down on a dresser and pulled off his shirt. As he let the towel drop, he glanced over at her and smiled. She smiled back, already anticipating the feel of him. Last night, moonlight through the windows had softly shadowed his long, lean torso as he lay above her, hands on either side of her head, supporting his weight. She'd felt completely carried away, subsumed by passion; her body spasmed now, recalling it. This morning, in sunlight, she'd seen the red marks on his shoulder left by her teeth.

He carried the food over to the bed and set it on the sheet between them.

"I feel incredibly happy," she said.

"Thai food does that to me, too," he said.

Edie reached into the bag, withdrew a pair of chopsticks and poked him in the shoulder. "That was a compliment."

"I took it as one." He brought her hand to his mouth. He kissed her fingertips and ran his tongue between her fingers and along her palm, tracing her lifeline to her wrist. "I'm very happy, too."

"It's possible I may never be able to walk again." She reached into the bag again, lifted out a carton of pad Thai, the other pair of chopsticks and a couple of paper plates. "Not that I'm complaining." The bag was still heavy with cartons of food and she peered inside, counting three, four, five more cartons. Peter had phoned for the food while she was still submerged in bubbles. "God, how much did you get?"

"Wild and frenzied sex always makes me famished."

"Really? And do you frequently find yourself famished?"

He smiled. "Serve the food, wench."

"Coming up." As she started to open another carton, she remembered something. "Hold on." Her purse was on the dresser and she climbed out of bed to walk across the room, feeling, and trying not to be, self-conscious about Peter's eyes on her body. Lying-down nakedness, she'd discovered, was far less intimidating than walking-around nakedness.

"Close your eyes," she said. A minute or so later, she climbed back into bed beside him. "Keep them closed."

She watched his face as the music started, his forehead creased in concentration, his head nodding slightly as though to the tempo. Moments passed and then a smile of recognition broke across his face.

"Ah… Mahler's Eighth. *Symphony of a Thousand*."

"What movement?"

"First. Just before the choral comes in."

"Key?"

"E-flat."

Edie lay back against the pillow, fighting to keep a straight face. "What I find most intriguing about the first movement is that it uses an essentially archaic text and key form. I'm also quite impressed by the use of baroque devices such as *melisma,* double fugues and…*ughmm.*" Peter had reached over, grabbed her and stuck a piece of chicken in her mouth. As she tried to wrestle free, he pinned her down on the bed. She shrieked, shot out from under him and climbed onto his stomach, legs astride.

"I will make a convert of you yet," he said.

"You already have."

"I'm talking about Mahler."

"What? You think I wasn't'?"

"Did I mention being hungry?" he asked.

"Want me to get off?"

"No." He lifted his shoulder off the bed to kiss her. "I want you to stay there and feed me. And then, for equality's sake, I'll feed you."

She reached for one of the cartons, opened it and dug the chopsticks into what appeared to be sesame noodles. The thick spicy aroma filling her nose, and the impassioned chorus of Mahler's Eighth—which privately she didn't like any better than the Sixth and wouldn't know one from the other if her life depended upon it—filling her ears, she fed sesame noodles into Peter's mouth.

"Did I mention before that I think you're wonderful?" he asked between bites.

"Three times." She leaned closer to lick away a sesame seed from the corner of his mouth. Her drew her down and kissed her so tenderly it left her breathless. "I think I may have said something similar to you."

"What if I said I loved you?"

"I'd say it's probably too early for that," she said, looking into his eyes as she said the words, "but I think I love you, too."

For a moment neither of them spoke. Edie kept watching Peter's face. *I love him.* She said the words over and over in her head. *This is the face of the man I love.* It seemed so amazing, she couldn't seem to process it somehow. All the years ahead of them, waking up beside him. Opening her eyes to see his face. *Peter Darling. I love Peter Darling.* She buried her face in his neck.

"Feed me," he said.

"Typical male." She sat up, dipped a fork into one of the other cartons. "Beef and broccoli."

"My favorite," Peter said.

"Mine, too." She fed him, fed herself. "But if I get bits of broccoli stuck in my teeth, I want you to tell me."

"Edie," he said after a moment. "You have what? Another week? Two?"

"Ten days."

"Have you thought…"

His voice had trailed off, but she nodded. She knew exactly what he meant. "I haven't stopped thinking. It's you, of course. But it's a lot of other things, too." She explained the whole thing with Viv and her concerns for Maude. She told him about Jessie and the baby. "I keep wondering if it would be better for her and Roger if I took them to the shelter…safer, I mean. But Jessie seems so happy at the house, and Maude loves having her and

Roger for company. It's like she suddenly has this purpose.''

''I'm sure that's true,'' Peter said.

Edie nodded, still thinking. ''Viv always talks about me just zooming in and zooming out again and maybe she's right, but things seem to be falling into place somehow…'' Chopsticks poised, she looked at him. ''Beef. Sesame noodles or pad Thai?''

''Surprise me.'' He waited until he'd finished the mouthful of noodles she fed him. ''Are you saying that you're thinking of staying in Missouri?''

She nodded. ''The thought's been kicking around for some time. Not necessarily that I'd stay in Little Hills— although I will until I'm sure Mom's not going to be forced out of her home—but just doing something…meaningful. That day I was at school and I heard you and Beth talking about affecting people's lives, it really resonated. And then talking to the kids about journalism, I felt fantastic.''

''You could teach,'' Peter said.

She smiled. ''That occurred to me too, but…it's such a huge stretch, Peter. My work has always felt like such an integral part of who I am. It would be like cutting off my arm or something.''

''You'd grow a new one,'' he said. ''Work is only a part of who you are. The essential you will still be you, no matter what you do.''

''Do you think the girls would accept me?'' she asked, and he looked at her for such a long time that she thought he was going to tell her something awful, so she broke eye contact and dug into the noodles. ''I mean, I know I'm not warm and cuddly…''

''Edie.'' He waved away the food she'd lifted to his mouth. ''This belief you have that you're an unlovable person...I suppose it doesn't surprise me. I'm very fond of Maude, but at the party she told me this story of how your father died. I can still hear her saying, 'If it hadn't been for Edith, he'd be alive today.' How often did you hear that while you were growing up?''

"Constantly. The whole litany of my evil deeds. Hiding my sister's asthma medicine, killing my rabbit. Mom only told me since I've been back that my rabbit actually died of old age."

"But don't you see what's happened?" Peter's face was impassioned. "You've internalized it. You've actually bought into all the rubbish so that now, on some level, you believe it yourself."

She sighed. "Intellectually, I suppose I realize that, but it's difficult to just...change what I've always believed."

He stroked her hair back from her face. *"'They say the owl was a baker's daughter...'"*

She smiled, waiting.

"Hold on. I'm trying to remember...baker's daughter, baker's daughter." He frowned, then his face cleared. *"'They say the owl was a baker's daughter. Lord! We know what we are, but know not what we may be.'"*

"Okay. At the risk of revealing my ignorance, I give."

"Don't remember. The line just popped into my head."

"Ah."

"I think it's very apt. I wouldn't even consider you for a wife candidate if I didn't believe—"

"Wife candidate?"

"Long story. When you meet my sister, Sophia, she'll tell you all about it. And, by the way, you have broccoli in your teeth. But it goes very well with pearls."

WATCHING EDIE FROM across the table at his home the following evening, Peter thought of her in her pearls and nothing else and wished very much he didn't have to return her to Maude's when dinner was over. He searched the faces of his daughters and his sister for clues to their feelings about this woman who had so completely captured his heart. Sophia was talking to Edie now, asking her, rather too pointedly, whether most foreign correspondents were unmarried.

"...because I imagine it would be rather difficult on one's—" Sophia hesitated "—one's spouse and children."

"It is." Edie looked squarely at Sophia. "But I have many, many married colleagues, some married to fellow journalists—which probably makes it a whole lot easier. Those with stateside husbands or wives say it's kind of like marrying someone in the military. You just get used to the lifestyle." She sipped some water and turned to Delphina. "My mother has one of your poems on the fridge that you signed just for her," she said solemnly. "And I have to tell you, I'm just a tiny bit jealous."

Peter watched Delphina's face turn pink. Around the table, everyone else was also watching Delphina; Natalie with a touch of envy, perhaps, because Edie had singled out Delphina and not her. He caught Sophia's glance and knew she was exercising great restraint by waiting for Delphina to respond and not urging, as she normally would, that Delphina offer to write a poem for Edie.

"I wrote it especially for...Grandma Maude," Delphina said, "because I like her face and her blue eyes. And she likes cats and so do I."

"I like cats," Abbie chimed in. "I like Tinkerbell."

"I like Poochie," Kate said. "He has white paws."

Elbows on the table, Edie nodded. "You know, Kate,

I can never remember whether it's Poochie or Panda who has the white paws.'' She looked at Delphina. ''Do you know?''

Delphina glanced uncertainly at Kate. ''Poochie has white paws,'' she confirmed.

''Cats are fun to watch, aren't they?'' Edie said and all the girls nodded enthusiastically. ''Once Tinkerbell climbed up my mom's drapes. All the way up, and then he just sat at the top of the window meowing for help.''

''He couldn't get down?'' Kate asked.

''I'm sure he could,'' Edie said. ''He got up there without help.''

Delphina chimed in then with a story about Marmalade, an ancient and obese ginger tom who, Peter recalled, never seemed to leave the couch. And then it was Natalie's turn and the twins were clamoring to tell their funny stories. The polite restraint that had marked the beginning of the meal gave way to the usual dinner-table bedlam. Peter, watching Edie, looked away for a moment to see Sophia watching him. She held his eye for an instant, and winked. Edie would do, Sophia was signaling. It would probably take some adjustment all around, but Edie had Sophia's seal of approval.

''…and there's a very famous book of poems about cats,'' Edie was telling Delphina now. ''It's called *Old Possum's Book of Practical Cats* and it was written by a man whose name is T. S. Eliot.''

Delphina nodded happily, hardly able to contain herself. ''He was born in St. Louis,'' she said. ''But he lived in England for a long time—''

''Like Daddy,'' Natalie provided.

''Hey,'' Edie grinned. ''You girls know more about him than I do.''

"I know one of the poems in the book," Delphina said. "'Mr. Mistoffelees.' Well, I know part of it."

"'Mr. Mistoffelees!' Edie said. "Wow! That's my favorite one of all."

"I can say some of it," Delphina said.

"I'd love to hear it," Edie said.

Delphina glanced over at Peter. He smiled.

She bowed her head for a moment, then looked up. She took a deep breath and began to recite the Eliot poem.

Peter thought his heart might burst.

TWO WEEKS PASSED, then three. Edie was vague about future plans, but as long as she remained in Little Hills, Peter was satisfied to let things progress at their own pace. The girls seemed to be growing closer to her, their conversations frequently peppered with things Edie had said or done. One afternoon, she'd loaded them all into Maude's car and driven them to the library for story time. Delphina had been ecstatic. "Edie is so nice," she'd confided.

"It's almost frightening," Edie whispered one night as she and Peter stood on Maude's porch, arms entwined, trying to say good night, but unable to actually part. "I look at Delphina and feel such an incredible connectedness, I keep thinking she could actually be my daughter. The other girls are wonderful, too, but Delphina just touches my heart."

Peter drew her closer, kissed her mouth, her neck. "God, I love you, Edie."

She pulled back to look at him. "You're kind of growing on me, too." She caught his face in her hands. "If I'm not careful, I'm going to get very mushy and sentimental…"

The scream came from inside the house, and then the sound of something falling. Edie fumbled in her purse for the key, turned it in the lock and threw open the front door. Maude lay in a crumpled heap at the bottom of the stairs.

CHAPTER NINETEEN

"Mom." Edie was down on the floor beside Maude, who was whimpering softly, her eyes half closed. "What happened? No, don't talk." She glanced up to see Jessie at the top of the stairs, her eyes wide and dark.

"Oh my God." Jessie came running down the stairs, crouched beside Maude. "I just got Roger off to sleep and I heard a crash. What—"

"I tripped over the baby's stroller," Maude said. "Didn't see it there."

"I'll call for an ambulance," Peter said.

Edie held Maude's hand. It's my fault, she thought. If I'd listened to Viv. If I hadn't brought Jessie here. *But you did, a voice taunted. You did it. Every action has a consequence, Edie. You killed your father. You killed Jim Morrison. You hid Vivian's asthma medicine. You're bad, Edie. Bad, bad, bad.* She shook her head to clear the clamor. "Mom. Do you hurt anywhere?"

"I *can't* comb my hair," Maude said. "I can't even get up."

"I don't want you to get up," Edie softly reassured her. *Bad, bad, bad.* "Just lie quietly. Peter's calling an ambulance."

"What's Peter doing here?"

"We had dinner with the girls." *Every action has a consequence. You're bad. Bad, bad, bad.* "He just brought me home."

"That man called again." Maude was making moves to sit up. "Fred? Red? I said you'd call when you got home."

"Don't move, Mom, okay?" Upstairs she could hear Peter's voice. "Twen*tee*-four Monroe," he was saying. "Yes, yes. Of course. Right," he said.

Edie closed her eyes for a moment. When she opened them again, Maude was watching her.

"You going to marry him?"

"Let's just focus on you right now, okay?"

"You're not too old," Maude said. "Women your age have babies all the time."

"Mom, please." Edie exhaled slowly. Her body seemed to be filling with an enormous emotional storm; huge gray banks of tears, thunderbolts of fear. Remorse, doubt, confusion, the culmination of all that had happened since her return to Little Hills. She felt it building in her chest, behind her eyes, clogging her throat. Peter was down on the floor beside Maude now. Long bony knees. His sweet face. God, she was going to cry. She smiled at Jessie, ashen and terrified. It's going to be all right, Jessie, she silently promised. It will. Just don't let the storm break until Maude's taken care of.

"I don't know, Maude." Peter was shaking his head. "This could mean an end to your ballroom career, you know."

Maude raised a hand as though to swat him. "If I were fifty years younger, I'd fall in love with you myself," she said.

Edie heard the distant wail of sirens. She squeezed Maude's hand. "I think help is on the way."

PETER SET DOWN a cardboard cup of vending-machine coffee and a package of cheese crackers on the small table behind Edie. She nodded thanks and turned back to her mother. They'd been at the hospital all night and now he could see thin gray morning light filtering in through the blinds above Maude's bed. She had fractured her hip and lay sedated, waiting for the orderly to wheel her off to surgery. Edie leaned close to Maude's face and began talking to her softly. Maude's eyes fluttered open, focused on Edie for a moment, then closed.

"Viv's gone to get some fresh air," Edie told her. "She'll be back in a minute."

Peter yawned, unfurled himself from the molded-plastic chair and came over to stand beside Edie. Her hand still in Maude's, she shot him a sideways glance. In silence, they watched the rise and fall of Maude's breathing. Behind them, in the lighted corridor, he heard the purposeful slap of rubber soles on polished floors, the ambient hospital noise of equipment and voices and bleeps and bells. He inclined his head toward Edie and her hair brushed his face like a caress.

"Bearing up?" he whispered.

"I'm fine." She rubbed her eyes, glanced at her watch. "It's late…or early, or whatever. Don't you have to be in school, or something?"

"I'll make some phone calls in a bit."

"Don't…I mean, I appreciate you being here, but I'm fine."

"Edie, I'm here because I want to be here." He stopped himself from asking whether she wanted him there. He wanted to believe she did. All through the night as they'd waited for Maude to be wheeled back and forth for various tests and exams, he'd held fast to the belief that his presence was a comfort. At one point, a resident had walked into the crowded waiting room and asked for Maude Robinson's family members and

Edie's hand had closed around his own. She was holding it still as the resident explained that Maude had broken her hip and would require surgery. "At your mother's age…" the resident had said, and Edie's hand had gone very still.

Edie leaned to kiss Maude's forehead. "Anything to get attention, huh, Mom?"

"Oh good, they haven't taken her yet," Vivian said from the doorway. "The damn elevator was stuck on the fourth floor. What is it about hospital elevators? Do they stick more often than other elevators, or does it just seem that way? How's she doing?"

"Out for the count, I think." Peter moved aside to let Vivian stand next to Edie. Chilled and drained by the long night and lack of sleep, he imagined collapsing under a weight of blankets, Edie beside him with her arms wrapped around him as they drifted off to sleep.

An orderly arrived with a gurney and a couple of nurses, and Peter walked out into the corridor to allow Maude's daughters a moment alone with their mother. He leaned against the wall and yawned again. When he raised his hand to his face, he felt the stubble of beard across his palm. Maude was wheeled from the room, the orderly pausing briefly for Vivian and then Edie to kiss their mother. Then the gurney disappeared into an elevator.

"Well…" Vivian sighed. "I guess now we just wait."

Edie, her lower lip caught between her teeth, seemed fixated on her feet.

Peter watched Edie shrug, then shake her head. And then she looked up at Vivian and both women embraced. Peter had the impression that it was Vivian comforting her sister and not the other way around. The realization surprised him, somehow. He would have guessed that Vivian would be the one to fall apart. A moment later, Vivian had produced a tissue; Edie took it, blew her nose, swiped the back of her hand across her eyes and appeared to mentally shake herself.

"Peter," she said. "You look exhausted. Go home, really. I'll be fine. Viv's here and I'll call you as soon as I hear anything."

He looked at her, trying to read into her face more than she might be saying. He saw only weariness and, he sensed, an enormous determination not to break down. "Edie…" He caught her shoulders and pulled her close. Her body confirmed his suspicion. She felt rigid, almost brittle in his arms.

"I'll be in the cafeteria," Viv said after a moment. "See you both later."

He waited until Vivian had disappeared down the corridor, then took Edie by the hand and led her to a patients' lounge. He removed a couple of magazines from one of the two armchairs. Edie sank into the chair, leaned her head back and closed her eyes. A moment later, she stood up again.

"I'm too exhausted to even sleep."

"Then don't try." He sat down in the chair she'd vacated, held out his arms. "Come here."

She hesitated before perching tentatively on his knee. "Peter, don't say anything until I've finished, okay?"

He nodded.

"I don't think I can do this…the whole commitment thing. I think I got kind of intoxicated by it all, the romance…whatever. But what just happened with my mom seems like a sign, a warning sign. I'm truly not given to the metaphysical, but it's inescapable. If I hadn't brought Jessie home, my mother wouldn't be in surgery right now.''

"If you hadn't brought Jessie home," Peter said, "she might have been beaten to death by her boyfriend and your mother might have tripped and fallen down the stairs, anyway."

Edie drew a long shuddering breath. "You can't possibly understand, Peter. I've lived with this my whole life. I killed my dad, I killed my rabbit—"

"But you *didn't* kill your father *or* the rabbit." Peter felt an edge of exasperation. "We talked about this, Edie. You've just heard Maude say it so many times that you've incorporated it into your own beliefs about yourself."

Edie got up off his lap and began pacing the room. "I understand what you're saying. I do. But I understand it up here." She tapped her forehead. "And then something like this happens…something that's directly or indirectly because of something *I* did, and…I honestly don't think I can deal with it." She sat down on his lap again, took his face between her hands and kissed him. "I love you, Peter," she said against his mouth. "But I'm going to take the Asia job. I honestly believe it would be better for all of us."

He watched her face for a moment. "You've been up all night, Edie," he said. "You're under a great deal of stress. I'll respect whatever decision you make, but get a decent night's sleep before you make it and then let's talk."

She shook her head, smiling as though he'd just proposed something kind but unrealistic. "I've made up my mind. I was happy with my life before I came back to Little Hills and I can return to it and be just as happy. I want to give the girls my copy of the *Old Possum* book.

I need to go by the high school to clear up some loose ends with Beth. I'll drop it by your office.''

And then she was gone. Peter leaned his head against the back of the chair and closed his eyes. Did Maude have any idea at all, he wondered, of the harm her careless words had created? He suspected not. He wondered if years from now, Natalie or Delphina, or one of the twins, would hold as true some false notion of themselves created by something he'd said or done. Too numb and exhausted to think anymore, he decided to go home and follow his own advice to Edie.

EDIE STOOD in the middle of the hospital cafeteria looking for Viv and blinking in the harsh fluorescent light. Her eyes felt gritty, her head floating free somehow. She kept waiting for the storm to break. It hadn't happened, as she was sure it would, when Peter drew her down on his lap, and it hadn't happened when she'd left him sitting in the patients' lounge. *A ridge of high pressure,* she imagined the weather guy on Maude's TV proclaiming, *is holding back a strong storm system. Once the high pressure breaks down, the forecast calls for heavy rains and gale force winds.*

The cafeteria had a build-it-yourself taco bar, a soup and salad bar, and an American grill—five kinds of burgers, and plain or chili-cheese fries. The mingled aromas were making her feel slightly sick. Maybe she should forget about finding Viv and go curl up somewhere and sleep. Maybe sleep would miraculously fix everything and she'd realize that Peter was right; she had merely incorporated the things Maude had always told her into the image she had of herself. But then Delphina would break her leg on the roller skates her new stepmother had bought for her, or one of the twins would choke on a piece of candy she'd supplied. Or Peter, without the blinders of new love, would see her for who she really was and be sorry he ever met her.

Aloneness might be lonely at times, but it had its advantages. You weren't responsible for causing anyone else's unhappiness. She'd been fine until she came back home and got caught up in everyone's lives. Maybe she would just leave now, take a cab to the airport. She'd call Maude and tell her...what? *You have Viv, Mom. Just don't let her talk you into selling the house if that's not what you want. I'll send you money...* She'd call Viv too. *Stop envying me. My life is not at all the way you imagine it. And stop filling the void in your own life with...stuff.*

"I'm waiting for an omelet," Vivian came up beside her. "You're not having anything?"

"Not hungry." Edie stuck a thick white mug under the spout of a coffee urn, paid for the coffee and carried it to over to a table by the window. The view outside was of a multilevel parking lot. She wondered groggily whether it was still breakfast time, or had the day slipped away into lunch?

"You should eat something," Vivian had followed her. "How about a muffin?"

Edie shrugged. She didn't care. "Fine, thanks."

"What kind?"

"I don't care, Viv...bran," she said, when Viv still waited.

"What if they don't have br—okay." She'd read Edie's face. "Whatever they have." Vivian walked toward the food line.

Edie sat with her head in her hands. Days seemed to have passed since she'd climbed into the ambulance with Maude. They wouldn't let Peter in the ambulance; only family members, the driver had said. But he had already been waiting in the emergency room when Maude was wheeled in. He'd hugged Edie and she'd leaned into his chest, aware in some distant way of his heart beating against her face. She banished the memory. If she allowed herself to dwell on such things, the storm would break right here in the hospital cafeteria. Right in front of Vivian, who was approaching the table with a laden tray.

"Okay, this looks pretty healthy, right?" Vivian set the tray of food down on the table. "I'm not real thrilled about spinach, but it's got all these antioxidants and God knows what else." She took a bite, chewed thoughtfully. "I don't think Mom ever worried about eating healthy, though, and look at her. Edie? Are you okay? Damn, I forgot your muffin." She set her fork down. "Hold on, I'll go—"

"Viv, sit down. I'm fine, really."

"You don't look fine. You've got circles under your eyes."

"We've been up all night, Viv. You don't look so hot yourself."

Vivian smiled and lifted the edge of the omelet to scrape away a layer of spinach. "You're probably right. Do I look too bad?" She leaned over to reach for her purse, but apparently changed her mind. "Oh, the hell with it. I'm not trying to impress anyone."

Edie eyed her sister for a moment.

"I know, I know. Don't even start." Carefully, as though it required great concentration, she sliced a piece of the omelet. "Edie...I know you're probably waiting for me to yell at you about Mom. About her falling over the baby's stroller and everything, and I just wanted to say I'm not going to do that.'' She looked at Edie. ''Do you mind if we talk a little?''

''Go ahead. I'm not sure how much talking I feel like doing, but I'll listen.''

Viv frowned at her food. ''I feel bad that we haven't been getting along too well since you got back. It seems like I'm always complaining about something you've done or haven't done. Just like the day after the party when I was going on about you and Peter…'' She eyed Edie. ''By the way, last night, with Mom and everything, really changed my opinion about Peter. When Beth used to gush over him, I'd think it was just her, but I tell you, the next time Ray starts bitching about him, I'm going to tell him to shut the hell up. *I* like Peter. And you must feel like you've just won the lottery, huh?''

''Oh…'' Edie cast around for something innocuous to say, but her brain seemed to have frozen. And then, to her horror, the tears burst through, filling her throat and her nose, gushing from her eyes. For a moment she couldn't breathe, she was crying so hard. She grabbed at a napkin, held it in front of her face and sobbed.

''Edie.'' Viv was beside her, an arm around her shoulders. ''What is it? What's going on? Is it Mom? She'll be okay. The doctor said she'd need a walker for several months, but…is it Peter? Yes? No? Tell me, don't keep it all bottled up. Come on…''

She pushed more tissues into Edie's hands. ''We'll go find somewhere quiet to sit. No? You want to stay here. Okay, you sit there and I'll tell you what I was going to say. Is that okay? You want to hear it, or you want me to just shut up and leave you alone? No? Was that a shake or a nod? Here…'' She reached across Edie for more napkins. ''So anyway, I think what it all comes down to is I'm happy with my life. I mean, most of the time I feel like an okay person. And then you get home and everyone's so impressed with everything you've done and I call Mom and it's Edie this and Edie that and Edie makes her these delicious breakfasts…forget that *I* cook her breakfast every time she stays with us. And before long I'm feeling that I'm in high school again listening to everyone telling me that it's a good thing I'm pretty, because Edie got all the brains and then I just felt like you didn't really…respect my life. It wouldn't be your kind of life even if you were living in Little Hills. But then I started thinking. I'm *not* dumb. I've never been dumb. I only feel dumb when Edie comes home, which is pretty dumb in itself, right? I mean, it's not like I pop a dumb pill before I go to the airport to pick you up, so why do I feel dumb the minute you get in the car?''

"Vivian…'' Edie knew suddenly that the worst of the storm had passed. She dropped her hands from her face, turned to her sister and pulled her close. It was an awkward embrace, both of them twisted at the waist, her mouth in Vivian's hair, but moments passed before she broke away. "I love you, Viv,'' she said. "And don't worry, I'm not going to get maudlin, but I just want you to know that. Now get back on your side of the table so I can drink my coffee, which probably got cold while you were blabbing away.''

"I love you too, Eed,'' Viv said when she was back in her seat again. "D'you feel better?''

"I'm not sure.'' Edie blew her nose into a napkin. "But I think I've lost about five pounds in water weight…''

"Yeah, that would be your luck. You have a crying jag and lose five pounds, I have one pig-out on chocolate to feel better and gain five pounds.''

"Thank you, Viv," Edie said. "I really mean that."

Vivian shrugged. "I just yakked."

"No, you just confirmed something I've always known on some level but didn't believe deep down." She leaned across the table. "You don't feel dumb unless I'm around and I don't feel like a miserable excuse for a human being until I come back home... So what does that tell you?"

Vivian grinned. "That it's all Mom's fault?"

"Yeah, let's just blame Mom."

"Poor little old Mom," Vivian said. "Up there in surgery while her two miserable excuses for daughters bitch about her."

"Well, I do remember coming home from school with all A's," Edie said, "and Mom would hardly look at me. But you'd get a C and she was beside herself." She saw something in Vivian's eyes and another piece fell into place. "And I thought she was ignoring me because she didn't like me."

"And I thought I was dumb, but she made excuses about my asthma just to make me feel better."

"But she did let me believe I killed Jim Morrison."

"*Jim Morrison.*" Vivian shook her head. "You've lost me."

"That lop-eared rabbit I had when I was fourteen."

"That was its name? I thought it was Elvis Presley."

"Oh *please*. Like I would name a sweet little rabbit after Elvis Presley."

"Well, *I* happened to like Elvis Presley," Vivian said. "Anyway, what d'you mean you killed him? He was ancient when you got him. I remember Mom telling you not to get too attached because he probably wouldn't be around for long."

Edie relayed the account Maude had given her.

"But you were a kid, Edie. Either way, it's so long ago. You can't still feel guilty."

"Can you still feel dumb?"

"Yeah." Vivian nodded. "I see what you mean. So what do we do?"

"I'm not sure, but I think just recognizing what's going on is a good start."

"Here's what we can do," Viv said. "You keep reminding me that I'm not really dumb, and I tell you that you're not condescending and sarcastic..." She met Edie's eyes for a moment and they both started laughing. "Okay," she said a moment later. "You're not a miserable excuse for a human being."

"That's a start," Edie said. "But it's going to take a while. We both need to really, *really* believe it deep inside to get rid of all the years we've believed the opposite. It's like getting a red-wine stain out of a white tablecloth. You can wash it over and over, scrub at it, throw in some bleach. Eventually, it might fade so you can hardly see it anymore, but the stain's never going to come out completely."

Viv was nodding, her expression thoughtful. And then, "When the hell have you ever laundered a white tablecloth, anyway?"

"MOM CAME THROUGH the surgery just fine," Edie told Beth later that afternoon when she dropped by the center. "She's still groggy, but Viv's with her. I grabbed a few hours' sleep and I'll go back there later so Viv can go home when the boys are out of school."

Beth nodded and Edie eyed the plate of cake and melting ice cream in her lap. Earlier, Beth had surprised one of the teen mothers with a birthday cake, a gesture that had caused the girl to break into tears because, she'd explained, nobody had ever made a cake for her before. In their heart-to-heart at the hospital earlier, Vivian hadn't mentioned Brad or his pregnant girlfriend. How it would eventually turn out, Edie didn't know, but she hoped the girl would find her way over to the center, just as Jessie had done.

Which reminded her of why she'd stopped by to speak to Beth. "I want to help Jessie get back on her feet," she said. "Financially, and whatever else I can do. I'm not sure about my long-term plans yet, but I want Jessie and Roger to have a home. Mom's going to need help once she's released from the hospital, and she likes Jessie."

"It's mutual," Beth said. "When Jessie dropped by yesterday, she couldn't stop talking about how sweet Maude was and how grateful she was to both of you. And your mother seems to have really taken to Roger." A moment passed and she reached over to touch Edie's hand. "I hope you realize what a wonderful thing you've done for Jessie and the baby. Having someone to listen and care means so much. And *you* were there to do that."

Edie swallowed. "Don't make me cry, Beth, because I haven't finished talking business..." She smiled shakily. "One crying jag a day is more than enough. Anyway, the doctor said that Mom will need help once she's discharged from the hospital. If Jessie would like to do that, I'll pay her a salary. She and Roger can stay in my old room, where they are now, or Jessie could have a little apartment nearby and come to the house every day. I'll let her decide. If Maude needs more help than Jessie can provide, I'll cover that, too."

"You've discussed this with Jessie?"

"Not yet. I thought I'd talk to you first. But I'm pretty

sure she'd agree to the plan. I just don't want her to have any reason to go back to the abusive relationship she left.''

Her face thoughtful, Beth leaned back in her seat. ''Okay, we've taken care of Maude and we've taken care of Jessie and Roger. Now, what about Edie?''

''Edie doesn't know about Edie.'' She exhaled. ''But I still haven't finished with business. Vivian's son Brad may have got this girl pregnant—''

''Melissa. She's already been in to see me. Brad's apparently not willing to take responsibility, but we're working on that. Meanwhile, Melissa's beginning to make some plans. She's talking about adoption.'' She smiled. ''*Now* can we talk about Edie?''

''If we talk about Beth first…and Sam O'Neil. When I last saw the two of you together, things looked very promising.''

Beth scraped at the last of the cake, tossed the plate in the trash and smiled dreamily. ''They are very promising.''

''I want to hear all about it.''

''Edie, I honestly never thought it would happen, but we just can't seem to get enough of each other. We talk and talk, late into the night, about everything, but we never seem to run out of things to say to each other.''

''That's great, Beth. I'm very happy for you.''

''I'm very happy for myself…but let's talk about Edie.'' She glanced beyond Edie's shoulder and jumped up from her seat. ''Uh-oh, what's going on out there? Excuse me…''

Alerted by something in Beth's voice, Edie got up too and followed her out of the glass-enclosed cubicle and into the center's main area. The normally noisy and hectic scene had frozen into a tableau, silent but for the wail of a baby. All around the room, clusters of girls stood, transfixed by the tall dark-haired kid in the flannel shirt with the gun in his hand.

"Somebody better tell me where my son is," he was saying. "Or I'm going to shoot this place up."

Edie felt the blood drain from her face. His son, she knew without a doubt, was Roger. Who, at this very moment, was probably sound asleep in her old bedroom.

CHAPTER TWENTY

IN THE MOMENT before he walked into the teen mother center and into the point of a gun, Peter had been thinking about Edie. Wondering whether she'd slept and, if she had, whether she'd had a change of heart. He'd been thinking of Edie's face; her amber eyes, her mouth. And then he'd walked into the center and seen a gun trained on that face. She'd been talking to the boy, her voice low and without inflection.

"And I'm sure you must miss him," she was saying as Peter entered the room. The boy with the gun had turned then, recognized him as the principal and pointed the gun.

"You guys got my kid hid somewhere," the boy said now. "My kid. I ain't leaving till I get him back."

"Well, let's see what we can do to help you." Peter took a few steps forward, his brain searching for the boy's name. Billy? Bobby? Something with a B and a Y. He took a chance. "Bobby, isn't it?"

The kid nodded. "You gonna tell me where my son is?"

Peter looked from the gun to the boy's face. Random thoughts and images zapped through his brain. He saw his daughters' faces. He remembered that just last week in St. Louis, a disgruntled student had shot and killed his math teacher. He knew that if he turned his head slightly, he would see Edie's shoulder. Edie, whom he half expected to, but hoped to God wouldn't, step forward and demand the gun. He imagined that Edie was probably exercising great restraint right now. If the gun went off and left the girls without a father, he wondered whether Edie would step forward then.

"I know you're concerned about him," Peter said. "I'm a father too, and I can't even imagine what I'd do if I couldn't see my daughters. What is your son's name?"

"Roger."

"And is Roger enrolled here at the center?"

"Yeah, my girlfriend brings him. I ain't seen him since she started playing games with me. I've had it with this crap." He waved the gun. "I want my kid."

Peter moved a little closer. "How old is he?"

The kid shrugged. "I dunno…six or seven months."

"Ah." Peter smiled. "That's an interesting time in a baby's development. What can he do? Is he crawling yet?"

"Yeah, kind of. He's real smart. Jessie ain't got no right to hide him from me."

"Jessie's the baby's mother?"

"She's playing some kind of goddamn—"

"Jessie's a student here at Luther?" Peter asked, raising his voice to be heard above a baby's insistent wail. Others were joining in, a loud chorus in the otherwise silent room. Behind Bobby, girls were shooting frightened glances at the playpen, where three of the babies had pulled themselves upright. Tiny fists locked around the canvas support, they rocked and screamed, clamoring for attention. Peter nodded in the direction of Beth's cubicle. "Would you like to find a quieter place to talk about this?"

"Crying babies don't bother me none." Bobby kept

the gun pointed. "Just tell me where my kid is and no-body's gonna get hurt."

"It's a good thing the screaming doesn't bother *you*." Peter wondered whether anyone had called for the po-lice. He smiled at Bobby. "I imagine Roger's a good baby, isn't he? Doesn't cry much?"

"He's tough," the boy said, pride in his voice. "Just like his old man."

"Does Roger look like you?" Peter asked.

"Carbon copy."

"Pictures in your wallet, I bet?"

"Yeah, my mom's always sticking a camera in his face. She wants him back, too. It's not right, keeping her grandkid away from her."

Peter nodded. "No, I'm sure she misses him, too. Look, I can only imagine how difficult this must be for you, but I really want to help you."

The kid said nothing.

"I mean that, Bobby." Peter looked directly into the boy's eyes. "Those aren't empty words. I want you to believe me."

With his free hand, Bobby scratched the side of his neck.

"Do you believe me?"

"I don't want no yak yak yak shit…"

"You want your son, right?"

Bobby nodded. His face had reddened. "I ain't per-fect, but I love my kid."

"I can tell." Peter kept his eyes on the boy's face. In the distance, he could hear sirens. He'd been listening for them, wanting to hear them, but they suddenly seemed less important than reaching this boy. "No one's perfect, Bobby. When I was your age, I was far, far from perfect.'' He held out his hand. ''Do you want me to help you see your son again?''

The boy scratched his neck again, and his chin crumpled. A moment passed and he nodded imperceptibly. Then he dropped the gun in Peter's hand. Peter heard the sirens grow louder, then stop. He put his arm around the boy's shoulder. By the time three uniformed officers burst into the room, he had walked Bobby into Beth's office and they were talking in private.

EDIE STOOD in Peter's office with the door closed. His arms were wrapped around her and they were locked in a kiss that just went on and on. The knock on the door didn't register at first. Dazed, Edie pulled away slightly to see the door open a foot or so. Then, like a hand puppet, Ray's head appeared around the edge of the door, goggled and withdrew.

Edie grinned at Peter and started laughing so hard she had to sit down. Looking amused himself, Peter scooped her up in his arms, sat down in the chair and deposited her in his lap. He kissed her again.

''Your reputation's shot now.'' Edie giggled.

''*Au contraire*. I think it will be enhanced. I can picture the headlines. 'Lowly High School Principal Captures the Heart of Dashing Foreign Correspondent.' People might have found that hard to believe, but Ray can now provide confirmation.''

''Except if I stop being a foreign correspondent.''

''The Asia job…''

''I'm going to turn it down.''

''I'm getting whiplash. Didn't you just tell me—''

''That I was going to take it? I know. I think I was so stressed out by Mom's accident and no sleep, I just kind of fell back on it because it felt familiar, but it's not what I want, Peter. I love you, I honestly do.''

"Say it again.''

"I love you.'' She twisted around on his lap to see his face. "I feel kind of relieved now that I've made the decision. I really do think I'd like to teach. I know it's going to mean going back to school—maybe I can do some freelancing to support myself, but it's kind of exciting to be starting something new. Tomorrow, I'll call—''

"That's tomorrow. Right now, I want to hear about the high-school principal capturing your heart.''

"You've got it.''

"Good. Because when I left you at the hospital yesterday, I wasn't entirely convinced that a good night's sleep would do the trick. I felt as though a little bit of my heart had been ripped out and it hurt like hell. I infinitely prefer having it captured.''

"God, Peter.'' She buried her face in his neck. "I was so terrified for you when that kid was waving the gun. I wanted to rip it out of his hand and tell him to knock it off because I had something very important to say to you.''

"I know. I heard your voice when I walked into the room, and I thought the hardest part about this whole drama might be determining who would ultimately be the one to talk him down. I half expected you to step in at any moment.''

"Trust me, I wanted to. But I could see that what you were saying to him was registering, so I restrained myself. What's going to happen to him?''

Peter sighed. "Well, brandishing a gun in a day-care center will obviously carry some consequences, especially since he's already on probation. It might be some time before Bobby's actually holding his son, but I promised I'd help him and I will. He's like so many of the kids here. He just needs someone to care about him, to be on his side.''

"I love you, Peter." She watched his face. "I know what you're saying, he's a lost kid and all that, but I have to say that when I saw him with that gun, I was so terrified that he'd panic and shoot that my whole body was shaking.''

"I had one or two of those moments myself. I'd think about the girls and what would happen to them if something—''

"Don't." Edie kissed his mouth to stop the words. "Don't even say it." She swallowed. "Listen, Peter, and I mean this with every fiber of my being. As long as anyone, you or the girls, wants me to have a role in their lives, I'll be there.''

His arm tightened around her and they sat in silence for a moment. "Thank you. I can't tell you what it means to hear you say that.''

"I mean it.''

"I know.''

"Viv and I had a long talk after you left this morning. She helped clear up a lot of things in my mind. If she hadn't, I'd have probably managed to convince myself that this whole thing—Mom's accident, the kid with the gun—was all my fault because I'd tried to help Jessie. But I've thought it through and I really don't blame myself. I've decided that my new mantra is, 'You're basically a good person, Edie.'''

Peter grinned. "Basically?"

"Well, I'm still working on it. This time next year, I'll probably dump the qualifier. Might even add an adjective or two. 'You're an amazingly, miraculously good person, Edie.'"

"I wouldn't overdo it," Peter said.

She punched his shoulder. "Seriously though, I'm very happy. A little scared, but definitely happy. You think the girls *will* like me? I mean, I'm not expecting them to immediately fall head over heels or anything, but I don't want them to think of me as a wicked step-mother and—"

"Shut up, Edie." He caught her hand, turned it over and kissed the palm. "The girls already *like* you and in time I have no doubt they're going to love you. How could they not? I love you and they're my daughters. Highly intelligent and intuitive about these things."

She considered this for a moment and smiled. "Which *must* mean I'm a good person, right?" She grabbed his hand. "Come on, let's go and pick up the girls and take them to see Mom. And then we'll tell her that sometime in the distant future, but probably in her lifetime, you intend to make an honest woman out of me. You think her heart can stand the shock?"

"Oh, I think so," Peter said. "Providing you don't snap at her."

"Or slap my head."

"Did I ever tell you I think you're wonderful?" Peter said.

"Yeah, but you know what?" She turned to look at him. "I don't think I could ever hear you say it too many times."

A Full House
by Nadia Nichols
(Superromance #1209)

**Dr. Annie Crawford's rented
an isolated saltwater farm in
northern Maine to escape
her hectic New York life and
to spend time with her
troubled teenage daughter.
But the two are not alone
for long. First comes Nelly—
the puppy Annie's ex
promised their daughter.
Then comes Lily, the elderly owner of the farm who wants
nothing more than to return home with her faithful old dog.
And finally, Lieutenant Jake Macpherson—the cop who
arrested Annie's daughter—shows up with his own little girl.
Now Annie's got a full house...and a brand-new family.**

Available in June 2004 wherever Harlequin books are sold.

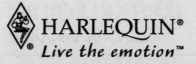

HARLEQUIN®
Live the emotion™

www.eHarlequin.com   HSRCOCAFH

Forrester Square

LEGACIES . LIES . LOVE .

**The mystery and excitement
continues in May 2004 with…**

COME FLY WITH ME
by
JILL SHALVIS

Longing for a child of
her own, single day-care
owner Katherine Kinard
decides to visit a sperm
bank. But fate intervenes
en route when she meets
Alaskan pilot Nick Spencer.
He quickly offers marriage
and a ready-made family…
but what about love?

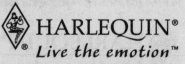

HARLEQUIN®
Live the emotion™

**Visit the Forrester Square web site
at www.forrestersquare.com**

FSQCFWM

HARLEQUIN *Super*ROMANCE®

The Man She Married
by Muriel Jensen
(Superromance #1208)

Men of
Maple Hill

Gideon and Prue Hale are still married—but try telling
that to Prue. Even though no papers have been signed,
as far as Prue's concerned it's over. She can never
forgive Gideon's betrayal. Too bad she still misses him....

Available June 2004 wherever Harlequin books are sold.

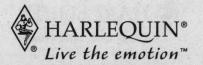

HARLEQUIN®
Live the emotion™

www.eHarlequin.com   HSRMOMH2

Beneath tropical skies, no woman can hide from danger or
love in these two novels of steamy, suspenseful passion!

UNDERCOVER SUMMER

USA TODAY
bestselling author

ANNE STUART

BOBBY HUTCHINSON

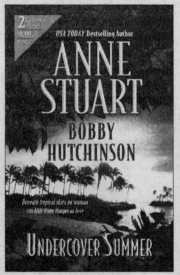

Two page-turning novels in which romance heats up
the lives of two women, who each find romance with
a sexy, mysterious undercover agent.

Coming to a bookstore near you in June 2004.

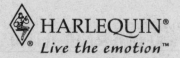

HARLEQUIN®
Live the emotion™

Visit us at www.eHarlequin.com

BR2US

eHARLEQUIN.com

Your favorite authors are just a click away
at www.eHarlequin.com!

- Take our **Sister Author Quiz** and
  we'll match you up with the author
  most like you!

- Choose from over 500
  author **profiles!**

- Chat with your favorite authors
  on our **message boards.**

- Are you an author in the making?
  Get advice from published authors
  in **The Inside Scoop!**

- Get the latest on **author appearances**
  and tours!

 **Want to know more about your
favorite romance authors?**

Choose from over 500 author profiles!

**Learn about your favorite authors
in a fun, interactive setting—
visit www.eHarlequin.com today!**

INTAUTH

If you enjoyed what you just read,
then we've got an offer you can't resist!

Take 2 bestselling love stories FREE!

Plus get a FREE surprise gift!

Clip this page and mail it to Harlequin Reader Service®

IN U.S.A.	IN CANADA
3010 Walden Ave.	P.O. Box 609
P.O. Box 1867	Fort Erie, Ontario
Buffalo, N.Y. 14240-1867	L2A 5X3

YES! Please send me 2 free Harlequin Superromance® novels and my free surprise gift. After receiving them, if I don't wish to receive anymore, I can return the shipping statement marked cancel. If I don't cancel, I will receive 6 brand-new novels every month, before they're available in stores. In the U.S.A., bill me at the bargain price of $4.47 plus 25¢ shipping and handling per book and applicable sales tax, if any*. In Canada, bill me at the bargain price of $4.99 plus 25¢ shipping and handling per book and applicable taxes**. That's the complete price, and a savings of at least 10% off the cover prices—what a great deal! I understand that accepting the 2 free books and gift places me under no obligation ever to buy any books. I can always return a shipment and cancel at any time. Even if I never buy another book from Harlequin, the 2 free books and gift are mine to keep forever.

135 HDN DNT3
336 HDN DNT4

Name	(PLEASE PRINT)	
Address	Apt.#	
City	State/Prov.	Zip/Postal Code

* Terms and prices subject to change without notice. Sales tax applicable in N.Y.
** Canadian residents will be charged applicable provincial taxes and GST.
All orders subject to approval. Offer limited to one per household and not valid to current Harlequin Superromance® subscribers.
® is a registered trademark of Harlequin Enterprises Limited.

SUP02   ©1998 Harlequin Enterprises Limited

Forrester Square

LEGACIES . LIES . LOVE .

**Secrets and romance unfold at Forrester Square…
the elegant home of Seattle's most famous families
where mystery and passion are guaranteed!**

Coming in June…

BEST-LAID PLANS

by

DEBBI RAWLINS

Determined to find a new dad,
six-year-old Corey Fletcher
takes advantage of carpenter
Sean Everett's temporary
amnesia and tells Sean that
he's married to his mom,
Alana. Sean can't believe
he'd ever forget such an
amazing woman…but more
than anything, he wants
Corey to be right!

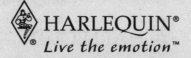

HARLEQUIN®
Live the emotion™

**Visit the Forrester Square Web site
at www.forrestersquare.com**

FSQBLP

Sometimes the best gift you can receive is the truth...

SECRETS & SONS

Two novels of riveting romantic suspense
from bestselling authors

JACQUELINE AMANDA
DIAMOND STEVENS

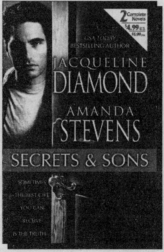

While unraveling the mysteries of their brothers'
deaths, two heroes discover an unexpected twist...
the sons they never knew they had!

Available in bookstores everywhere in May 2004.

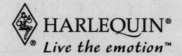

HARLEQUIN®
Live the emotion™

Visit us at www.eHarlequin.com

BR2SAS